DEDICATION:

THE COLONIAL CLUB is dedicated to my beloved husband Roddy, without whose help, my life or this book would not have been possible. All my love, now and forever.

Diane.

W0013716

EPIGRAPH:

'Necessity makes us perform what is needed most'

The Author

BY DIANE McDOWELL

THE WEEKENDER

*

THE COLONIAL CLUB

*

THE ASHINGFORD SERIES - BOOKS 1 - 7

AMELIA'S LEGACY – BOOK 1

THE DAY OF THE BUTTERFLIES – BOOK 2

THY WILL BE DONE – BOOK 3

MOONLIGHT ON THE LAKE – BOOK 4

DREAMS OF TRUTH – BOOK 5

THE PATH TO MATURITY – BOOK 6

THE DAY OF RECKONING – BOOK 7

*

NAMES IN THE MIST - BOOKS 1 & 2

NAMES IN THE MIST – BOOK 1

CRADLE IN THE VALLEY – BOOK 2

*

MA'S BAIRNS - BOOKS 1 & 2

DRUMMOND - BOOK 1

MACAULAY - BOOK 2

CHAPTER ONE:

Previously...

Twisting and turning the narrow track made its way skyward affording little scope for stopping at any vantage point. "Between a rock and a hard place," she muttered... but in this case it was between hard rock and a sheer drop. Near the summit, Michael managed to squeeze the jeep onto a narrow strip of greenery rewarding them with a superb panoramic view of the verdant valley below. Relieved to have found somewhere to stop, she saw him grin.

"Race you to the edge," she yelled.

"No contest," he called back.

What was happening far below? Nothing... except for those things which accompany silence; the noise of wind in the atmosphere and the hazy sounds emanating from the cosseted lush valley beneath.

Suddenly, Michael detected movement… far below a pick-up truck turned off the road onto a sandy track leaving clouds of billowing residue. There followed another, and then another… each heading along the same track, leaving similar clouds of dust in their wake. The realisation that squashed in the back of each truck sat groups of people in uniform made him salivate with interest, and her quiver with fear. Dropping to the ground, he pulled her down beside him, and together they slowly inched back from the edge.

"What's all that about?" she asked, her voice full of innocence.

"Give me a moment, Prue," he snapped, as his mind spun through the available alternatives. He then twisted around on his belly, crawled back to their jeep, and prised a pair of binoculars from the glove box. After slithering back to where she lay, a quick look through the lenses confirmed his worst fears. Michael passed the binoculars to her… which she fumbled and dropped. He picked them up and handed them back to her thankfully without comment. Once focused, her eyes locked onto the men in the pick-up trucks; they were wearing combat gear, with rifles and heavy ammunition belts slung over their shoulders. She was shocked. The pair lay in silence watching, as truck after truck turned onto the sandy track, each adding to the increasing clouds of dense dust. The convoy headed towards a copse of trees whose foliage swallowed them into its innards, like an animal with its prey.

Prue noticed something glistening in the rays of the noon-day sun… she pushed the binoculars back into Michael's eager hands, and watched as he raised them to his eyes. "Damn," he muttered, "let's go. I don't have a clue what's going on, but it looks like they've either spotted us or our jeep!"

"What now?" she replied, alarmed and confused. "We can't go back down that way." To her ears, her voice sounded pathetic and weak, which perfectly matched the feeble feelings presently swimming around in her mind. Michael reached over, gave her his hand, and pulled her towards their yellow jeep. It shone in front of them, its cheerful exterior matched only by the blazing sun. It had been her pick! Not one of her better colour choices, she thought in the circumstances... but they were supposed to be on holiday.

"Come on, we need to shift our butts, and get the hell out of here," he urged.

Thank goodness she wasn't expected to drive... her nervous system was already shot and couldn't have coped with the slightest of emergencies.

"For God's sake Prue, stop dawdling, and get that lovely butt of yours up on the passenger seat," he shouted. "Now!"

She could hear the distant sounds of an engine as it groaned and laboured its way upwards. If Michael was aware of its progress, he didn't say, but made it clear by his words, that they were not hanging around to provide a welcome.

*

The Present...

Her memories of that event were still vivid, and she could almost taste the acrid diesel fumes in the air.

But that had happened years ago... and since then, a whole decade had passed, stuffed full of similar out-of-the-ordinary experiences. Michael had always insisted on taking their breaks in the most bizarre locations, none of which could be considered normal holiday destinations.

Today she sat with her feet dipped in their apartment's rooftop pool. It was bathed in warm sunlight, which reflected her current mood perfectly. Most things in her world at present were basked in a rosy glow. They had not long left the wintry wet weather behind and had arrived in this paradise... now that was something for which she was so very thankful!

She opened her eyes and watched as he sauntered towards her. From his gait, she sensed something was amiss. "We've got to go back," he muttered, as he came to a standstill beside her, his eyes scanning the water to avoid her gaze. The words had been so faint, that she'd heard little more than their vibration coming from his throat.

"If you've something to say, say it out loud and clear," she replied. "You know how I hate your under-the-breath scenarios. Give it out straight, Michael."

"You got my gist, or you wouldn't be making a fuss," he whispered, "like I said... we're heading home."

"But why…we've not been here that long?" she protested. "It's only been three months, and I like it here… I feel… relaxed."

"Don't bloody ask why, Prue. I haven't any answers to give you," he again muttered, before turning and walking away, leaving her sitting like some wet discarded rag-doll.

The pool momentarily lost its sparkle as a cloud temporarily covered her sun. She rose, and sat at a nearby vantage point, worldly wise enough to realise that he'd soon be on his way out of the building. It was not long before she was proved correct. The top of his head became visible, and she watched him make his way along the path through the gardens towards the exit gate. He'd not taken his car or called a taxi, and it was strange to see him leave on foot… she could not recall this ever happening before. As she watched from her perch she felt that he was not only distancing himself from her, but also from the Michael she knew and loved.

Confused and angry, she returned to the pool and lowered herself over the edge. "Damn," she muttered, as she immersed herself into the deep waters which cooled her heated body and brought her a degree of instant relief. She didn't want to leave here… no, this place suited her just fine.

A few minutes later, she was back out of the pool. She dripped all the way to the elevator, where she descended the short distance to their apartment. She felt ashamed that she'd left it more than slightly damp and could only imagine the comments it would undoubtedly attract... but never mind... she wouldn't be hearing them.

Their spacious and light apartment had clean modern lines, while its furnishings enjoyed a certain quintessential crispness. She slid the *terrasse* door open and headed for her favourite lounger to dry off. The wide expansive *terrasse* was awash with heady varieties of exotic perfumed greenery and lush tropical plants. The Garden of Eden itself could not have been blessed with a sweeter air or more luxuriant surroundings.

CHAPTER TWO:

His side of the bed remained empty that night, which was of great annoyance to her, as she desperately needed to talk to him. That morning, she was due to meet her new friend Kate in their favourite coffee shop, which in truth resembled not a shop, but more of a palace... hence its name *The Coffee Palace*. The establishment would shame any *palazzo*, and had more gold than Fort Knox, or so her friend would utter each and every time they entered its opulent interior. Despite its overt decadence, they loved sitting surrounded by layers of glitter, while being served by staff who made them feel extra special.

Before leaving the apartment, Prue checked her mobile for messages, but found zilch from her beloved. How could he be so damned mean as to keep her blanked out over their future... and where the devil had he disappeared to this time? No time now to wonder, as her taxi had arrived.

Once seated at their usual table she tried to relax, but her mind kept returning to Michael. She would have loved to be able to discuss her situation with Kate, but with no explanation to give her, she would have undoubtedly been mocked. Her friend wouldn't understand their strange relationship... how could she... for Prue didn't understand it herself!

Kate arrived, and once settled chattered on in her usual fashion about a load of old rubbish. Then it happened, over her shoulder Prue glimpsed him standing by the door. "Kate, something's come up... I'll have to go," she interrupted her friend, "I'll phone you later."

"What—?" called out Kate.

This made Prue stop in her tracks, turn, wave and shout "Bye!" to her bewildered friend.

By the time she resumed her rushed departure, she saw that the doorway was now empty, with no sign of Michael. She nevertheless continued towards the exit, which she calculated would be easier than trying to explain to Kate.

Once outside in the busy main Square, her heart began to thump as she called out, "Michael, Michael, where are you?"

"How old is Michael?" asked an elderly lady.

"Why do you want to know?" she replied.

"Well, it makes a great deal of difference. Boys are interested in different things at different ages, or at least they used to be in my day," the woman replied.

"I'm sorry... I wasn't thinking. I know exactly what you mean, but Michael's not a boy... he's my husband," she stammered, with the realisation that by now, the odds of finding him were probably zero. Despite having had this thought, she smiled at the woman, who smiled back, then reached out and took hold of her hand. She stated that husbands did not normally get lost, unless they were of a certain kind... but then quickly tried to reassure her that this would surely not be the case with her Michael.

"Husbands only get lost if they want to, or have a reason to get lost... is that what you're trying to tell me?" queried Prue.

"I'm sorry, my dear, I can see that I may have upset you," she replied. "I'd better go now, as I've things to do... but it was nice to meet you, and I do hope you find your Michael soon."

*

Prue stopped calling out Michael's name, as to continue would be pointless. She crossed the Square, desperately looking for a place in which to hide from Kate. Her eyes settled on a shop with a faded exterior, which directly faced *The Coffee Palace*. Wedged between two larger units, she felt strangely drawn towards this petite enterprise, and as she pushed open the door, was greeted by an empty interior.

15

"Hi… try and squeeze in, if you can," called out a guy who was busily wiping tables. They both laughed as she plonked herself on the nearest seat.

"Is it okay to sit here?" she asked, with a cheeky grin. He nodded, and then chuckled when she asked him that if he wasn't too busy... could she order a coffee and a few slices of toast? She felt she needed to chew on something, while she tried to recover her composure. Her eyes darted back and forwards across the Square to the entrance of *The Coffee Palace* and was rewarded by seeing her leave a few minutes later. Kate did not look over, but Prue instinctively ducked out of sight. The man laughed at her antics, and she willingly joined him.

This guy was priceless to her in her moment of need. Next, he played a happy tune on his music machine, whilst she wriggled her butt into a more comfortable position. Her new friend brought over her coffee first, which she appreciated, and a few minutes later her order of well-done toast arrived... singed to perfection. The café took on that delicious aroma, which can only come from singed toast.

"My compliments to the chef," she called over, as he took up his stance behind the counter.

"He'll be pleased, when I tell him," he replied, giving her a pretend salute. They smiled at each other in the way that only friends usually do. "Just passing through?" he asked.

"Might be… I'm awaiting orders," she answered.

"Are you in the military?" he asked.

"Something like that. I take orders... well, at least I did," she answered, "but no longer."

"So you've done your time, as we say in the trade?" he stated.

"Might have," she replied, "you, my friend, have been very helpful... and I'm now thinking straighter than I've managed in a long time."

"Glad to be of service... to the Service," he stated in a laughing voice. "Was it the coffee or the toast, which brought you this clarity, or a combination of the two?"

They laughed once more, then she noticed with disappointment, that a young couple had entered their world, and were about to sit at one of the window tables... all good toast must come to an end, she thought.

CHAPTER THREE:

Prue checked her phone for missed calls, texts, or messages... for anything at all from Michael... but there was nothing. Damn him! What gives him the right to treat me this way, she thought, always dangling her from the edge of the hairy precipice which bore his name? She was now back at their apartment, having walked from the café carefully checking behind her at every twist and turn. She had been checking she was not being followed... although by whom... she had no idea? She blamed Michael for her furtive behaviour, for he was the one who had bred into her the need for some most peculiar practices over the decade they had been married.

Twist and turn... that made her memory snap back into grappling mode once more, as she wrestled with their joint history. Her mobile began to play its ditty... it was Kate's name on the display. Of course it was her... by now she'll be totally steamed up and demanding an explanation. She would not be getting one... instead Prue stuffed it under a cushion and sat on the little blighter.

What the devil had Michael been doing standing watching her? Or was it Kate he'd been watching? None of it made any sense, but she hated him at that moment, and not for the first time either! "I hate you, Michael Lambasto," she screamed at the room, and had her mouth in gear for her next outburst, when she heard a noise... someone was knocking on the apartment door. Tiptoeing to the door, she listened, and then looked through the spy-hole... it was Marcel. Why was he hovering out there? Why could he not do his hovering and hoovering outside someone else's apartment?

She then heard him utter... "*Madame* Lambasto, is you all right? Is it not good with you?"

The knocking continued. "Hell's bells, is there no bloody peace from ringing phones and people banging?" she muttered, as she jerked open the door. "Hello, Marcel," she greeted him, with her voice pitched as high as she had ever heard it before. She smiled at him with the best fixed smile she could muster. "How can I help you?"

"I listen you scream; are you no good?" he replied. "What I speak... is all okay with *Madame*... you made me... okay then... all?"

"Never better, Marcel," she replied, "things couldn't get much worse."

"So, you… that good to hear… how *Monsieur*?" he asked. "He busy man… I see him in town… he pop in many places… yes… no?"

"*Mon Mari* is… indeed a busy man. I'm glad you've seen him popping in many places," she replied. "Sometimes Marcel, I wish he'd pop back here. Never mind, I now know I can count on you to take good care of him, wherever he pops up next."

"*Oui, Madame*... I think," he said, "can I you help, *Madame*?"

"Not at the moment, Marcel, but I'll let you know if I think of anything… Nope, can't think of anything I need from you at the moment," she replied. "Not anything you can help me with anyway, but who knows, times change don't they, and you'll be my first port of call in a storm."

A confused Marcel turned to resume his vacuuming.

Back inside the apartment, Prue felt mean… how was the poor man meant to follow that confusing train of a conversation? "It's all your fault, Michael; I should've drowned you in the pool yesterday. I should have grabbed you by the leg of your fancy suit, or just given you an almighty push," she muttered, then thought better of it. "Don't be so immature Prue, why don't you try to have more grown up thoughts for a change?"

CHAPTER FOUR:

Kate kept ringing every five minutes or so. What a bloody pest! Prue now could only hear her mobile faintly whine, as she had now heaved it amongst a basket of wet clothing through in the laundry-room. She didn't want to speak to her or anyone else... only Michael. Thoughts developed in her mind... nagging doubts.

She moved outdoors, and as she lay in the sun on the *terrasse*, she thought of Kate, and what she knew of her. She had met her three months previously, not long after they'd first arrived on the island. Michael and she had gone to a certain bar by the harbour, and Kate had been there with her husband. He was seemingly one of Michael's bunch of seedy associates, an unattractive man, who went by the name of Bart. Bart had appeared scruffy to her, not that he did not have expensive clothes to wear, it was just that he did not manage to dress himself properly. Prue had instantly decided that if he was her Bart, she would have bartered him long ago... but as they say, horses for courses. He may have had hidden qualities which Kate saw as redeeming, as she had never heard her say anything negative about him... but then again, neither had she said anything positive.

It was on that first evening that the two women befriended each other. Kate was a native of this peculiar island, which made her of interest to Prue. They started to meet for coffee soon afterwards... although like herself, Kate never gave much away on these meetings, always keeping her cards pressed tight to her more than ample bosom.

Now, as Prue lay on the lounger, a niggling embryo began to mature. How did Michael know she would be at *The Coffee Palace* that morning? She hadn't told him... of that she was positive, so who had? Perhaps it was Kate he'd been watching... they could have arranged to meet there? If that was a possibility then she should have followed Kate, as she may have led her to Michael? Instead, she'd made the mistake of dodging into that little café... no, that wasn't a mistake. The guy there had been so sweet. He'd lifted her spirits during her short visit, and as she thought of him, she remembered their easy rapport. This made her smile and put such silly thoughts about Michael and Kate out of her mind... for the time being at least!

Could that be a faint knock on her door? She raised her head and listened intently; yes, someone was there gently knocking. Michael wouldn't have knocked; no gentle tap from him, no, he was a founder member of the straight-to-the-point, no-nonsense Club, it would have been loud knocks from him. No, whoever it was, it was not Michael.

She rose from the lounger, and this time enquired who it was through the intercom?

"It me… *Madame* Lambasto… it Marcel… I give gift to you." She opened the door on hearing the poor man's dulcet tones, whereupon he handed her an enormous pineapple... "I want say I sorry… for this morning, *Madame* Lambasto," he continued.

"Oh, Marcel, that's so sweet, but you were only doing your job. It was my fault. Once again, thank you," she said. "Are you still on duty?"

"No, I go," he replied.

"Then come in and cut the pineapple for me," she requested.

"No come in," he replied, "no come in… no inside," he answered, repeatedly glancing over his shoulder.

"Okay, then let me buy you a drink down in the bar?" she suggested.

"No, *Madame* Lambasto… I sorry… no… no," he replied, "no drink… if go… I no more the job." He then turned and hurried away leaving her hugging her pineapple.

Prue secured her door and smiled as she thought of Marcel and his kind gesture. Her smile suddenly changed to a grimace. Poor man… she felt so sorry for him. The strict list of do's and don'ts were obviously dished out to the staff in a blunt and brutal fashion.

*

She took her pineapple through into the kitchen and laid it on the counter. It was a fruit that Michael absolutely loved… it was such a pity he wasn't here, as she always shied away from handling such large over ripe examples as this. She then became truly concerned about him. Her inability to deal with a pineapple had brought the reality of a missing Michael to her door. They were far from home in this strange foreign island. God alone knows where she was… or more importantly where he was, and as she looked at it she realised she was being frightened by an oversized, over ripe pineapple!

She felt alone. She was used to him and his escapades, but had expected him back by now, or at least to have received a message. He always managed to get a message to her. "Michael, come back, I need you now, if for nothing more than to deal with this damned pineapple," she shouted. "You know I can't phone you."

*

She had met Michael ten years previously on her first day at Cambridge University. He belonged to the upper-class, science buff brigade, his speciality being chemistry; whilst she was from a very different breed, being a fresh-faced farm kid geared to read philosophy of all things. She had straw behind her ears and dangling from her hair, whilst he had been well-groomed, extremely good looking and exceptionally mature.

Michael had lived for nineteen and she for seventeen years, when their paths unexpectedly met. If they hadn't met then, their paths would probably never have crossed.

Not being used to busy traffic, or the noise made by excited young voices, she'd found herself clipped by a cyclist, as she stood chatting to some new acquaintances. The impact knocked her to the ground, and Michael arrived first on the scene to help her. He gently checked she was unhurt, and then did a very strange thing; he took hold of the young student who'd been riding the bike and pinned him up against a nearby wall with considerable force. It had happened in a busy student precinct, and everyone stopped in their tracks to stare. The young cyclist began to shake, such was the ferocity of Michael's attack. "I'm sorry, I'm sorry, I'm sorry," the poor guy screeched, repeatedly.

"Too right you're sorry. You watch where you're fuckin' going in future," she clearly remembered him replying. No one present moved, as Michael's actions, language and tone had stunned them. He then lifted the terrified young man off the ground before dropping him with a thud. The crowd had watched like helpless stooges, as this scenario played out in front of them. Michael then stooped over and picked up the guy's bike. Those present began to groan, expecting him to mangle its frame. Instead, and to everyone's surprise, he checked it over, and then helped his victim up and returned it to him. "Show's over," he shouted, dismissing the crowd with a wave of his hand.

"My, somebody really likes you," said one of her new group of friends. Prue didn't reply... but did wonder if this could really be the case?

He was well travelled, while she had never been anywhere foreign. His father was someone in the Diplomatic Service, while her folks ran a small farm in the West Country; on reflection, perhaps they balanced each other perfectly?

Two months later, at a pace dictated by Michael, and shortly after her eighteenth birthday they became Mr and Mrs Lambasto, at a ceremony only attended by them, and a few of their new friends from University...

Suddenly it dawned on Prue that her phone must have stopped ringing some time ago; she'd been so deep in thought that her ears had stopped receiving signals. Thank goodness! She retrieved it from the damp laundry basket and took it through into the lounge to check her texts. She glanced at them, then, for no apparent reason, heard Michael's voice ringing in her head, reminding her not to become... dehydrated, of all things!

"Thanks, love," she replied, and headed for the kitchen. With a glass of water in one hand, and her phone in the other, she returned to the lounge to check her messages properly. There were a few that stood out as not being from her regular sources... however scrutinising them found nothing positive. Michael's list... would have to be her next step, so she collected it from its secret hiding place, and after a lengthy check and cross check, the outcome was still the same... nothing fitted. The emergency phone was her last resort... she picked it up and sighed. "Blast," she cried, it needed charged. "You should have checked it Michael, what's the point of leaving me a dud?" She went to put it on charge, but just in time, remembered Michael's words. "Don't charge that phone in this apartment Prue... go somewhere safe." What kind of phone could not be charged in your own apartment? Why had she not asked him, because she already knew the answer... a Michael Lambasto phone! Go somewhere safe? Where was safe on this island of low-life creatures? This island paradise was outwardly wonderful, until you scraped beneath its veneer. This beautiful place where nothing was as it seemed...

"Why bring me here, Michael? Why couldn't we live a normal life, in a normal place, and have a normal family?" she groaned. Her thoughts then flicked back to Kate once again, and she realised Michael had not been there to meet her. Of course, he hadn't, and she subconsciously apologised to him. Kate had been seated with her back facing the door, so she wouldn't have known he'd even been there. He'd wanted her to see him, and to leave the premises...

"Thanks, Michael, sorry for what I thought earlier," she whispered. "You've looked out for me ever since that first day we met, and I love you so very much." Her thoughts then returned to the task which lay ahead. Where could she charge the phone safely? She had no true friends here, certainly not Kate.

"Close your eyes and let your mind wander free," is what Michael would say, "and the answer will always come..."

CHAPTER FIVE:

Prue allowed her mind to wander overnight and came up with a most strange decision… she wrapped up the large pineapple and placed it into a green holdall, together with her sharpest knife… whilst keeping the emergency phone and charger on her person.

She then left the apartment before the sun rose too high in the sky… would she walk or take a taxi? Walk, it had to be; she couldn't trust taking a taxi, not with her head in the place it was this morning, or indeed at any other time on this damned island. Get a move on before the sun turns on its unbearable heat.

Her walk was pleasant enough, the light producing a marvellous glow that reflected off the white buildings and the blue sea. What a beautiful island, such a pity it had to be spoilt by horrible people. "Michael, where are you? Why are we here?" she muttered, as she continued on her way. As ever, he had left her with no knowledge of what game he was involved in, or where he was playing it out…

"Don't, ask Prue, you know I can't tell you, however much I want, I just can't…" she could hear him stress these words, as if walking by her side. Her eyes started to water, and for the first time in a long while, she wished for the cold comfort of her folks.

"Yousa besa all right, little missy?" a passer-by asked.

She smiled somewhat pleased that someone had cared enough to ask. "Eh, yes, I'm good… thanks," she replied, the old man having restored her faith in some of the island's humanity, but certainly not all.

There were fewer people out and about than expected, so it surprised her to see that the little café was crowded. She viewed it from the other side of the Square, and as she began to cross, he looked out of the large plate glass window, smiled and beckoned her inside. It was full of customers, which for him was great, but to her a disappointment; that hadn't been in her plan. He waved his arm once more, beckoning her inside...

Prue then noticed a girl helping him, which caused her to hesitate… this may not be one of her better ideas, she thought? However, before she had time to ponder any more, he beckoned her for a third time… what could she do but accept his invitation?

The noise hit her as soon as she entered, as did the fact there were no vacant tables, so she threaded her way to a high stool at the counter. "If you can hang on, for a little, the place will shortly clear? We usually get a bit of respite for an hour," he said, leaning over the counter, "before it builds up again."

"Your friend," she asked, "is she your boss?"

"No, she's not... this is my palace and whilst it may not be golden, it suits me just fine," he replied, the warmth of his voice giving her an inner glow.

Prue ordered a coffee from the girl assistant and he called over to say it was on the house. The assistant gave him a frown, to which he mouthed... "she's family" as way of explanation.

His family? Now that felt nice and brought her yet another warm glow. While she sat and sipped, she used her time to survey her 'cousin'. There was nothing about him that stood out as special, except for his mop of unruly hair. Michael always came over as suave, with clean-cut lines, but this guy's voice did have a special sound, a certain smoothness mixed with passion, and a large dollop of understanding.

She turned her attention to his girl assistant, who dealt with the clientele well enough. She was young and pretty, so would probably put extra bums on seats. Prue then closed her eyes, and let her mind wander once more...

"Hello, are you still with us?" he asked. "Please remember, you're perched on a high stool."

She opened her eyes... she hadn't considered the dangers of the stool. "Thanks... I've brought you a pineapple," she replied, reaching into her holdall.

"That was nice of you," he responded, whilst his hands operated the coffee machine on auto pilot.

"I thought you'd be someone who'd appreciate my spiky friend," she stated.

"Give me time to think about that remark," he replied, with a smile.

"Don't take too long… pineapples can go off quickly," she remarked.

"Really? I didn't know that," he replied.

Marina… whose name she'd heard being called out, gave them a strange look. "It's a family trait," he explained to her, "to speak a load of rubbish."

"That's true," Prue agreed, "me and your… boss, have inherited some peculiar genes."

"Nothing bad, Marina, just some little tweaks in our nature that make us say crazy things at times," he added.

"When there's a full moon, or when the earth is in certain positions… these sorts of times," explained Prue.

"I'm not so sure about the certain positions," he added, his face lighting up with a smile that warmed the room.

"Don't knock it, these genes have got us this far in our lives," replied Prue.

"Can I get served, please?" called over a slightly irate older woman, "I thought this was a café, not a nonsense talking shop?"

"I don't think we'll come back here again, Jennifer, there's plenty of other eateries," added her friend, "where they actually serve you!"

"I'll be right over ladies," he said, carrying his smile with him.

Spinning around on her stool, Prue saw the women melt at the sound of his voice. They'd be back for sure, she thought... they wouldn't be able to stay away!

CHAPTER SIX:

It took a while, but after eleven the café did eventually clear... not a stampede, more of an orderly dispersal. Prue hadn't moved from her stool during her wait and was numb down under! A reluctant Marina was sent to order supplies, and after she'd left, he came over and helped her down from the high stool. "You shouldn't have sat up there for so long, it's a killer," he said.

"Not too sure what you're meaning?" she replied.

"Wait until you get settled in one of my comfier seats, and all memories of the stool will soon fade," he replied.

"What's your name, 'cousin' dear, it's slipped my mind," she asked, "Marina called you Fuzz, which, don't get me wrong, is fine... but it's not a proper name?"

"It suffices as a handle," he replied, which left her a shade unsure as to what to say next. She didn't want to call him Fuzz. She wanted to call him Steve, John, or even Brian... anything but Fuzz. "What's the story with the pineapple?" he asked, with a puzzled expression.

The mood in the café suddenly changed; it didn't feel right to ask him to slice it up now, not if he wouldn't tell her his proper name. She also thought it strange that he hadn't asked her for her name. She made a snap decision to take the pineapple back home, and not to charge up her phone here, not in his café. It was too late now for that anyway, she should have put it on to charge as soon as she had arrived... but she hadn't expected it to be busy. She had assumed it would still be empty. Why had she thought such a stupid thing?

"What's the story with the pineapple anyway?" he repeated.

"Just take it as a joke," she replied, "I have to leave... I need to get going."

"Fine," he answered.

She strode out of the café carrying her holdall, deliberately not giving a backward glance. She had only taken a few steps onto the *Place de l'ocean*, when it dawned on her that people didn't ordinarily walk around here with holdalls... for fear of being stopped by *la police locale*. What had made her bring a large kitchen knife, of all things? For goodness sake, she'd been headed for a café of all places, so, needing one to slice up a pineapple would not serve as a plausible excuse. If the police did stop her and found the knife, she'd be arrested, detained overnight or longer, before being taken before the beak. There was no jury on this island, and only one Judge, a certain Maurice Wiseman Stoker. She hadn't been here long, but long enough to hear the tales that circulated about the infamous Judge Stoker... and a tale woven around an overripe, outsized, pineapple, and a turquoise handled long kitchen knife, wouldn't cut with him...

Why in heavens name had she brought a knife? She could just visualise how the following day's edition of *La Belle Post*, would read...'W*oman arrested with knife in her bag... known to have been a patron of a café where B.Y.O.K seemed to be the order of the day.*'

The police wouldn't stop her... surely not? She clutched her holdall, and now feeling guilty, turned into the *Maison Victoria,* where she soon realised she'd made a big mistake. This was definitely an alley in which one did not loiter, and definitely not with a large holdall pressed tightly against your chest...

Just then, a shadowy figure slid out from an equally shadowy doorway, followed by two other figures, "Good day, Missy," said a burly guy dressed in an ill-fitting police uniform, fondly eyeing her green holdall...

He could be a police officer, or he could be anyone... anyone at all; it seemingly wasn't a crime to impersonate an officer of the law in these parts, no crime at all, unless of course the real police themselves got miffed with you. He stretched out his hand for her bag.

"You're not looking in my bag. My husband has given me instructions, and I mean to obey him," she replied.

"A woman who obeys? I ain't never heard of such a thing before. Samuel, you ever heard the likes?" asked the first officer of his comrade, who was doubling up with laughter.

"Why no, Jerome, I ain't never heard of no woman doing what she's been told neither," he replied.

"Take the bag, keep it! It's only a stupid old bag," she snapped. "That's if you're such a desperate trio?"

"The lady sure ain't never heard us songbirds sing, but the Desperate Trio… what a cracking name for a band," replied a laughing Jerome.

The two doubled over with laughter once more, whilst simultaneously eyeing her up, as though she was tonight's dinner. She knew they were sussing her, trying to work out to whom she may be connected on this island? Who you knew around here, was all that mattered.

Prue then thrust the bag towards them once more and stamped her foot with some force.

"Hey, Missy, don't you be getting yourself all stampie footie with us," said the third man, who had remained silent up until this point.

"Stampie footie? What kind of dumb language is that?" she asked. "Do you not have to pass some kind of competence exam to join the police in this God-forsaken place?"

The three men burst out laughing once more, "You be one feisty ladybird, Missy," replied Samuel.

"Now, now, Samuel, I'm guessing here, that this lady's a visitor to our island paradise. What kinda words is that to be using to a foreigner?" replied the third man.

They continued to guffaw, but she sensed that the third man was the boss. She turned and handed him her bag, which he took, and bowed his head. He then annoyed her, by tossing it over to Jerome, in a manner which was less than gracious, who in turn, tossed it to Samuel. Having no fresh meat to pass it on to, he held it up above his head. Prue turned to walk away...

"Missy, Missy, back here you come, or you're for the black pit. Come back over here or you'll go before the Judge," ordered the boss man. Prue swung around, terrified, but showing them only a confident pout. She thought she knew what was coming, but then to her astonishment, her holdall was returned unopened.

She thanked them the best way she could in the circumstances, by taking to her heels and making a hasty retreat, followed by peels of laughter... loud reverberating laughter.

CHAPTER SEVEN:

Once back at the apartment, Prue locked the door including its secondary secure mechanism, and then did the same with the doors which led out to the *terrasse*. These locks were stiff as they'd rarely been used, and her shaking hands made her task all the harder. She was a wreck by the time she'd finished. "You fool, how is Michael meant to get in when he arrives home?" she muttered. "He'll only have one key with him... idiot, let your brain engage."

She now felt put down and abandoned as she shivered in this land of wall-to-wall sunshine and warm sparking waters. "What... who the dickens is that—?" she spluttered... and without daring to breathe, listened intently... It was muffled, but sure enough, there it was again, a voice from outside rising through the heat haze. For goodness sake get up and listen properly, she silently commanded herself, and with that rose from her sofa and put her ear to the glass of the *terrasse* door.

"*Madame* Lambasto… *Madame*," the voice called.

Did she want to see Marcel, for she knew who it was? She supposed she did, as he was after all a kind man, and she hadn't experienced much kindness of late. She unlocked the door and stepped out onto the *terrasse*, from where she could see him below. "What is it, Marcel, what's so important?" she asked.

"*Madame* Lambasto, I sad about you… is *Monsieur* with you?" he asked. Prue told him that she couldn't hear him properly, and to wait there. She then nipped into the kitchen, took out the knife from her holdall and slipped it back into the cutlery drawer. The bag already stank with an aroma of sickly sweetness… its walk in the heat having done its job well. She next made her way back out onto the *terrasse*, "Marcel, can you come up to the apartment, I've something for you?" she asked.

"*Madame* Lambasto, I tell you, I no come to apartment… I lose job, and we no eat. *Madame*…," he replied.

"Just come to the door, you're surely allowed to do that?" Prue insisted before leaving him standing in the area below. She then made her way to a position behind the front door, from where she could peer through the spyglass. A few minutes later, Marcel arrived looking every bit as a fugitive would. Throwing open the door, she thrust the holdall into his arms,

"Marcel, take the pineapple away, please. I don't want it or this bag, but thanks for your kind gesture."

She then closed the door before he had time to protest, and Marcel did not knock again. Why had she done that, the poor man would not and could not possibly understand? He didn't deserve such rudeness, as he'd always shown her genuine kindness and consideration, unlike some other members of staff, whose faces were mere facades with their fixed smiles and disingenuous lip service. Performance... what a performance she had delivered, and all because of the gift of a now over-ripe, blinking pineapple!

"Not, by me Michael, this is entirely your fault," she screeched into the emptiness of her apartment, "you should be here with me, not wherever you are."

*

In the heat of the afternoon, he rested his shoulder against a rock, and glanced down to see a pool of blood forming around the bottom of his trousers... "God, not here, not now!" he groaned, "I'm fucked."

Michael slithered further down the rock face until his leg reached the stony ground and winced as he fell over. He pushed himself up and wrenched at the fabric of his trousers to better see the extent of his leg injury, then wished he hadn't! All he wanted was to be with her... the love of his life, which he'd known ever since their first meeting.

During one summer vacation when both undergraduates, he'd ventured into this murky world he

40

now inhabited, and completed his first bit of business... collateral damage included. He recalled Prue having rented a jeep as a surprise, and managed a watery smile through his pain, as he thought of her and that damned jeep. Bright yellow it was... an obvious target under the azure sky... but all of which added to the danger of the hunt, and the thrill of the chase. Michael Lambasto was hooked, his only concession to sanity being to keep Prue safe. Danger that day had become the opium coursing through his veins, and when mixed with his life-blood, was the fuel that drove his addiction. He slumped backwards, his head striking the stone cliff edge... it was not so much the pain but the sickening dull crack of bone meeting stone...

Prue... Prue... I'm so... so sorry—

CHAPTER EIGHT:

Night had fallen, when a man of imposing dimensions strode into the building where the Lambasto apartment was situated. He headed straight for the near slumbering Concierge and demanded to see *Madame* Lambasto...

He told him that she had since vacated the apartment, and as far as he knew, the island. The man spun around on his heels and disappeared back through the revolving front entrance door, before quickly returning with another equally imposing man in tow. "Can you tell us when she left and why?" the second man asked.

"Two days ago, but I'm not in a position to tell why," he replied, politely.

"How did she leave?" the first man asked.

"I don't understand what difference it makes how she left, the fact is she did," replied the Concierge.

"Don't get smart with us. You're nothing but a jumped up janitor, standing there in your fancy uniform. You don't fool us as to who you really are," snarled the second man.

"And who might that be?" replied a now agitated Concierge, his hand hovering over the emergency button which connected him to his boss… and the island police.

"A jackass peasant, who's lucky enough to have had a good English schoolteacher," he snarled once more.

Marcel appeared unannounced at that moment, "Please'cuse… I put *Madame* Lambasto in taxi; I take her bags," he interrupted. *"Madame… is good lady."*

"Who the hell's this," snapped the first man, to the Concierge, "another peasant upstart?"

"Minus the good English teacher, by the sound of what we've just—," sniggered the second man.

"I help guests," interrupted Marcel, looking to the Concierge, who readily nodded in agreement, and then took over…

"His name is Marcel; he looked after *Madame* Lambasto during her stay here," he advised.

"I bet he did," said the first man, "service her well, did you?"

They laughed once more, while the Concierge and Marcel held eye contact with each other for support.

"Get me the name of the taxi firm and driver… also find out where he took her," demanded the second man.

The Concierge and Marcel exchanged glances, "I need to ask who you are, and what right you have to enquire about *Madame* Lambasto?" quizzed the Concierge, with an air of renewed defiance.

"Just do as you're fuckin' told or face the bloody consequences. I'm Inspector Hurangee, and this is Inspector Siad. I thought you'd have recognised us," replied the second man.

"I'm sorry, but I've already pressed the emergency button, as I didn't recognise either of you. My apologies once more," replied the Concierge. "You can explain to your colleagues when they arrive… they shouldn't be too long."

"You can bloody explain that to them yourself. We've other pressing matters to deal with, and can't afford the time to hang around here," snapped Inspector Siad.

"If you are sure," replied the Concierge sarcastically, "then you can depend upon me to give them the information you requested."

The two men then headed back for the revolving door and disappeared out into the night. Marcel raised his eyebrows in the direction of his colleague, "You press button, Eugene?" he asked.

He shook his head, "I almost did, but I didn't. The boss will be pleased with us for not involving the police. Thanks Marcel, for coming to my aid... it needed the two of us. I'm going to phone the boss man now, to tell him what's happened, and request an armed guard be posted on duty here," replied Eugene. "*Madame* Lambasto... do you know if she's still on the island?"

"I no know she nice lady, but *Monsieur* Lambasto no good man," replied Marcel.

"I think I know what you mean," said Eugene, with a smile. "Now get off home; I will tell the boss how you helped me... and Marcel, here is a phrase for you to try and learn... I will put a good word in for you."

"Put good word for you... is that good?" he asked.

"Near enough, now you keep your ear to the ground," laughed Eugene.

"My ear on ground?" Marcel repeated, puzzling over this phrase as he left... still, he knew he had done a good job.

CHAPTER NINE:

The unwashed piles of dishes seemed never ending a couple of evenings before. It had been busy, and with Marina on her half day, Fuzz knew that he could do with some help. Coincidently, he had just finished dishwashing, when she knocked on the door of the café. Despite the 'closed' sign, he could not leave her standing there.

"Fuzz, I've left two bags over at *The Coffee Palace*... I've slipped them behind the gold and white curtain near the front door. Can you fetch them for me, before anyone discovers them?" she urged, "I mean like now... please." He didn't make any attempt to move. "Fuzz, go now... this is serious," she repeated sternly, and in her most matronly of voices.

What the hell is going on, why me, he thought? But he went and was back almost as soon as he'd left. "Here they are *Madame*," he announced. "It's just as well I know the doorman… he's a decent guy, so I don't think he'll blab."

"It's nothing secret; it's only a few changes of clothing… you can surely imagine," she replied, with a smile.

"Yeah, I think I can," he said, looking at her with a grin, "or perhaps not?"

"Get over with you; you know exactly what will be in the bags, well not exactly, but near enough," she replied, also smiling.

"You're one strange lady," he said. "Let me rephrase that, one amusing lady. Would it be rude of me to ask what exactly's going on with you and your bags?"

"It's complicated, so I'll need a coffee, and—," she began.

"And how many slices do you want?" he interrupted.

"Ehm… two, can you—?" she started to ask.

"It's the only kind I do," he replied once more. "I wasn't expecting to see you again after the last time. My name's Billy by the way, but please don't hold that against me, use it, or tell anyone, as I like Fuzz much better."

"So do I, now I've gotten used to you as a Fuzz," she agreed. "I'm Prue, by the way. Well, since we're bearing souls on names… it's actually Prudence."

The expression on his face revealed all, "Nice name, I'll also agree to keep Prudence under my hat, since you're keeping Billy safe for me."

This humour and banter of theirs was fast becoming a shared pleasure.

*

She was now in hiding in the back room of the café; washing the dishes helped to pass the time during the evenings, however, during the day her only entertainment was the books and magazines Fuzz had thoughtfully brought her. He'd also told Marina that he'd taken on an evening dish-washer, and that he'd locked the door to the back shop as there was a problem with the drains.

That first night, Prue told him of her dilemma... "Why did you leave your apartment?" he'd asked.

What a profound question... why indeed? First, there was no sign of Michael, which made her feel he was in serious trouble, otherwise he would have been in touch. Second, she no longer felt safe, and whether this was true or not, she no longer wished to remain there. Third, she also needed to charge her damn phone somewhere away from the apartment. This was her only remaining link to Michael, and she had no one she felt she could trust... not one person in this whole God-forsaken paradise, except for him.

She had told the Concierge that she needed to leave in a hurry but had booked a taxi herself. Marcel had subsequently loaded her luggage into the taxi's trunk, with a face so glum and actions so exaggerated, that his performance was mighty close to deserving an Oscar. Once the taxi had left the apartment grounds, she'd asked the driver to take her to *The Coffee Palace*, and as they say, the rest was history...

*

Fuzz had taken her in without the slightest hesitation. He could have been married with a mountain of children; she did not ask, and he did not say. That evening they charged the special phone, but there was nothing on it... no messages, no nothing... dead, and the silence was eerily blood curdling. This whole sorry mess had now taken on new and serious dimensions...

Fuzz took great pity on her, and apart from letting her stay, tried to make her cramped accommodation as comfortable as he could. Marina had never had the opportunity to venture through into the back shop, as he'd made it his main task to deal with the dishes himself. What story he'd told her as to why she was barred from venturing through, must have been convincing, as he merely laughed, shrugging it off whenever Prue asked.

How long this arrangement would or could continue, and what her next move would be remained a mystery... to both involved parties.

CHAPTER TEN:

Marina was now due a weeks holiday. "Thank goodness," said Fuzz to Prue, "you don't know how damned difficult it's been trying to keep her out of here. She's wearing me down, wanting to come in for this and that."

"What's she doing about toilet breaks?" Prue asked, with a smirk. She had given some thought to this. "Also yourself, what have you been—."

"Oh, she's quite adaptable... she uses the customer's toilet, as do I," he replied. "We're not reduced to a bucket in the corner, or anything like that." They each smiled at this remark; she knew she should have worked that one out for herself. "I told her that there was a really bad plumbing situation, but I suspect she knows I'm keeping something from her... so thank goodness she's due a week off."

"Keeping something… or rather someone from her," stated Prue, and could tell from his expression that the dreaded moment had now arrived.

"Prue… we need to have a chat about the someone who's staying in the back-shop," he replied, looking down at the floor.

"What do we need to say to the someone in the back-shop?" she asked.

"You know very well, Prue. I've done my best for you, and I think it's now time for some answers and explanations," he replied.

Crunch time had indeed arrived! She looked around her domain… her twelve by six dwelling. It was now her home, and she'd become rather fond of it during her short stay. Her memories of the outside world had become fainter as each hour passed. Any traffic noise from the café or the outside world had mysteriously morphed into music by the gurgling sounds of the dishwasher, whilst her bed, which composed of a few cushions scattered on a wide wooden counter-top, had become more comfortable each time she'd lain down. She had food, somewhere to perform her ablutions, and the added bonus of Fuzz playing her favourite tunes in the café. The melodies wafted through into the back-shop, helping to soothe and entertain.

Prue recounted to him what had happened in her life recently. Her tale sounded pathetic, even to herself, and she could see from his facial expressions, that he was amused, concerned and confused, all baked into the one pie. "Well?" she asked, once she had finished…

"Well, what?" he replied.

"You know what I mean; help me out by saying something… anything," she asked.

Fuzz took her hand and squeezed it gently, "*Madame* Lambasto, that was some tale… sorry, not so much a tale, but more of a harrowing reality," he replied.

"You're welcome," she said, with a shrug of her shoulders.

"Michael… your husband, is he… reliable?" he asked.

"He is to me… he's always returned home before, although in truth, I've never known from where exactly," she revealed.

Fuzz gave her a sneaky smile, and she responded with one of her own. "What does your Michael do?" he then asked, "I mean, what does he actually work at; how does he earn his crust?"

"I don't really know, in all honesty," she replied. Fuzz smiled, and she responded likewise once more.

"You mean to tell me that you've been married to this man since you were eighteen, and that you really don't know what he does for a living, is that correct?" he asked, seeking clarification.

She nodded… she felt like a stupid child who didn't know her home address.

"Do you love him?" he asked.

"Yes, very much… he looks after me, and gives me the best of everything, with no worries or problems," she replied, "until now that is."

"Nice," stated Fuzz. His reply made her laugh; actually, more than laugh, as she rocked back and forward vibrating with mirth. He joined with her; she liked this guy, he was one of the best. "Are you… in some kind of danger?" he asked.

She shrugged her shoulders, by way of response. He shrugged his in her direction, and they sat and shrugged their shoulders together, while she searched for an answer. "I don't know," she eventually replied. "I didn't feel comfortable in the apartment… the staff seemed fine, but I wasn't sure about them, and Michael told me to leave."

"Michael told you to leave? Now that is really interesting… how did he do that?" he asked.

"Well, he kind of speaks to me in my head… in my thoughts," she answered.

"Really?" he said, raising his eyebrows.

"Stop it, Fuzz, I know this all sounds ridiculous, but it's true to me, and it's all that I have to keep me from tipping over the edge," she replied.

"Sorry Prue, but at least you see the funny side, which does help," he said.

She could never call this man Billy… to her he was Fuzz, through and through. He was her Fuzz… or was he? "Are you married?" she asked. A long silence followed in which she watched him pull a face and pout his lips. "Are you... yea, or nay," she repeated, "it's a straightforward enough question?"

"She left me... that's why I'm here in this bad-land paradise. We came here because of a dodgy job I'd landed, but the firm went bust big time almost immediately, and she blamed me. One day she flew off into the sunset without warning, and I later learned that she'd filed for divorce. After a while, I managed to scrape up enough for this little palace of mine," he explained.

His tone was dull and lifeless, and all Prue wanted to do was to make it better for him. So they were both disasters; well, she supposed that was unfair on Fuzz, at least he had his own business and was not travelling light like her... with her two bags, and a useless mobile phone connected to nowhere... "Could you not have gone home, back to—?" she began to ask.

"No, I'd rather be a failure here, in this place where no one cares, instead of somewhere where people feed off the miseries of others," he interrupted.

"Thanks for being so frank with me, Fuzz," she said. They started to laugh again; the truth was that she'd never laughed so much in her life. Everything they said to each other brought a fresh smile...

"If we were musicians, we could form a trio... The Frank, Fuzz, and Prue Trio?" he suggested.

"Or maybe just Frank, Fuzz, and Prue?" she replied.

"We could always get rid of Frank as he's not been pulling his weight recently," he suggested. "I like the sound of the Fuzz and Prue Duo."

"So do I," she agreed. "Let Fuzz and Prue, play for you. Now that sounds grand."

"Are you a musician?" he asked.

"No… are you?" she countered.

"What do you think?" he replied. When they'd finished laughing, Fuzz then surprised her by changing the subject. "I live in a cabin out of town."

"Nice," she replied, "do you have a garden?"

"Yeah, of sorts. I've lived there since Sonia gave me the big elbow," he replied. "It isn't on the same planet as the Blue Ocean Apartments, but it's all I can afford. I can squeeze you in, if that's what you want… you have to leave here, you know that, as Marina's on your trail, and who knows who else? Each time the café door opens, I think it could be the *Sérénité* Police or worse. On reflection worse would be infinitely preferable."

He looked really worried, and her alarm bells flexed their muscles… if Fuzz dropped her, where would she go? She could go back to the apartment as it belonged to them, and Michael would expect her to be there when he returned. Perhaps she'd been selfish and stupid, and should have stayed put and waited for him? Why in heaven's name had she left, and come here of all places? Nothing had happened back there that she knew of, except... Michael himself had told her to leave!

When Fuzz spoke again, it was in a hushed voice, "Prue, there were men across at *The Coffee Palace* today asking about you by name. My doorman friend told me and said that they were of the menacing variety. He didn't mention anything to them about your bags, but I don't know him that well, and he might be susceptible to being squeezed sometime in the near future. You really need to leave here... you can see that can't you?"

She was relieved that it wasn't Fuzz who wanted her to go, but alarmed at the actual reason. His words injected fear into her veins... she wanted her Michael, and began to cry... Fuzz rushed, grabbed some paper towels, and she smiled a big watery thank you.

"I'm going back to the apartment," she suddenly announced. "If Michael comes back, he'll expect me to be there, so I've no option... I have to be there."

"You said, if he comes," he replied, "do you have doubts?"

"No, how dare you think that he won't come back... of course he will," she answered. "Fuzz, I'm going to phone for a taxi right now."

"Don't be so petty," he replied.

"I'm not being petty, how dare you! The sooner I'm out of here the better," she stated. She phoned for a taxi using the café pay phone, then went and shoved any items of clothing that were lying about, back into her two bags. When all zipped up, she went and sat out in the front shop, in what was now a silent, frosty atmosphere…

They never got the chance to speak to each other, to put things right between them as the taxi arrived at the toot. The taxi driver must have been hovering around the corner, or even ranked outside the café door, as it only took what seemed seconds before he was banging on the door.

Fuzz stood up, ready to carry out her bags, but she already had them organised. "Bye," she said, as she strode towards the door. Fuzz nodded, by way of response.

*

The bob of his fuzzy head was the last thing she saw, and it didn't take long before the taxi swept her up the drive towards the Blue Ocean Apartments. This island was beautiful, but also bijou!

Marcel was seated on a bench near to the entrance foyer, contemplating or simply taking in the view. On seeing her in the taxi, he rushed over to greet her, and enthusiastically took control of her luggage. She gave the driver a sweetener of a tip, and held her head aloft as she re-entered the building.

There was no one at the front desk, which was both a surprise and a relief, so she hurried Marcel into the lift. He didn't speak on their way up, which was unusual, nor would he accept a tip, after he had delivered her and her bags outside her apartment door.

She had herself to blame for that, rejecting as she had his gift… that blooming over-ripe pineapple, the one that had led her on a real humdinger of a dumb adventure.

Marcel made sure there was no one within earshot before he spoke, "*Madame* Lambasto, it is good you come home," he whispered, opening up at last. "I miss you, *Madame*."

She thanked him for his kind words, and that she'd manage her bags from here. He walked a few steps ahead along the corridor, and then swung around and returned, "*Madame*, where have you been?" he whispered. "Have you seen, *Monsieur* Lambasto?"

"Not tonight, Marcel," she replied, "not tonight… perhaps tomorrow." She put her finger across her lips, and hoped he understood the gesture.

Once the door closed behind her, she engaged the dead lock, then switched on the lamps, and checked out each of the rooms… just in case. There was no sign of Michael or of anyone else. She turned on the radio, but when she couldn't pick up a decent station, reverted to her own hi-fi for music. This breathed some much needed life into the apartment, and went some considerable way to sooth her frayed senses. In the kitchen, she filled the teapot from a boiled kettle, and a few minutes later sat hugging a mug of black tea, it being the only thing she had to hug. "Michael, come home, and never go away again… ever," she groaned, "and buy some damned milk on your way home, please."

Would he do that if she asked him... not buy her milk but not ever go away again? She'd never asked him to give it up whatever it was he did, but didn't know why? He'd led her a merry dance over the last decade, accompanied by a merry tune, and she'd willingly danced and skipped along without any words of protest.

She knew by his actions since the first day they'd met, what type of man he was, or would turn out to be... but why had he taken her on-board his ship? Perhaps he now regretted their marriage, and looked upon her as a shackle around his ankle, holding him back, and making his life unnecessarily difficult. He could fly like an eagle, whilst she was as delicate as a gold-crest, who could only flutter her tiny fledgling wings.

Prue continued to hug her mug, gripping it almost to breaking point. She then thought of Fuzz. Why had she left in such a horrible manner? What a child she was! He'd been so good to her, so kind, and yet she'd repaid his kindness by acting as a petted mare. She wished she could redo her departure and change history...

CHAPTER ELEVEN:

Early the following morning, Prue heard what sounded like a timid knock on her apartment door. When seeing who it was, she opened it. He looked at her gingerly, probably wondering if she would accept his gift? She could see from his face that a certain pineapple still weighed heavily upon his mind. However, he put his finger to his lips, in the same way as she had last night…

"Thanks, Marcel," she whispered, as she accepted his gift of a freshly baked baguette.

"You need more? Whisky… sweet bread… fruita?" he asked quietly.

"No, this is fine," she whispered, "it smells delicious. Wait Marcel, perhaps milk please… if possible?" He nodded, then slowly backed away, pressing his finger to his lips.

What was going on here? Did she not wish to be seen, and did Marcel appreciate that fact, she wondered? Does he know more than herself, which wouldn't be difficult, as she felt a prisoner in her own apartment? She slid open the door to the *terrasse*, and as it was not overlooked, decided it would be safe to venture out. On returning to grab her sunglasses, she heard another tap on her door, and was delighted to find a small container of milk looking up at her. "In you come my little friend," she whispered. "Marcel, you are an absolute star." She then made her way through to the kitchen, picked up some breakfast items, and was soon back outside again, on her favourite lounger, from where she ate breakfast.

Who were the men who were looking for her at *The Coffee Palace*? Had they been here to this building asking questions? She relaxed a little… my dear friend Marcel, might be able to shed some light on that?

*

Fuzz was upset. He'd gone home to his cabin but couldn't sleep. That crazy woman had attached herself to him as a limpet does to a rock, and as a consequence was upsetting his cosy world. Ever since Sonia had left for pastures new, he'd settled into a lifestyle of simple, uncomplicated contentment.

What a miserable farewell that had been between him and Prue! He couldn't work out who was most to blame, and concluded that they'd both behaved like kids… who was this crazy woman anyway? He jumped out of bed, fired up his computer and googled the name Lambasto. It was a strange name, but just as he thought, no one with that name appeared on his screen. He chastised himself for even thinking that the name would appear. Her and her beloved Michael... now there was one hell of a guy! What kind of man was he, living a life dodging and diving? How she'd described him, made him seem like some tango-dancing musketeer... and what kind of woman was she, who'd never asked the man questions about anything? Talk about an odd couple!

Fuzz would normally have made himself a mug of hot milk at this stage, but couldn't because he'd forgotten to bring any home. "Damn you, Prue," he yelled. She had knocked him out of kilter... he had never forgotten to bring milk home before. Notwithstanding, she was good company, he had to admit that, and cute... yes, as cute as another man's wife can be cute. He then downed a glass of water, and headed back to bed... he didn't have Marina to help in the café tomorrow, and tomorrow had already arrived.

"Christ, not now," he exclaimed, as he lashed out at the wall. Someone, a few cabins beyond, had decided to throw an impromptu party, and the heavy beat of the music throbbed in time with his aching head...

CHAPTER TWELVE:

The noise was overpowering, and then there was silence. He went to move his arms, but couldn't... he was trussed up like a parcel, and there were no people that he could see, in fact, he couldn't see anything! God, where was he... was this heaven... or was it hell? He wouldn't have expected heaven, so concluded he was in hell. Prue wouldn't join him here... of that he was certain... and also glad.

Then he heard voices, but not loud enough to overhear what was being said. This was torture... he strained with all his might, but couldn't make out the spoken words. Then the noise came again, only to fall quiet once more, apart from the indistinct voices...

Suddenly, the air changed and then he heard the distinct sound of someone breathing... "Good morning, Michael. Welcome back to the land of the living. We're extremely relieved that you live to serve us another day," said the voice. "The dressings on your eyes will come off soon, so don't you worry about that, old man."

CHAPTER THIRTEEN:

The moon shone in her bedroom window that night. It was full... an absolute round of a thing, dangling low in the sky. Its brightness awakened her, but she could not be angry as it was beautiful. Prue rose and slipped quietly out onto the *terrasse*, but did not stay long as she felt she was intruding into the domain of the creatures of the night. Whilst she could not see anything, she could sense them... out there, surrounding her in the darkness.

Once safely back indoors, she shivered and comforted herself with the thought of a mug of steaming hot cocoa, then remembered she had used the last of the milk. Surprisingly, as she rummaged around, she found a packet of biscuits in a tin... Michael must have bought them, for she hadn't. "Thanks love," she muttered, "you must have known I'd fancy a nibble."

A furtive search in the fridge, found it lacking to say the least. She said a short prayer, asking as nicely as possible, for Marcel to pop by in the morning and offer to do a shop. As there was no milk for cocoa, she decided to settle for a whisky and coke. There was plenty of whisky, but this was her last can of the other...

This wasn't going to work! She was out of her depth, alone here on this crazy island. Her thoughts turned to her mum and dad, safe and living a normal rural life down on their Somerset farm. Her eyes watered... could she perhaps phone them... and if she did, what could she say? More to the point, what would they say? She could almost anticipate with a high degree of certainty what her mum would say, "Jim, look at the map, and see where the devil she is this time." Then she would continue, "Why can't you live a normal life in a normal place, like normal everyday folks, Prue?"

The phone lay tantalisingly within arm's reach, and at this moment she could have been easily tempted! When Michael and her had first ventured to the farm to tell her folks they'd tied the knot, she remembered being told quite forcibly by her mum, how easy she was to tempt. There followed no congratulations; she didn't even say it was a surprise. Instead, all she'd received was her mum shaking her head and her dad standing silently by.

"You'll no doubt be pregnant?" she suddenly announced over lunch, and when Prue replied that she was not, this seemed a source of disappointment and annoyance.

"Can I ask why you've married in such haste?" asked her poor long suffering dad.

Prue could detect genuine interest in his eyes. "Because we love each other; is that not why people marry?" she replied, looking to Michael, who'd been gazing out the window towards the fields and beyond.

He had been taking in the conversation however, and moved to her side to support her. "Yes, we married because we love each other, and I wanted Prue to be my wife," he reiterated. "You must know how that feels?"

Her folks merely looked at them as if they lacked intellect, "Marriage is not all about love you know, you surely must've learned that with all your years of education," her dad replied, much to her surprise.

"Huh, love should be banned," added her mum.

What answer could Prue give to that statement? Even Michael, with all his charm and wit, was lost for an answer. They hurriedly finished their meal making polite inane conversation, and as soon as they'd finished, they left...

*

Six months later, after no further contact with her parents, Prue, out of the blue received an invitation to a family wedding, which her mum had forwarded to Cambridge. Her cousin June was seemingly marrying a delightfully suitable young man, who was established in a local law firm, and could well afford to get married. Her mum finished her covering note with the hope that

67

Prue would attend the wedding on her own, which would enable her to have a much overdue private word!

Michael laughed when she showed him the invitation and covering letter; his reaction demonstrated to Prue that her parents views, were of no consequence to him. As a result she made no attempt to attend, and her cousin's nuptials slipped by without further mention.

Two and a bit years later, and true to form, her parents consented to attend Prue's graduation ceremony; but declined an invitation to attend Michael's. His was a happy affair, whilst hers was melancholic.

Prue had met Michael's parents not long after they married. Mr and Mrs Lambasto senior had been visiting Cambridge for the day, and asked them to join them for lunch. They were pleasant enough, although somewhat detached. The following Christmas, saw them invited for dinner at Michael's family home. Prue, who had been dreading the occasion, stuck close to him, doing her best not let her surroundings overwhelm her.

"That was well done," commented Michael, turning to smile at her as they drove home. She didn't reply, but simply smiled in return, relieved that no overnight stay had been arranged.

*

Prue decided that one whisky was more than enough, and retired to her lonely bed. She did not reach for the receiver to call her folks, deciding to leave that for another day. Next morning she waited and waited, but Marcel did not knock as she had hoped, so she gave up and took herself out onto the *terrasse*, subconsciously stooping behind the expanse of greenery.

She hadn't long taken a seat when she heard a familiar voice being carried upwards on the warm ocean breeze... "*Madame*... later... I come later, *Madame*..." wafted Marcel's voice.

She hastily scribbled a shopping list in her best large print, and waited. Eventually, she detected the lightest of taps on her door. It was Marcel. She threw the door open, and thrust the list into his hand. He looked puzzled. "*Madame,* I no read," he whispered.

"Come in, Marcel, you have to come in," she whispered back.

After furtively checking around, he stepped gingerly inside. Once in the hallway, he stood, feet apparently nailed to the floor. He shook his head when asked to come into the lounge... "*Madame* say," he said, "and I know..."

She took that to mean he'd remember by heart, and so reeled off her list of needs. "It will cost money... cash, dollars," she added.

"Sorry," he replied, "I have no the money... I no good help you."

Marcel you are a good man, she thought, as she handed him more than enough cash for the items on the list. After carefully counting it, he stuffed it into his jacket pocket. No problem with his arithmetic, she thought, with a wry smile.

"You look *Madame,* please," he said, pointing with two fingers to his eyes. "I bring when I come." Prue opened the door, checked no one was around, and he slipped back out into the corridor, and disappeared from view. As she re-closed the door, a thought struck her. She would soon run out of cash, and doubted if Marcel would be able to deal with any other form of payment.

Fuzz also floated through her mind, and she wondered if he'd thought about her? The café did have the phone installed, the problem was that she didn't know its actual name, as it didn't have any sign on view. Then she had an idea, so she looked up *The Coffee Palace*, called and asked if they could give her the phone number of the little café opposite?

"Do you mean Fuzz's place?" asked the girl who answered.

"Yes," she replied.

"Just hold on, please don't hang up, I'm going to fetch him," she said.

Prue was surprised to say the least, and it seemed an age before she heard a familiar voice boom across the wire. "Hi, who is it?" he asked.

"It's me, Fuzz... I need your help, and can't leave my apartment," she replied.

"For God's sake, Prue, I've had to leave the café to its own devices… you know Marina's still on holiday," he stated, "why not just phone me at the café?"

"I would have, if I'd known the number," she stated.

He thankfully obliged, and asked her to phone him there.

"Anything else I can help you with?" asked the girl, probably sarcastically, but perhaps not?

"No," Prue replied, "but thanks for your help; it was very much appreciated."

She then made herself comfortable before calling the café. He answered quickly enough, but then asked her to hang on until there was a break in the demands of his clamouring customers. She did as bade, and hung on contentedly listening to the comforting hubbub of voices in the background, punctuated by the clanking of dishes. He then came back on the line, and asked her to phone back at four, which was when he began his clearing up operation, and preparations for the following day.

Prue got the distinct impression he thought she ought to have known to call at such a time… which she probably did, and now would have to be extra nice, if she was going to have any chance of redeeming herself!

*

71

Marcel hadn't returned by four, which was worrying, so when she comforted herself by phoning Fuzz, found that they were somewhat reserved with each other at first... "Any news of... Michael?" he asked.

"No, but I found a half opened packet of biscuits he'd bought," she replied.

"That sounds impressive," he stated.

"I don't know why I told you that," she responded.

"It's all right, I understand how your mind works," he said, failing to conceal a giggle.

"That's good to know," she replied.

"Come on, tell Fuzz all," he said, and so she did.

It felt much better now, as she'd managed to unburden herself, although probably by doing so had over-burdened him. When he told her not to worry, and that it would all work out, she had no other choice but to believe.

*

At around five, there was a familiar light tapping sound on her apartment door, and on looking through the spy-hole, found nobody there. After waiting a short time spying and listening, she tentatively unlocked the door to find a solitary bag standing to attention in the hallway. Checking to see if anyone was around, which there was not, she whisked it indoors, and with the door re-secured, checked its contents. It was stuffed with all her requested items, plus a few extras for good measure. "Thank you my dear friend," she muttered, as she carried the goodies through into the kitchen.

*

During her earlier conversation on the phone, Fuzz had asked her back to the café. However, in order to achieve this, she would need Marcel's help. Nobody, but Marcel knew she was presently encamped in her own apartment, and it would be best to remain that way. Fuzz had also advised, she ought to leave without too much delay, and she knew he was right, as strange men could come looking for her there, or even the *Sérénité* police! She was a fugitive... only she had no idea what she had done, and this bizarre situation prompted a giggle...

"Get serious girl," she told herself sternly.

"That's going to be mighty hard to do," she replied.

"Don't be such a wimp," she ventured.

"Why? I like being a wimp," she replied.

"Grow up, Prue," she concluded, as she terminated this one-sided conversation...

She looked around her prison; it was very pleasant, particularly the *terrasse*. She slid the door open, and sneaked outside. There was one large palm tree that she could hide behind, which would afford her an excellent view of the concourse below. As she made her way over, she muttered... "Michael, Michael, please guide me out of here! This kind of situation is your forte, not mine... give me a clue, at least."

The sudden sound of a car door being slammed far below caught her attention. Peering over the parapet, she saw a police car, with two burly officers standing alongside. "Michael, I asked for a clue, not a blooming shock-wave! For God's sake, guide me please," she mouthed into the prevailing breeze, as she ran back indoors. Grabbing her pre-packed bag containing passport, papers, cards, and the little cash she'd left over, she exited the apartment remembering to snatch her lightweight jacket from the hall peg...

Had they come for her? Better to decide that they had, and get a move on... which way... right or left? Being left-handed, she decided left, as midway along the corridor there was a door, with steps which she had always believed led down to the staff quarters. However, when she switched on the light, she saw it was actually a cupboard, stuffed with cleaning products, and towels. She was about to leave, when the sound of the lift being operated, and heavy footsteps echoing in the stairwell a few floors below, struck fear into her heart.

They were closing in with every step... with one hasty glance, she tried to memorise where things were in the cupboard, switched off the light, then squeezed herself behind a large trolley, before carefully moving a few items in an attempt to conceal herself. She was not at all comfortable, but it was more important to concentrate on the fast developing situation outside, not her comfort. Scarcely daring to breathe, she heard the doors of the lift open, followed by voices and tried to count the approaching footsteps... there were exactly ten!

"Chief, this door's not locked," said a loud voice.

"That guy downstairs said she was a whimsy little floozy, I'll second that. Can't even remember to lock own her ruddy door," replied the Chief.

Their voices disappeared, and she knew where they'd gone. It pained her to think of them in her flat, touching her and Michael's things... their mementoes, gifts, and the special little items that had no value to anyone except for them alone...

The sounds of footsteps on the stairwell were getting ever closer. She had not been in the habit of walking up all these flights herself, being that they lived on the uppermost floor of the building. Michael however was well acquainted, and would run up and down them every day for exercise.

Judging by the footsteps and their chat, it sounded like two people... then it went silent as the chatting stopped... one may have gone into the apartment to speak with the others, but one had certainly remained in the corridor as he began to whistle...

Prue closed her eyes; she was so afraid, and imagined the blood draining from her brain... just stay put, don't move she urged, groping around in the blackness until her hand came into contact with a wall socket and plug. With no obvious power switch, she traced the cable from it with her hands... where did it go? There was a slim chance it might lead to the makeshift overhead light, so she wrenched the plug out and waited with bated breath…

The whistling had now stopped, and she toyed with the idea of making a run for the stairs… but stopped when she detected the distinctive pungent smell of a cigar, or an extra strong cigarette… and a rasping cough confirmed he was still present. Footsteps began to come her way and the door was suddenly yanked open… thank goodness for the dim, ambient lighting in the corridor… the light switch was flicked up and down, but to no avail, so the door was slammed shut… by now, she had all but lost her ability to breathe…

"Check every room on this damned corridor," a voice instructed.

"What are we looking for, Chief?" asked another.

"Don't be so fuckin' smart with me, or you'll find yourself back picking crops in the fields," replied the Chief. "You know damned well who we're looking for… his damned bit of skirt. Once you're done, get down to the next floor, and check there. And don't use the fuckin' lift, take the fuckin' stairs… I'm not encouraging your damned laziness."

The clunk of footsteps resounded on the marble stairs, initially sounding like thunder-claps but then faded like distant drums... "What a pair of fuckin' no hopers you've got there. How did we land up with them in tow?" remarked the Chief. "George, it's your job to surround me with a team of hard men... men with brawn and a brain in their heads."

"I'll sort it, Chief. These guys came recommended by Jean-Paul Baston," replied George.

"Baston the bastard... I should've known," responded the Chief.

They were now on the move... coming ever closer. Footsteps stopped outside the cupboard for a second time, the door jerked open and the light switch tried once again. The staccato clicking on-off, on-off, on-off, punctuated the gloom. "What kind of top-notch apartment is this anyway? They can't even manage to change the fuckin' light bulbs?" remarked George.

"One that accommodates the dross... the dregs and those monied bastards who have no loyalty to anything or anyone other than to themselves," replied the Chief.

Slamming the door shut was their final act; and then the voices faded, along with their footsteps... until all fell silent once more...

*

Absolutely stunned by their words, it took a moment before she had the courage to wriggle in an attempt to make herself more comfortable. She'd never heard such derogatory words before, and the shock that they were being used to describe her and Michael, wrenched at her very core. Michael, dross with no loyalty, how dare they! Her, a whimsy floozy... was that really how she came across to others? Okay, it may be true that she'd lived all her married life cosseted from the harshness of the outside world, so perhaps she was everything they'd called her? But no more... that had been a short sharp reality shock, and from which the will to change everything in her life was born.

Her thoughts returned to the here and now, and her predicament hit home... no more would she ask Michael... no, from now on she would have to take care of herself.

All was now quiet in the corridor, but she decided to stay put for as long as possible. She then started to silently sob, as was her habit... "Grow up," she muttered, then crossed her arms, and squeezed her body as hard as she could, in an effort to force circulation and feeling back into her numb limbs. This made her feel foolish, and didn't stop her tears... then she heard a noise in the corridor, which made her tears freeze...

"*Madame, Madame,*" said a soft voice. Was it him? She concentrated... "*Madame, Madame...,*" the voice repeated. She was tempted, but didn't succumb, instead, squashed herself down as far as she could; something wasn't right about the voice, although she didn't know quite what? The calling out may not have lasted long, but her waiting did... suddenly, and without warning, her world was consumed by an inky blackness...

When she awoke, some hours may or may not have slipped past... but she couldn't hazard a guess which... perhaps it had only been minutes? Sore, and barely able to move, she found her feet to be a combination of numbness mixed with pins and needles.

Nevertheless she persevered, and managed to grope for the door handle... slowly, ever so slowly she turned it and tentatively pushed the door ajar. If anyone was still in the corridor the game was well and truly over, but she didn't know what else she could do?

It was difficult to judge the time, as the light in the corridor shone with the same eerie glow irrespective of whether it was night or day. Time didn't matter anyway, the main thing was that no one was around, so she took her chance and slowly limped back to her apartment. What a stroke of luck, she wasn't the only oaf who hadn't locked the door... so she slipped inside, cranked shut the dead lock, and gingerly pushed open the door leading to the bedroom...

Whoever these men were, they had made a mess; even the bedsheets had been pulled back, Michael's clothes lay sad and scattered across the floor, yet her things hadn't been touched? Who and what had they been looking for?

Where to now? She chose the kitchen... things had been messed around in there too, but they hadn't touched the bag of provisions Marcel had brought.

To quench her thirst and feed her hunger was her first priority... it was too late to phone Fuzz, as the café would now be closed. She had stupidly never acquired his mobile number, which was unforgivably remiss on her part. She forgave herself, and tried to think out of the box... whatever that meant exactly?

As she helped herself from Marcel's bag, she remembered about that voice in the corridor, the one she thought might have been his... had it been him? She just didn't know, and that gave her the creeps. She decided that she now had to rely on her own wit and was not going to hang around the apartment any longer!

She had access to the lift, which was only ten of her steps from the apartment door; it could either go up or down. Why go up, unless for a swim? There were fire escapes from there, and also from her own *terrasse*... but she was no James Bond, and the thought of having to use the fire escape had always filled her with trepidation. There would be no *'Body found at bottom of fire escape'* headlines in tomorrow's local rag if she could help it. A better idea... and a more simple solution was to boldly walk out of this apartment block...

Prue headed for the bathroom and emerged a short time later a changed woman... it was the best she could do in the circumstances. Raking around, she found some items of clothing she'd never worn... nothing too bright, but not too dowdy either... a French blue jump suit came to hand. She could wear that together with her plimsoles, as she would need to walk into town. Thank goodness, it was not too far...

Into her backpack, which already contained her personal items and a little cash, she added some of life's other little necessities. Then over a cup of hastily brewed coffee, she pondered what time it would be best to leave? Her decision was made by the time she had drained her cup; she would leave shortly after breakfast the following morning when there were lots of people milling around downstairs. She then considered picking up a taxi outside, but decided it best to revert to her original plan, and walk...

Nervousness was not a strong enough word for what she felt. She tried on a pair of dangly earrings, after managing to find the long lost piercings in her earlobes. Now if she spiked her now cropped hair with gel to accentuate the change in her appearance, even Michael would probably walk past without recognising her... well, perhaps not? She re-checked herself once more in the mirror, shocked that she was going to venture outdoors without her waterproof mascara; how long had it been since she had done that? Yes, she was confident she could walk past herself, after viewing the reflection of this stranger in the mirror...

CHAPTER FOURTEEN:

By half past seven the following morning, she was washed, dressed and ready to go. She brewed herself a final strong black coffee to help calm her nerves, then picked up one of Michael's cigarettes. Never having smoked before in her life, she quickly decided to refrain. Opening the doors to the *terrasse*, she slipped out to breathe the scented morning air. She loved this place; it was her oasis, and the weather... perfect as usual, made for another lovely day in the paradise that was this godforsaken island.

Just before eight, dressed in her jumpsuit and with her backpack secured, she headed out, leaving the door unlocked just as she had found it yesterday. Once into the lift, she managed to reach Reception without anyone recognising her. The lift had stopped at most floors collecting passengers, which including a guy she and Michael had spoken to on many occasions. He smiled in a way he wouldn't have, had he realised who it was. Prue found his lack of recognition reassuring...

She could see Marcel, standing waiting to carry luggage or any other items out to the various resident's vehicles. He glanced her way in the passing, but didn't appear to recognise her as she continued to drift along in time with the others. Her group was about to reach the steps that led to the revolving door, when she heard a voice call... "*Madame, Madame.*"

Prue momentarily froze... "*Madame,* mind steps, *s'il vous plaît,*" called out the instantly recognisable voice.

"*Merci,*" she replied, without turning around.

Once outdoors and in the sweet fresh air, she made her way along the pedestrian path, whilst most other folks headed for the car park. She could not help but admire the flowers and lush shrubbery... so manicured, so perfect. The outside world was now in view, and when she reached the wrought iron gates, she was a free woman, but had paid a hefty price for that lift ride to freedom!

Her legs gave a jelly like wobble at first, but soon steadied, allowing her to launch into a confident swagger. The magnificent turquoise ocean ahead beckoned, as she headed in its direction. Leaving the tarmac behind to follow a more discrete sandy path, she pulled off her plimsoles and carried them. Never had she felt such a feeling of freedom as she did at that moment, and her pace quickened as she hurried towards the ocean...

All around, the sandy bay stretched out in a semi-circle, and in its midst stood the centre of the little town with its central Square and harbour. She rubbed the sand from the soles of her shoes and slipped them into her backpack, leaving her hands free to dip in the clear waters. Her feet were now submerged and with cupped hands, splashed the salty water onto her face, arms and neck. This place was without doubt paradisal, or it would have been if it had not been for… she paused and thought of Michael… he had not been living within her head recently, which was unusual. She did not have time to consider why as her main objective was to reach the safety of the café… and Fuzz.

It was not far to the central Square, as the town was of doll's house proportions. After lingering for a short time on an old jetty, drying her feet in the warmth of the early morning sunshine, she continued towards the edge of the town Square. Beside the small harbour, Prue took a seat at a makeshift milk-bar, checked what little cash she still had, and ordered herself the luxury of a vanilla shake with extra ice. From here she could view the world that was this place in reasonable comfort.

Fuzz's little café bar was open; it sat surrounded and overshadowed by its glitzy bigger siblings. He'd done well to build up such a regular clientele despite the competition. Just then, a police car circled before pulling up at an adjacent waterside café. The two occupants demanded coffees from the owner, then lit their obligatory cigarettes. She had no reason to think they would pay her any attention, but nevertheless found their unwanted presence a strain. There was a sun shade at her table, and although still early, she angled it to shield her from their view. Just sit tight, and observe, she told herself. It might take some time, but she reckoned she could master this taking-care-of-herself lark. The two officers were thankfully soon on their way to deal with whatever deviousness they had up their rolled up sleeves that day. This was her signal to make her way to Fuzz's.

She could hear the aged air-conditioning unit from the café, struggling to cope above her head, as she peered in through the window. It was busy inside, in fact busy enough for him not to turn as she creaked the door open. Her eyes were drawn to a lone vacant table set against a far wall. This required her to squeeze past a number of other occupied tables. Once there, she struggled off her backpack, which in such a small space was duly noted and felt by those seated nearby.

"On holiday dear, are we?" asked one of the old colonial ladies, who'd probably found herself abandoned on this island after the flag had been pulled down.

"Something like that," she answered. "What about yourself?"

"Oh, no dear, I live here," she replied.

"There are a few of us who stayed on," added another, "you know… after the—,"

"Do you like living here?" interrupted Prue.

"We make do, but it's not like the old days," added a third.

"Why, what's changed?" asked Prue.

"Oh, absolutely everything, dear," replied the second lady.

"You have no idea. Back then, well it was... more civilised," whispered the first old dear.

"Never mind, the good old days may yet return, and you do have the lovely weather as compensation," replied Prue.

"Can I get you anything, Miss?" he asked, without looking at her.

"Can I give you any help?" she replied.

"*Je suis désolé?*" he answered, as he swung around.

Lifting her backpack high above her head, she squeezed past to the serving side of the counter, where she immediately donned an apron, pecked him on the cheek, and whispered in his ear, "It's me, Fuzz, and with no Marina today, you're in much need of my help."

"Stand there and do the drinks for me. I don't think my hand would be steady enough to pour, after the shock you've just given me," he whispered. "Good to see you, but for goodness sake Prue, it's a bit drastic, is it not?"

"What's done is done," she replied, "what do you think... of the main event?"

"I'll tell you later, when I'm over the shock," he replied, with a shake of the head.

For the rest of the morning, Prue busied herself behind the counter, with one eye on her task and the other watching him, as he moved around his domain charming his customers. She could see the colonial ladies adored him. Perhaps he reminded them of an old-time *beau*, or perhaps the son they would've loved and treasured? Whatever it was, he had them firmly under his spell.

The café experienced a quiet spell at around eleven-thirty, and as they sat at a table for their break, he examined her... "Well, what do you think?" she asked.

"Couldn't you have just covered it up with a head scarf," he countered, "or something like that?"

"What? Oh, I see what you mean. I never thought of doing that," she replied.

"You're a danger to yourself," he stated.

"Thank you very much, my friend," she replied, "for having such confidence in me."

"Prue, at least you got here in one piece... and it is growing on me," he said, with a grin.

"I wish it would grow on me too, but it's going to take a fair bit of time to do that," she replied. "Of course, I'll need to get it tidied up by a proper hairdresser. I just gave it what people would call a rough chop."

"You look lovely, even with your rough chop, so stop fishing for compliments," stated Fuzz.

"I wasn't fishing for anything," she protested, "unless there's a spot of lunch going spare?"

"You just sit where you are and allow me to serve you," he joked. "You've been in the wars, and have had a bit of a hairy time!"

She smiled, and he brushed against her hand with his, as he rose. She didn't know what would happen next, but she knew she no longer felt alone.

CHAPTER FIFTEEN:

"Where the devil—," he asked...

"You're safe, Michael, that's all that matters," came the curt reply.

"But what about my wife, Sir?" he asked, turning to face the voice.

"I'm sorry, it can't go on... this marriage of yours. This dragging her from place to place must end. Let her go... let her get a life of her own," came back the dispassionate reply. "I'll leave you to think it over... but think long and hard. If you love her, let her go."

*

When closing time arrived, they stopped working, and put up the 'closed' sign. "What the devil do I do with you now?" asked a puzzled Fuzz.

"You decide; I was invited here, so I'll leave it up to you," she replied.

"I told you to leave your apartment... I didn't invite you here," he protested, then saw her happy expression evaporate, and hurriedly came to her rescue... "Only joking... where else would I expect you to go, but here?"

Her happy expression returned... she was easy to please, he thought, she is indeed a naive young woman, trusting and loving... especially if her loyalty to this Michael bloke is anything to go by? Fuzz wanted to hold her close, but resisted the temptation.

"Prue, I live in a cabin out on the Green Plantation Road site," he continued, "way out beyond the outskirts of town on the coast road."

"Is that good?" she asked.

"Probably not; it will be a shock to your system if I take you there," he replied.

"It takes a lot to shock a system like mine," she answered. "Living with and keeping up with Michael has never been a picnic."

"Okay, I'll take you... if you're sure?" he agreed. She merely laughed in reply, and gave him a delicious smile.

Once they'd cleared up and prepared for the next day's business, they went out to the backyard, where stood his trusty old Vespa. "Are you game enough to sit behind me on this?" he asked, pointing to his mechanical steed.

"Michael's trained me for most things, so that isn't a problem my friend," she replied. And it was true; she was an excellent pillion passenger, and also fast becoming an enigma.

When they reached the cabin, he expected her to show disapproval, but on the contrary, she found it cute. Once inside, she looked around, and didn't display any signs of dismay at its small dimensions or dowdy appearance. "I'll soon brighten this place up for you," she announced. "Have you any land out the back?"

"A fair bit, although I haven't done anything with it. Most folks here have fruit and veggies growing, and some even have flowers, but I haven't bothered," he replied.

"Well, I can sort that out for you as well," she announced.

"You? You're an upmarket woman, not a peasant farmer," he replied.

"I'm a farmer's daughter, not quite a peasant but not far off, and for your information, I have the land in my blood. I didn't think I had until now, as I feel it pulsating through my veins at the very thought of your plot," she announced, wrenching open the back door to survey the land. "My, it's almost the size of a small holding at home."

Fuzz looked at her with wonder. He didn't know much about her, but in this moment wanted to know everything. He disappeared into his bedroom, while Prue remained outside assessing the plot's viability. She could see it all in her mind's eye; how she would divvy things up for maximum yield and efficiency. Prue laughed to find herself so enthused with a fallow, hitherto neglected patch of scrub land covered in rough grasses.

*

Stood in his only bedroom, Fuzz was at a loss as what to do as he'd only one set of bed sheets? He intended giving Prue the bedroom, but his sheets had reached the stage when they were way past needing washed.

Prue stepped back inside all excited, only to find him with a face which resembled that of a naughty little boy. "What's wrong?" she asked, and when he explained his dilemma, she made a sympathetic face, "Poor Fuzz, please don't take it so hard... leave it to me," she responded and went back outdoors where she looked at the adjacent plots. She then left by the front, and walked past three of the cabins, before knocking on the door of the next, where she introduced herself to the occupier.

The neighbour, a large woman, wasn't slow at inviting Prue inside, and after hearing of Fuzz's dilemma, could only laugh at his predicament. "Him be a nice man that Fuzz, but he be a man on his own," she stated. "Fuzz be in need of a good woman... that be what Bernice thinks."

Shortly afterwards, Prue left with an armful of clean sheets. "You bring them back to me for the washing after you done sleepin' in them, Prudence," she called after her, "bring me his dirty ones now, and I'll boil-wash them for the boy."

"I will, and thanks, Bernice," she replied.

"How did you do that?" asked Fuzz, on her return.

"By asking nicely," she replied. "You have such nice understanding neighbours, or at least Bernice is."

"They're all good folks, but why Bernice?" he asked. "How did you know she's our best laundry lady?"

"Well, I looked for someone who had lots of washing hanging out to dry, but it was too late in the day for that," replied Prue, "so, I looked for the cabin with the most area given over to drying clothes."

"I would never have thought of that," said a stunned Fuzz

"Just you leave it all to me, I'll look after you, my boy," she replied. "Bernice agrees, as she's of the mind that you need looking after."

Prue stripped the bed, replacing them with the clean sheets. She then gathered up the soiled laundry, plus a plate of café leftovers that Fuzz had brought home, and was about to return to Bernice's, when she also lifted a bottle of soda from a rack in the small kitchen annex. "Payment, for her work," she explained to him as she left.

"Good idea," he replied. "I'd never have thought of that either. I might have thought of the leftovers, but not the soda. That will certainly be a shock to Bernice's system!"

Prue didn't follow his meaning, and merely shrugged her shoulders. When she returned, she brought with her a bottle of Bernice's homemade wine, which they later sat on the back step to enjoy. "I like it very much," he muttered.

"What," she asked, "the wine?"

"No, what I mean is that I do like the wine, but I was talking about your hair," he replied. "Long or short, I think it's lovely."

"Michael liked my hair long," announced Prue, and that comment served to end their pleasant conversation as far as Fuzz was concerned, as she began to witter on about Michael, his likes and dislikes, whilst he allowed his mind wander…

"Prue, I think it best if you stay here… at least for the time being. I can manage the café on my own. It's just a few days until Marina returns from holiday… what do you think?" he asked.

"Fine, as long as I can get on and change some things around here," she replied.

"That's fine by me… do whatever you want. I will have a listen on the vine to see if anyone's still on your trail. Mind you, you may have been reported as a missing person by now… I'll no doubt hear from one source or another," said Fuzz.

"I don't have a problem with staying safe; but I think it's all to do with Michael," she replied. "I think it's him they're after, whoever they are, and not me?"

"So do I," he agreed.

"So do I, what?" asked Prue.

"Think it's all got to do with that husband of yours," he answered. He sounds like a right pain in the butt, he thought.

"Right, let's make ourselves some toast and milk, and then we can turn in. I'm whacked," replied Prue. "Fuzz, thanks for everything, you're the only one I have that cares about me, except for Michael of course."

Bloody Saint Michael, thought Fuzz, where's the rat when she needs him?

Prue handed him a fresh sheet, and he looked at her with a bemused expression? "If you want, we can share your bed. Just wrap yourself in the sheet, and keep to your own side," she suggested.

He nodded at her with a wry smile… well, that's me told… my own side of my bed, he mused, at least it's not on the floor, which was where he thought he was heading. At the very least he would get a comfortable night's sleep, that's if sleep was an option with her lying alongside…

CHAPTER SIXTEEN:

The next morning they were both up early, and Fuzz scurried off on his scooter to open for business. After he'd left, Prue managed to give herself a full body wash, and then dress into her only change of clothes, before venturing outdoors. She was certainly not alone, as she found most folks around didn't appear to have jobs. They moseyed along, cultivating fruit and vegetables, keeping the obligatory hens, and supplementing living costs with whatever opportunities came their way.

Prue picked up a rusty spade from the back door to test the ground for hardness, whereupon it sprung back against her leg, "Ouch, damn it!" she shrieked.

A man, who was sitting on the back doorstep of the adjacent cabin, laughed loudly, and although her eyes watered, she soon joined with him in laughter. "You tryin' to dig over Fuzz's plot, little lady?" the man asked.

"I'm trying," she replied, still laughing, "but it's going to be a tough ask."

He stepped over the low border fence to join her, then shouted something over to another couple of neighbouring men. She couldn't understand... no matter... for whatever it was, they jumped the wooden fence to join them...

"Give them pretty sticks of yours a rest, little lady, and we'll... wait little lady, I be wonderin'... does Fuzz be wantin' his whole plot worked," asked the neighbour, "he ain't never lifted no tools before?"

"Marlon, this here is Prudence... she be here to look after our Fuzz, so you men mind your words and take good note of what she says," called over Bernice. "You give my friend Prudence respect now."

"Right you are, Bernice, we gets the message clear like," replied Marlon.

Prue waved her thanks to Bernice... good choice of friend, she thought, as she seems like a powerful woman in these parts. She then sat back on the doorstep to watch as the men began to flex their muscles. They dug, in what almost seemed like a competition, with each turning occasionally to see how much the other had managed, and if Prue was watching. Prue knew their wives would no doubt be around, and didn't want any problems, so went indoors to have a good look around.

The living room was okay, although it could do with some colour... just a few splashes here and there. The washroom however, left much to be desired and she decided she would start by giving it a God Almighty bleach and scrub. Fuzz was in dire need of some cleanliness lessons, and the bed sheets she'd taken last night to Bernice had been an absolute disgrace; they could almost have walked on their own filthy little legs...

Her thoughts then turned to Michael... in contrast, he could go by the name of 'Mr Clean', or even 'Lord Squeaky Clean' as he smelled divine and always looked hot. Tidiness to him was of paramount importance, and she knew what he'd think of her being here. This was certainly not his kind of place. Nevertheless, she felt nothing at the moment, only acceptance of how it was. Indeed, she felt exhilarated as she looked outside to see how the 'big dig' was progressing. If the truth were told, it was going rather slower than expected, so she fetched a few sodas from the cool box, and delivered them to her troops, together with some words of extra encouragement.

"Little lady, you knows do you, this not be the season to be doing this diggin'?" remarked one of the men, as he took a swig from the bottle.

"No, I never realised that. Are you telling me you can't manage?" she asked.

"Well, no... but only' cause you be in luck and have us. There be few other men on this here island who could do this job for you," answered Marlon.

"For Fuzz, not me," corrected Prue.

"Ah yes, girlie, I was meanin' for Fuzz," he agreed, which prompted Bernice to let out a mammoth howl of laughter, causing Marlon to blush through his dark weather-beaten skin.

Prue then made her way back indoors to keep out of the way. She was keen to sort out the washroom… aided with an almighty bucket of bleach and a bristle brush. She cleaned and flushed until it eventually cried submission! It had been a long time since she'd felt this good… she had done something so basic, and yet so rewarding.

"Hi there, little lady, it's me here. We men be goin' to fetch us somethin' to eat, and then havin' ourselves some shut-eye," called Marlon in through the open back door. "What you be doing, Missy Prudence? Have you been usin' that bug killin' stuff, 'stead of soap? I never smells me the likes."

Prue made her way to the door, "It's like what Bernice said, Marlon. I'm here to look after Fuzz, and one thing that desperately needed looking after was his washroom… which is fixed now," she replied. "How's the 'big dig' coming along?"

"The 'big dig' as you say, is goin' real good… tell Fuzz and don't you be a worryin'… we'll be back tomorrow to finish what we started," he replied.

"How much do I owe you?" she asked, "I mean, how much does Fuzz owe you?"

"In this place, we don't use many buck bills, or even that clinkin' stuff. We all knows what we each owe, and we all owe Fuzz aplenty," he replied.

"Okay Marlon, thank you for this morning's work; it's looking really good out there," said Prue. "See you tomorrow."

She went back indoors, and checked out the kitchen. There was hardly any food in the cupboards... but it was clean and tidy enough, thank goodness, just empty. Prue moved an upturned box, so she could sit where she could benefit from the cool breeze, and wondered what she ought to do next? It wasn't that she wasn't used to occupying her own time, God knows, she'd sat on her own many, many, times over her ten years of marriage to Michael... but not in these kind of surroundings.

After a while, she rose and went back outside, where she looked up and down the neighbouring plots. They stood silent; everyone having gone indoors for their dose of shut-eye, and she was about to do likewise, when Bernice appeared with a basket of freshly laundered clothing. She waved, motioning for her to come along to her cabin. Prue decided to take what little cash she had, to offer payment for the laundering, as she'd nothing else to use in this bartering game.

"You be puttin that away. I hope Marlon didn't take any of your bucks. We have our own rules here... we share not take," announced Bernice. She then handed Prue her sheets, which looked and smelled as good as new. "This is what I do, Prudence... this is my role; you'll find that you'll get one too, that's if you hang around long enough. You be either passin' through or you be one of us... which are you, my friend?"

"I don't quite know, Bernice. Yesterday, I never even knew this place existed," replied Prue.

"You look fresh tanned, my girl. Where you from? No don't go tellin' me; it be better I don't know. If Fuzz bring you here, he judge you as bein' okay," stated Bernice. "I do likes you girl, you be fresh... different like. Good work too, gettin' that lazy Marlon to dig your plot." She then roared with laughter, "This ain't no season for the diggin'... they're just the show-off kind, takin' on a hard dig to impress a pretty lady."

Bernice laughed loudly again, and slapped two glasses down onto the table, "We'll have ourselves a drink to that, Prudence child," she continued. "That be one real good move you made on our Marlon. That makes me laugh, yes, I really likes that. Now drink up, my glass be needin' fillin' already."

Here we go, thought Prue... how do I get out of this, without causing any unnecessary offence? This woman will drink me under the table, if I let her ply me with whatever's in that bottle? She looked around the room, and in the corner saw a harvest of bottles stacked up in a bumper crop pile... and the last thing she heard was Bernice... "Drink up Prudence, let's have a few before we nap..."

Her head began to swim... and when she awoke she found herself in bed in Fuzz's cabin. How she'd got there, she had no idea?

CHAPTER SEVENTEEN:

Michael's head was full of Prue. Not only was he confined to bed, supposedly to aid his recovery, but he'd received orders from the very top... to let her go. That was the establishment trying to be understanding, which in no way came natural to these pen pushing bastards. They were bloody-minded, dictatorial hard-nuts, but then he remembered... they were his bloody-minded, hard-nutted bastards...

That day when he'd first met Prue, he knew she was the one for him... the special one, and he knew what he had to do to keep her. He had to get married before anyone talked sense into the gap between his young ears. With the deed quickly done, what could they do? It was discouraged to form strong attachments to anyone; he'd always known that, but by marrying her so young, he thought he had found the perfect way around that situation...

It had been fine when they were at Cambridge, where they'd been so happy. However, once they'd left, and he'd begun to go on missions, it had torn at his heartstrings every time he had to leave her... and that had been on far too many occasions. She'd wanted children but that could never happen, or at least not until he was finished, washed up, or plain burnt-out. By then it would probably be too late anyway. Poor Prue, he'd inflicted his lifestyle upon her with all its rules and limitations, something which he had no right to have done. In essence, he'd been a bloody, selfish bastard...

The door suddenly swung open, and in he came once again... the very top of the tree. It had surprised Michael of the level of interest being shown in him, but the stark realisation soon struck that as they'd ploughed so much time and money into him, they did not want their investment to flounder. He was one of their most valuable assets, and in truth, he would not have it any other way...

"Well, Michael, it might surprise you to know that I'm not without feelings... but I always manage to rise above them for the common good," stated Sir. "Have you come to a decision? Are you going to let that little lady of yours have a life of her own, and allow you to concentrate fully on your tasks?"

For a brief moment... a still silence ruled...

"What news do you want to deliver to her? That I'm dead... is that to be my demise?" asked Michael.

"No, my boy, nothing quite so drastic; just missing... presumed dead... doing his duty for Queen, Country, and all the rest," replied Sir.

"And what if she re-marries, and I'm still alive?" he asked.

"But to her you would be dead; you surely would not risk causing an upset by popping up again... that would be cruel... and we could always come up with some evidence to support your untimely demise. Better to let the little lady down gently, before we crush your pod so to speak... you know I'm right, don't you?" replied Sir.

Michael didn't answer with words, but found himself agreeing... while at the same time using all his strength to hold back his tears.

The door closed as abruptly as it had opened, and he lay back on his pillow with the darkest of clouds bearing down upon him.

*

Fuzz arrived home to find Bernice sitting on his back step talking with some neighbours. What the devil's going on here, he thought? "Is something up, Bernice?" he asked.

"Prudence fainted before I could do anything, Fuzz. We be doin' fine, her and me... we just be talkin'... that kinda thing. I went to give her a drink of hooch, and she goes and hits the floor before it even reached her pretty lips," she replied.

"What... how is she," he asked, "and where?"

"She be lyin' on your bed, Fuzz... sleepin' like a new born," replied Bernice. "The folks 'round here were making their usual jokes, until I puts my hand up and told them to stop. I told them not to mouth out about my friend Prudence. I told them to mind my words, and leave well alone."

Fuzz shook his head in disbelief as he entered his bedroom where she lay under a sheet, sound asleep. He immediately began to worry in case she may have concussed herself... if she had, what should he do? Did he need to get her to hospital? He didn't want her to go there or anywhere... he wanted to keep her safe... but what had made her faint? "Bernice, what do I do now?" he turned and asked.

"Leave her be, she'll be fine. She'll sleep it off, whatever it is," she replied, following him indoors. "I never heard no crack or bang, so that be good news. Come and get yourself some fodder. Herbert has some fine beef, and we intend havin' ourselves a feast."

"Here Bernice, take my basket out, it's only bread today, but that will go down well with Herbert's beef," said Fuzz. "Where did he get it from anyway?"

"Now don't you go askin' me such dumb questions, Fuzzy boy. It bloody fell from the sky... same as everythin' else around here does," she replied.

He kept checking on Prue every five minutes, but it was not until nine when she finally stirred. "Sorry Fuzz, I don't know what happened," she groaned.

"Bernice served me some kind of drink, and all I remember was looking at a great big stack of bottles in the corner. That's it... that's all I remember."

"Have you had anything to eat?" he asked.

"I don't think I have," she replied.

"We saved you a plate of beef and bread, plus we've plenty of fresh veggies," said Fuzz.

"Maybe a little, you take most... you've been working all day," she replied.

"I've already had mine, and I can see that you've been working too... I've seen the washroom! I feel so ashamed of the state it was in, but to tell the truth I don't use it much, as I shower outside," he said. "But I can see and appreciate the difference... and Prue, let me say, I'm sorry again about the state of my sheets."

"Fuzz, you're free to do whatever you want with your sheets. You didn't expect me to be here, so you haven't anything to be ashamed of... honestly," she replied. "If you don't want to wash your sheets, and like them all grubby and full of germs, then that's your choice."

"I know I've let things slide ever since Sonia left me. Thanks for making me take notice again, I guess I was on the edge of a slippery slope," he answered.

"You were not! Look how you've got the café up and running, and against all the odds," replied Prue.

"Thanks for being kind; now let me try and get you fed," he said.

*

From then on, Fuzz treated her like a little bird with a broken wing, softly and gently, and she found herself refreshed by his efforts. His world was very different to the one she had come from... here the neighbours were caring.

Next morning, Prue found a number of large muscle-bound guys tiptoeing around her, as she sat outside in the early morning sunshine...

"They be goin' to leave the diggin' until tomorrow. That be a real good excuse you gave them lazy bums. We can't dig or we'll disturb Missy Prudence... that be the kind of tripe talk I be gettin' from them," stated Bernice, who had turned up just as Fuzz was about to leave for work. "I'll mind her today, you just do your job, young Fuzz. You is about the only guy round here that's got himself a proper job," she added, as he mounted his trusty old scooter.

She watched him go, until he was no more. "Now that he be gone, we can maybe find us out what made you faint yesterday?" she remarked to Prue, then asked her to come indoors, away from all the flappin' ears.

Prue didn't mind as the sun was rising fast on another hot day, and she'd decided to give its rays a miss. The inside of the cabin would suit her just fine.

"You feeling sick, Prudence? Look at me child, have you been caught short?" asked Bernice.

"Caught short... at what?" she replied, somewhat puzzled.

"Come on Missy, you ain't that innocent. Is that why Fuzz brung you here?" she asked.

"I can't tell you, it's a secret why Fuzz brought me here," replied Prue.

"You got me that confused way now, Prudence, with all this secret talk," she stated. "I thought that a little one might be on the way, that be all... my God it happens all the time?"

"A little one... do you mean a baby? I don't know anything about that," replied Prue. "Bernice, can I tell you something, but you must promise to keep it secret... come close, while I tell you... I'm married and have a husband."

"A husband? What you go and do that for, Prudence? How long have you had a husband?" she asked.

"Ten years," she replied.

"How old you be?" she asked.

"Twenty-eight," she replied.

"I thought you to be about twenty. You look well cared for... no hard labourin' for you Missy. You've had a husband for ten years, and you ain't got no little ones… then maybe you just fainted from the heat or somethin' like that?" announced Bernice. "What you doin' with Fuzz? You be sleepin' in his bed, so where's this husband of yours? Has he gone and got himself a new woman?"

"No, nothing like that, it's far more complicated. I can't say much, but Fuzz's sort of sheltering me," she replied, "and Bernice, for your information, I have my own sheet wrapped around me in the bed, as does he."

Bernice shook her head, "I ain't never heard of that kinda arrangement before… all wrapped up in sheets," she repeated, as she poured herself a black coffee and coughed to clear her chest… "Who's Fuzz hidin' you from?"

"That's the whole problem… I don't know! There are groups of different people searching for me… I don't know who they are or why," she replied. "I only know the police——"

"Not the bastard *Sérénité* police too… Stoker's chokers? I thought you be a smart cookie, but it seems you ain't. Most folks at least know who be lookin' for them," concluded Bernice.

"My husband's missing, so I think it's got something to do with him," explained Prue.

"You sure you done nothin' to get rid of your man?" asked Bernice, with a frown.

"No, he's gone missing, and different men are looking for him… and for some unknown reason, me too," stressed Prue.

"For some unknown reason! I knows the reason... first they find the woman, and then they gets their man. We don't take in no fugitives here, but I suppose we be havin' to make an exception with you Missy... now we knows you. Where does Fuzz fit in with all this secret stuff?" she asked.

"Nowhere, he's just my friend," replied Prue.

"Prudence dear, I be needin' to have myself a lie down. You've weighed heavy on me. You take yourself for a lie down too, as we don't want no more of that faintin' game," she answered, before taking her leave.

Prue nodded... what else was she to do but comply...

CHAPTER EIGHTEEN:

The café trade was ticking over, with the elderly colonial ladies being the backbone of Fuzz's clientele. Their presence brought in passing trade, and he found he had cultivated many returning customers. With his lack of space, this current number of customers was probably his limit… and all he could realistically cope with.

That morning, Fuzz was distracted by thoughts of Prue, and how this delicate situation between him and her had come about, and so quickly? He'd never cared about his wife Sonia in this way. Prue dazzled his senses, and whilst she may be someone else's wife, he felt that she was now his lady!

By chance, Marina looked by the café, and Fuzz pounced, literally dragging her behind the counter, "Could you cover for me for an hour, Marina?" he implored.

"Is it important?" she asked, expecting him to give her a reason.

"It is to me," he replied, and she could see from his face that his mouth was not for explaining further.

"Okay then, I guess I must strive to keep the boss-man happy," she stated, "please don't be any longer than an hour though, as I'm meeting friends at the beach."

"Thanks Marina," he replied. "Bye ladies, I've to nip out for a bit, but I leave you in Marina's capable hands. I'll not be long."

"Bye Fuzz," came the collective chant from around the floor.

He raced out, jumped on his scooter, and headed out of town. He was nearing the forest track, when he heard the sound of a siren followed by the breathing of a pursuing police car. Fuzz watched them saunter towards him in his side mirror, with the sun glinting on their oversized badges... "Hey you, with the fuzzy top... where you be boy-racin' to, going at that speed?" asked one very familiar officer.

"Just needing to see a woman, in a hurry like," Fuzz replied. "I'm kinda desperate."

"That be a good one, I likes that answer. The boy's desperate; methinks we need to let the pup get on his way. We don't want to keep the little lady waitin'," he said, laughing with his colleague. "You go easy now Fuzz, you know fine well what happens to young pups who get themselves all heated up, and drive too fast? God gets some, whilst Judge Stoker gets the rest."

Fuzz nodded, while they continued to laugh. He knew only too well of the fatalities that took place on the island's rough tracks, and also the rough judgement handed out by the Judge. He took off at a steady pace until he reached the forest track, from where on he opened up the throttle ignoring the officer's warning.

*

Back at the cabin, Prue was resting, when she heard his scooter arrive. She rose as he entered, and for a moment they just looked at each other. "Prue, I haven't much time, I just wanted to make sure you were all right?" he stated.

"I don't feel too bad, Fuzz… just a bit strange. Bernice thought I might be in the family way, but I put her right on that little notion," she replied. "What about the café, you haven't left your old ladies in charge have you? That, I would find amusing."

"I think I'd find it amusing too; no, Marina was passing, so I kind of persuaded her that she was missing the place," said Fuzz, with a shrug.

"That's what we call a busman's holiday at home," replied Prue.

"Oh yeah, well we don't have no buses here though." stated Fuzz.

"Why's that?" she asked.

113

"I lie... we do have two old twelve-seater ones, which is all the roads and tracks can handle on this island," he replied, "but you don't see them on the roads that often."

"I'd like a boat," announced Prue, suddenly.

"Wouldn't we all?" agreed Fuzz, which made them laugh. He then said that he needed to get back to the café.

"Thanks for taking the trouble," she said. She felt humbled.

"No trouble, no trouble at all... it was my pleasure," he replied.

Once back in the saddle, his mind was in free fall. He hadn't even mentioned to her he'd been pulled over by the island police. This happened many times, but today it had shaken him up inside, because he knew they were looking for her. More importantly, she had floored him when she'd told him about what Bernice had been thinking! That had shaken him up even more than the police. What was going on? He'd left his business at the busiest time, and for no good reason other than a desire to see her face. He now was developing a phobia about the island police, something which hadn't bothered him before. More importantly, there was that delicate matter that Prue may be in the family way...

Bernice was one hell of a knowledgeable lady, and rarely wrong about anything! If Prue was expecting, then it was the dastardly Michael's. This made him pull on his brakes with a sick feeling gnawing at his stomach, and it was a dazed Fuzz who returned to the café. Marina had to hurry off, and didn't have time to notice his condition, but his colonial ladies did…

Veronique told him to take a seat, whilst she made him a brew of herbal tea… something that she swore by, and just happened to have in her handbag. The smell of it alone brought on his nausea all over again, so she quickly changed it for a regular coffee. The ladies were most concerned about him, as he sat and watched them keep the café ticking over on his behalf. They were in their element… there was more life left in them than he'd ever imagined or given them credit for. "Just you sit tight Fuzz, we can manage; just help us out with some of the prices," called over Amabelle.

It was a mentally confused Fuzz, whose scooter later limped back to his cabin that evening.

*

After he'd left to return to the café at lunchtime, Bernice brought Prue a bowl full of fresh vegetables, "Make the boy some peppery pot tonight," she suggested.

"I would if I could, but I can't," she replied.

"Why can you not, girl," asked Bernice, "you still feelin' sickly?"

"No, it's just that I don't know what it is, so I don't know how to cook it," she replied.

"Lordy be, where do you come from, Prudence? No, don't tell me… I'll show you," said Bernice. "I can see me havin' to become one of them proper teachin' ladies, if I'm goin' to make a real woman out of you, Missy."

Prue smiled at her remarks, and Bernice started to laugh her loud cackle. "You sure 'bout what I asked you Prudence, 'bout you havin' a little one comin'?" she asked once more.

"Yes, I told you. I've been married for ten years, so yes, I'm sure," she replied.

"If you say so," said Bernice, with a shrug of her shoulders.

*

"This is delicious Prue, is there any more?" asked Fuzz. "Did you make this?"

"Yes, there's more, I didn't know how much you'd manage, with you being at the café all day," she replied, "and no, Bernice brought me the ingredients and showed me how."

"I didn't eat much today at the café. It was a strange day. I didn't feel too good myself this afternoon, but my colonial ladies helped out. In fact they were great," confessed Fuzz.

"What did they do, your… colonial ladies?" asked Prue.

"Veronique and Amabelle sat me down and took charge. They were amazing Prue, and in their element," he replied.

Prue smiled as an idea popped into her head, "Fuzz, as you don't have a name for the café, I've just had an idea for one," she said.

"Well, what is it, don't tease?" he replied.

"I wouldn't tease you on something so important, I just thought that *The Colonial Club* might hit the right mark," she suggested.

"It might just do that Prue; good thinking, I get it, I really do," he replied. "The word *Club* makes it personal to them… but, would that not put off other customers… what do you think?"

"No, it's the same old place, the name's just to recognise your ladies worth," stated Prue.

"Right, I'll get onto it… I'll ask one of the guys from here to do the deed," replied Fuzz.

"Do you know someone who's got that kind of talent?" asked Prue.

"Oh, sure, they've the talent for most things… they just don't have jobs," he replied.

CHAPTER NINETEEN:

Michael was recovering fast in both body and mind. He'd asked to see Sir again, and he'd not long arrived in his room... "I need to know that she'll be all right," he announced. "I need to know that she'll be let down gently, and receive things... like my pension, and all else she's entitled to as... my widow."

"Of course Michael, we are honourable people who look after our own... and their loved ones. Normally under such circumstances, pensions are awarded to parents or siblings, but in this case, arrangements will be made for yours to go to your wife or should we say, your widow?" replied Sir. "You will of course, receive your own pension at the end of your usefulness."

"My usefulness? I'd almost forgotten that one day I'll be a past-my-sell-by-date kind of operative.

Maybe I should call it a day now, and keep my wife?" said Michael.

"You could, but you won't Michael Lambasto, and you know why. This is what you do, and what you'll continue to do as long as you've the strength," came back the dispassionate response.

CHAPTER TWENTY:

Prue wasn't feeling one hundred percent when she arose the next morning, but she certainly had improved. He'd already left for the café, which left her puzzled as to how she hadn't heard the noise of his scooter. She worked out that this was because he'd probably walked it to the end of the road, so as not to disturb her. He'd also lifted the quilt from the floor, and replaced it over her fragile sheet wrapped body. A single sheet was not enough in this season, when the night temperature could drop drastically...

Prue made some fresh coffee, and then decided she didn't want it. They had a jug of mango juice in the cooler, which she sipped instead. Then she peered at the covered bowl of yesterday's pastries which Fuzz had left, and decided against eating any. Instead, once dressed, she'd take them to her neighbours, Joel, Marie and the kids, who would appreciate them.

They were more than pleased, and Joel gave her some seeds, a few seedlings, and said he'd come and help rake the soil into a fine tilth in preparation for planting. There weren't many seedlings, but the thought touched her. He went out to prepare the soil, while Prue lingered, and helped Marie get the little ones washed and dressed... baby Jean-Paul wrestled and wriggled when a wet cloth came in his direction. "I think this little one's allergic to water," laughed Prue.

"*Bien*," began Marie, and then remembered that Prue would not understand if she continued, "he be needin' the water on his skin, he bein' a *Sérénité* babe." She waved her hand in the direction of the ocean.

"That's true, when you put it like that," agreed Prue. She had enjoyed helping with the little ones. It had been many years since she'd even been near children or babies. Michael and her lived in a world of adults, who talked adult talk, and did adult things...

"*Combien de temps*... you and your man?" asked Marie.

"Ten years," she replied, concentrating hard to recall what little French she'd learned at school.

"Ten, *dix... mon dieu, et not you one bébé!*" exclaimed Marie."*Comment tu fais ca...* how?"

"My husband... *mon Mari...* doesn't want any... I think? He works away from home most of the time," replied Prue.

121

"*Et il ne vous touchera pas...* when he be... *avec toi*," said a laughing Marie. "You understand... he no touch you?"

This bit of freely given news would soon circulate around the cabins, of that Prue had no doubt. She could hear their earthy laughter resounding. She could not find a word to describe the feeble way it had sounded to her own ear. Prue had never thought of it like that, and Marie did have a point; there were so many things that Michael and her had never talked about, with having children being one of them. Prue made a quick retreat before being caught up in a conversation that could leave her with more questions than answers.

As she crossed back to Fuzz's cabin, Joel called her over and said that he would be happy to plant the seeds and seedlings for her if she wished? "Thank you," she replied. It was a start... these folks were so kind.

"It be giving me something to do, then I'll fetch Marlon and the others to finish diggin' the plot for you... sorry for Fuzz," he corrected himself.

"*Merci, s'l vous plait* Joel," she called back.

"You been talkin' to my Marie, Missy Prudence? She no speak good English like us workin' boys," stated Joel. This made him belly laugh. She decided to smile and laugh back... it being a tried and tested formula that appeared to work well.

*

Prue was used to an easy life, Bernice had noticed that, and had brought it to her attention the first

122

day they'd met. "Your soft hands make mine feel like that sandpaper stuff," she'd observed with a toothy smile, whilst thrusting her hands out for her to examine. Prue had taken them in hers and looked them over... they were indeed rough, red and swollen. However, Bernice had merely laughed when she'd asked if they were sore?

Today, back inside the cabin, Prue remembered the condition of Bernice's hands compared to her own, and went back outside to ask Joel if she could help sow the seeds? She wanted to dirty her hands by doing something useful, and from now on, she was determined to do Fuzz and her own laundry in a token effort to help heal Bernice's hands. She secretly also wanted to rid herself of their silky softness.

She helped Joel, and then went on to rake the dry soil while the guys continued with the digging. They chatted and laughed, talking to her occasionally, whilst the rest of the time, spoke in their own lingo or French. In fact, the way they spoke was akin to a bag of dolly mixtures... small bursts of mixed-up words... which everyone, with the exception of her, understood. They were talking their men's talk, which was their private thing to do, and she didn't mind one bit.

Marlon called over from time to time, as did Joel, with words of encouragement about the good job she was doing. She took each compliment graciously, and responded with a sweet smile.

Herbert arrived late during the afternoon, wheeling his scooter around to the back of his cabin, his pannier bag bulging with tonight's meat. "Missy, you come to my cabin and get Fuzz's share in half-an-hour," he called over.

Prue smiled when she saw some of the folks already heading for his cabin, but before she could join them, she heard Bernice, "I always gets first pick, so I picks a piece for you... to save you going into his cabin, girl."

"Thanks Bernice, but are you saying that I shouldn't go into his cabin?" she asked.

"You can, but I think you wouldn't like what you'd see... his knives be clean though," she replied, half choking on one of her hearty laughs. Prue smiled and asked how she should cook this piece of meat? "Just cut it up and fry it, girl... don't you know nothin'?" she responded, with yet another throaty laugh. However, on seeing Prue's expression drop, she quickly put a matronly arm around her shoulders. "I be sorry," she added, "why should you know, you ain't from these parts."

CHAPTER TWENTY-ONE:

Fuzz had called Marina the previous day to ask what she had planned to do on her break. He thought there was an off chance she might be available to help out in the café? "I'm not doing much," she replied, "I've run out of cash, and almost wish I was back at work."

"Back you come then, 'cause I need you Marina, or my colonial ladies will soon take over the place," he replied.

"What do you mean?" she asked.

"Oh, they think I need their help, and they're sure providing it for me, but it's becoming embarrassing," he replied.

"For goodness sake, where's your pride?" asked Marina. "Don't worry, I'll be in tomorrow to rescue you. What about that problem in the back shop?"

"It's all fixed… you can go in there now," he replied.

"You were up to something, I could tell… plumbing problems my backside!" she said.

"Now Marina, you remember about them colonial ladies. None of that gutter talk from you in the café please… these ladies are old stock, and should be treated genteel like," he joked.

"I'll be in tomorrow, first thing," she replied, "and I'll be sure to bring my posh voice and words with me."

*

They were soon back into their old routine, and Fuzz felt a sense of relief. He detected a trickle of disappointment on the faces of his ladies when they arrived and saw that Marina had returned. "Well, ladies, I can see that normal service has been resumed," announced Veronique. "Remember, we will be watching you, Marina, and we now have experience in running this café."

"You never told me it was a complete takeover," whispered Marina to Fuzz. "Please tell me they didn't cash up at the end of the day?" Fuzz dropped his head and looked away. "What a poodle you've turned out to be… wag your tail for me please?"

Fuzz laughed, as he thought that remark funny, "Later," he whispered…

*

That evening, when they'd eaten her attempt at boar stew, Fuzz and Prue walked through the pines to the beach. Once there, they sat on a fallen log and gazed out onto the oceanic expanse. "It was better today," he suddenly announced, "my hired help managed to keep them in their seats."

"I think it's sad that they're not allowed to help anymore," replied Prue.

"You would," he remarked. "It was horrendous watching them weave in and out with their laden trays, just waiting for the inevitable to happen."

"And did it happen... the inevitable?" she asked.

"No, but it could have quite easily," he replied. "It could have, if you think about it... Oh, for goodness sake Prue, they're not in their first flush... or even their second, they're elderly ladies."

She was looking at him with a smirk, forcing him to offer more and more reasons or was it excuses, as to why it had not been an acceptable scenario? He had to laugh when she suddenly tweaked his nose, and took off towards the ocean, tossing her borrowed sandals back in his direction. Before he knew it, she was in the water, floating on her back.

"That was a damned stupid thing to do," he yelled, as she walked back towards him, her wet clothes clinging to her body like transparent rags. For goodness sake, what would Michael say, he thought?

He saw an almighty grin on her face as she joined him back on the log. "I'll dry," she announced, "what's all the flipping fuss for?"

"That wouldn't be easy to say, but you managed your f's with ease," he replied.

"Managed my f's with ease? You're beginning to sound like a flipping fussy fool, my fine fellow," she laughed.

"Don't you worry about Fuzz's flipping fussiness, I'll soon take care of that," he replied. "Prue, you're cold... you've started to shake, and the sun's dipping fast. Let's get you back. I would give you my tee-shirt but unless you take your top off, it wouldn't do any good... and I'm sure you won't be doing that."

She suddenly fell silent and slumped against him, and he had to physically help her to her feet and carry her to his cabin. He'd never seen anyone go downhill so fast. Once inside, he sat her down, then ran and thumped on Bernice's door."Who the— Fuzz, why you come here," she asked, "you knows this is my one early bed night?"

"It's Prue... I need your help... come quick," he replied.

Luckily for him, Bernice had not yet changed into her night attire or whatever she wore in bed... so came immediately, and was shocked at the state of Prue. "Why the hell is she soaking wet Fuzz... what have you been doin' to the little lady?" she yelled.

"I haven't done anything. She ran into the ocean and soaked herself. She was fine when she came back, and then all of a sudden this happened," he explained.

Bernice stripped Prue of her wet clothing as she spoke, and asked him to fetch some large warm towels to wrap around her. She glared at him, when he handed her a small used facecloth. "Christ, Fuzz, get your butt along to my cabin, and bring me some big clean ones. I've some warmin' near the stove... now move your ass," she shouted.

At that moment, Joel's frame hovered just inside the back door, "What be goin' on?" he asked.

"Get out, you ain't needed here," yelled Bernice, and he didn't wait around to argue. Fuzz returned with an armful of towels. "Now get out... no... stay and boil me some hot water, but keep that nosey nose of yours out of here."

Bernice had temporarily wrapped Prue in an old curtain and when Fuzz returned, she set about drying her with the fresh warm towels. "Get a bloody hurry on with the damned water, and have some of our special tea ready, in case she be wantin' some," she added.

Fuzz was confused, what did she want him to do first, boil the water or make the tea? He didn't wait to ask, for fear of receiving another rollicking from her ladyship. He quickly worked out that it must be boiling water first, and felt really silly for thinking otherwise...

Back in the living room, Bernice was glad that Prue was slightly built, as her back was giving her gyp.

She couldn't have managed anyone heavier, not today anyway. Her knees cracked as she bent... was there no end to this ageing and decaying of this body of hers? At least her mouth still worked, and she praised the Lord for small mercies...

When Prue was eventually safely tucked up warm in bed, she let Fuzz into the room. "First she faints, then this, Fuzz. This girlie of yours only just got here in time, my boy. What be her story?" she asked.

"I really don't know, and I'm not making excuses," he replied.

"What's her other name... Prudence what?" she enquired. "Have you any idea?"

"At the moment, I'd rather not say. I want to try and trace her husband... this Saint Michael she worships," he replied.

"I hear a plateful of jealousy comin' from you, Fuzz. You watch you don't get yourself all mangled and hurt," she warned.

"Not so much jealousy, it's more like... confusion," he replied.

Bernice laughed one of her loud laughs, which caused him to glance across at Prue, but she was oblivious to her surroundings. She then informed him that it was most likely shock that had caused Prue's sudden fever... shock which had stemmed from stress to her system.

"Is it not more likely to be the baby thing?" he asked, tentatively.

"From what our Prudence be sayin', that just ain't possible," replied Bernice, with a grin.

"Then what do you think's causing her problems?" he asked.

"A bit of the both," she replied.

"Even after everything she's said?" he asked.

"Yes," she replied.

"Are you telling me you still think she's... in the family way?" asked Fuzz.

"That be what I said, wasn't it? You need to wash out your ears, young Fuzz."

*

When she had left, Fuzz wrapped himself up in his sheet, and decided to try and slip into the far side of the bed, which was his allocated space. He wouldn't need much room... His side of the bed? Why was he thinking that... it was all his bed? How had she managed to take it over, and who was she anyway? She was only a customer, wasn't she? How had he become involved with this seemingly crazy woman, who worshiped Saint Michael? He then rechristened him Black Saint Michael, a man who seemed the most selfish of husbands.

Fuzz then became emotional, and thought he'd better give the bed a miss and sleep on the floor. Perhaps a chair would be a better option, just in case she awoke confused and in need of a drink of water, or the toilet? He then began to cry, which for him was a new experience. It was not a tearful cry, more of a holding-back-the-tears routine. Why had this creature stirred up so much emotion in him when his wife never had? He'd never felt for Sonia the way he felt for Prue... and then remembered that she was not his to feel anything about. All his woeful roads led to... Black Saint Michael!

He tried lying on the edge of the bed, and then closed his eyes in an effort to drift away. "Prue, I'm sorry, but I need to go out in the morning... I've supplies for the café, you know that," he whispered, so low that she couldn't possibly have heard. "G'night and God bless my darling Prudence..."

He'd never called her that before, not her full name, but it did have a certain charm... there was a certain godliness about it, a wholesome quality... for goodness sake Fuzz, keep calling her Prue, as that sounds far more like the woman who's lying beside you.

These thoughts continued, keeping much needed sleep from his door. He couldn't just leave her in the morning... no, of course he couldn't, but if he didn't leave her, how could he open the café? Marina would be annoyed if he phoned, and asked her to run his empire for him today... there again, perhaps she'd enjoy being her own boss? When could he phone her though? It was now the middle of the night, or at least the early hours of the morning...

His mind continued to race, churning up one thought after another, until he was thoroughly exhausted and…

Bernice woke him in time for work, "Fuzz, wake up," she whispered, "you needs to get yourself to the café. You be the only one here who has somewhere to go each mornin'. You be the one who gives this place a sense of pride, so don't you be frettin' over her, someone will look in later and tell you how she be doin'."

He was too tired to reply… it would be useless anyway, as she was not the type of woman with whom you argued.

*

Marina fortuitously arrived early, for which Fuzz was grateful. "Have you been up all night?" she asked, looking him over. "You look dreadful."

"Maybe I'm just having a dreadful looking face day?" he replied.

"I was just making a passing remark," she answered, "no offence meant."

"None taken," he replied.

"How's that cousin of yours?" she asked. "You could've wheeled her in to help, when I was on holiday? I'm sure she would've managed, as she watched us work for long enough, perched on that stool of hers."

Fuzz was taken aback… he felt Marina had gone for Prue in an unnecessarily aggressive manner, which he didn't like or understand. "She actually did help out a little, but she's busy and not available," he replied.

"Why, what's she up to?" she asked.

"I don't know… I don't see much of that side of my family," he replied.

"I've not heard of you having much to do with any of your family," she retorted. "I thought you only came to this island to take up some dodgy job? Your wife departed, so how have you any family here anyway, it's not like it's a weekend destination?"

They were busily stacking shelves, and Fuzz was about to tell her to mind her own damn business and to get on with her work. However, when he looked over, her shelve filling was nearly finished, and he was the one lagging, so he kept silent. The one-sided conversation eventually fizzled out, much to his relief, and when he finished, he nipped into the back shop to splash his face with the coldest of water he could muster…

*

Soon they were busy with the ladies, and the various other customers, but Fuzz couldn't concentrate, he kept on thinking of her lying in his bed…

"You're not with us today, Fuzz," observed Veronique, "what's wrong?"

"I'm here alright… feel my hand," he replied.

134

"You know exactly what I mean… I think a little love-biter's been nibbling at your collar," stated Veronique.

"Oh, you are a one, Veronique," replied one of the other ladies.

Fuzz looked around and saw that all their eyes were now upon him, their interest fuelled. He felt like a patient being examined by a *docteur*, with a roomful of amused students looking on. First Marina, and now the ladies of the newly founded *Colonial Club,* were spoiling his day; a day which was hard enough to take as it was.

Joel sauntered in a little later, and sat himself up on one of the high stools at the counter.

"What news?" whispered Fuzz.

"She's fine; I saw her when Bernice was givin' me my orders to come here," he replied. Fuzz could feel Marina watching with renewed interest, her head cocked, straining to catch any loose snippets of their conversation. What was with that girl?

"Marina, serve Joel here with whatever he wants, and give me his bill," announced Fuzz.

"Another relative?" she asked, with all the nonchalant charm she could muster. Joel looked at Fuzz, obviously expecting an explanation of some sort, but none was forthcoming.

I'm the boss here, I don't need to explain my actions to anyone, he tried to tell himself, but without much success."Marina, will you also give Joel a bag of pastries to take away with him," he added, "and include mainly these apricot jam ones... please."

He whispered in Joel's ear, that they are her favourite ones, and to make sure she received her fair share. Joel understood and nodded in return.

*

When their quiet time came, Marina sat herself at one of the vacant tables for their coffee break, and gazed at him without saying a word."What's wrong with you... you're usually gassing on about something or other?" asked Fuzz.

"Gassing, is it? At least it's open gassing, not a secret-spiders-web-of-lies type of gassing," she replied.

"I beg your pardon, I don't know what's gotten into you today? A little manners wouldn't go amiss," he stated.

They glared at each other, neither saying anymore, while they finished their coffee. This frostiness continued for the remainder of the day, unless it was work related.

By the time he got home, Prue was sitting outside under a make-shift sunshade."Hi, how are you feeling?" he asked. "I like the sunshade, who made it for you?"

"Bernice brought some of the guys over, and they made it for me," she replied. "She thought I'd benefit from the fresh air."

"Bernice decided. Now that's not like her," stated Fuzz. They both laughed. She looked so sweet, so vulnerable sitting there. "Did you get your apricot pastries?"

She nodded, then stretched out her hands towards him. He took them, and caressed her fingers. He needed to protect and look after her. She had captured his heart, he now knew that for sure. "Fuzz, I'm sorry for getting myself wet, and bringing on that fever thing," she said. "Thanks for the pastries, and yes, I got most of the apricot ones… Joel made sure of that. I was impressed you remembered they are my favourites."

"I have to confess, they're my favourite ones too, so it wasn't easy to forget," he replied.

"In a few days, when I'm well enough… do you want me to come to the café to help?" she asked. "I'd like to come and help."

There had been no mention of Saint Michael up to this point, and Fuzz hoped he was fading… probably not though? He reckoned he would not get rid of Black Saint Michael that easily. "Prue, I think you should just stay here, out of the way," he replied.

Her smile faded. "Out of the way of what?" she asked.

"I don't know… just generally out of the way. We've never got any further with finding out who was looking for you, and I'm sorry to remind you, but you did have that horrible experience at your apartment," he replied.

One hand strayed up to her hair… it was cute the way it was… but when it had been long, it had been her crowning glory. "Does it look a mess Fuzz, tell me the truth please?" she asked. "I've never had the opportunity to get it professionally cut."

"It looks lovely, and you know it does," he replied. "Let's keep you safe here for a little longer, okay?"

She nodded in agreement, and he smiled back, with his fingers still entwined in hers…

*

Marina was annoyed and disappointed with Fuzz. She worked hard for him, and until now, he had been a truthful and straightforward boss. No more however; he was up to something… of that she was sure. He had gone to great lengths to guard his back-room secret, and she wished now that she'd tried harder to get a peep inside. He was now telling her lies, which was not in his nature, and he was rubbish at it! There had been the saga of his so-called cousin, who'd perched herself on a high stool in the café, staying there for hours, eating and drinking for free. She was sure he had lied on that occasion, then had capped it today, with his treatment of the guy who'd arrived and perched himself on the same blinking stool. He was certainly not their usual type of customer, but he too got his food free. This guy had even left with a bag of booty, which was not exactly a king's ransom, but it may as well have been due to the trouble it had caused with the regular apricot pastry eating customers! It had been hard work trying to keep them sweet by offering alternatives, and to make matters worse, most of the colonial ladies were of the forthright variety, and their displeasure had been aimed at her, and not him!

Fuzz seemed oblivious to the problems she was having trying to pacify and sweeten his customers. He'd acted as if he was not even in the building. It's that woman, thought Marina... or was she a girl? She was probably somewhere in between, but was definitely the cause... that so called cousin! "His cousin, my backside," she muttered, "but who is she?"

She knew who she was; she was the someone who was driving him to distraction. That then made her think of something she found insulting. She, his sole trusted employee, had not even been deemed fit enough to be told where he lived, and on this tiny island, that was quite extraordinary!

"Down the Green Plantation Road," was all he would say, and would never expand upon. She made up her mind that she was going to find out exactly where he lived, even if it meant following him... elaborately disguised of course. Why was she bothered about Fuzz anyway? Why, because she had just realised that she might be in love with the guy. Whether this was true or not, she certainly didn't want anyone else taking advantage of his sweet nature. No, she wanted his sweet nature all to herself...

*

139

At close of day, Fuzz grabbed what food was left over, stuffed it into his twin panniers, and rode off on his scooter. Marina was upset. There had not been even one backward glance to see if she had waved. Also, he had taken all the day's leftovers, without asking if she wanted a share. Okay, she always said no, but that didn't matter, he ought to have asked. She then gave an inkling of a smile… at least she did have the satisfaction of knowing that there were no apricot pastries in his panniers. What in heaven's name did he do with all the food he took home? Marina had never thought about this before, but now that she had, she knew it would gnaw away until resolved. That was something else she needed to investigate, and her investigations would be for his own good!

Fuzz hooted his horn to let the folks know he was home from work, and that he had some extra food. Prue found it amusing when the children came running over to his cabin to collect their share, they were so cute. He watched her with them, and it struck him that if she was expecting a baby, she would make a marvellous mother. He then looked in the kitchen, and saw two newly gifted fish lying beside the sink, waiting to be filleted…

She came and appeared at his side, "I couldn't Fuzz, I just couldn't," she stated, all watery eyed.

"Of course you couldn't. If you had, I would've been disappointed," he replied.

"Really?" she answered.

"Yeah, really," he replied. "You wouldn't have been my girl, doing that kind of thing."

She looked at him with a look which was hard for him to read. He'd called her his girl; how could he have been that stupid? He wanted her to be his girl, of course he did, but how could she be, while still Mrs Lambasto? He wondered if she was thinking of the dastardly Michael at this very moment?

"You're so good to me, Fuzz. Are you going to fillet the fish?" she asked, with a grin.

"Starting the job as we speak," he replied.

"I'll leave the kitchen then, if you don't mind," she said.

Fuzz then got to work on the fish, and was surprised when he turned, to find her back standing behind him. "Fuzz, I'm really worried about Michael, it's been a while now and I hope he's all right? He's never been gone this amount of time before. I just don't know what to do. The last thing he said to me was that we had to go back. In fact, he just sort of muttered it under his breath, and when I asked him to explain, he said that I'd obviously heard and had got the gist. He didn't want me to question him anymore."

Fuzz spun around on his heel, knife in one hand and fish in the other, "Prue, why exactly were the two of you here on this island?" he asked.

"I don't know, he never told me why we went anywhere… Fuzz, I've told you all of this before," she replied.

141

"Prue, you know that this is a shady island, full of dodgy folks. Why do you think Michael would have come to a place like this?" he asked… and the thought, why did he bring you here with him, went through his mind?

"We always went to these sort of places. My mother and father just couldn't understand how he had a job that took him to so many strange places," she replied.

"Neither do I, Prue. I'm with your folks on this one. I came here to work with a company that suddenly collapsed, but I knew they were cutting corners, taking risks, being dodgy. I made a mistake taking that job, but it was a one-off for me. Your Michael, on the other hand, appears to be some sort of serial dodgy character," he stated.

She looked at him like a hurt child. In her eyes he saw that Michael had now been promoted to an Arch Angel. "Prue, I'm sorry, I've spoken out of turn," he said, "forget everything I've just said. Please don't let it spoil things between you and me."

She smiled again, and started to prepare some vegetables.

"Are all the apricot pastries I sent back with Joel finished?" he asked.

"I've saved us two," she replied. "I know how you like to have one after your meal. They do seem to be very popular with everyone."

142

"Yes, I know they are," he said. Marina had been on his back all day for giving away so many to Joel, and he supposed she'd a point.

After they'd eaten, Prue felt well enough to walk slowly down to the ocean with him. He made her promise to take his hand, and not to let go under any circumstances.

"I promise you not under any circumstances, will I let go of your hand," she replied, with a smile.

If only that were true, he thought... but if Saint Michael called... she'd no doubt go running off after him...

CHAPTER TWENTY-TWO:

Saint Michael had great powers of recovery and was convalescing, before he once again would be called upon to enter the fray. He hated hanging around being served with his every need, although he had to confess, there were some very attractive nurses in this place...

He knew however, it was a ploy by Sir and the Organisation, to cleanse his mind free of his past, and show him what his future could hold, that sort of thing. He could almost read their every move; it was a game which both sides knew how to play!

Michael was teetering on the brink of succumbing to their ploy, as he was desperately in need of company. Then he thought of her... he knew they were having difficulty locating her, and he needed to know she was unharmed. He had threatened to search for her himself if none of the Organisation's jackasses could do such a simple task. They knew for sure she had not left the island by plane, and it was highly unlikely that she'd done so by any other means.

Something bad must have happened, or someone must be helping her? He had no desire to go back there, where everything had so nearly ended for him, but he would if he had to, and no person or Organisation would stop him...

*

Meanwhile, back on the island, just before opening time, a delivery was made to the café, of small shrubs and bushes. Fuzz told the delivery man to take them into the back shop, as it would be too hot for them to remain in the back yard.

"Why the plants, Fuzz... I never knew you had a garden?" asked a puzzled Marina.

"The garden's new, I now want it to be pretty where I sit. Is there anything wrong with that? They're just for a little piece of my plot near to the back door," he replied.

"A plot? You've never talked about having a plot before. How big is it?" she asked.

"It's just normal sized," he replied. "Why the sudden interest in my plot anyway? Can a man not try to improve his lot, his plot and his environment? I like flowers... and these sort of things... so, what's wrong with that?"

"Nothing, I suppose... I was only wondering why now, after all this time," retorted Marina. He turned his back on her, and unlocked the café door...

"What are you doing, it's too early? It's not as if we're even ready," she exclaimed.

"Marina, this is my café, so I can do what I want, and that includes opening when I like. I would appreciate it if you respected my right to privacy, especially in regard to my private life," he replied.

Marina sarcastically clapped her hands and cheered, much to his annoyance. "Brilliant speech, Fuzz... there's definitely something going on with you, and don't try to deny it. I won't be fooled," she announced. Fuzz relocked the café door, and went through into the small corridor that led to the back shop. "That's right, go into your secret room, the one your hard working assistant was barred from... heaven knows what you were up to in there? I'll get on with what still needs done out here, while you sit on your backside and sulk."

He slammed the door to the corridor shut. "Temper, temper," she shouted. "Who's acting like a big baby now?" She waited, but nothing happened... had she gone too far? She thought she perhaps had, and could be heading for the chop? Undaunted, she continued to ensure that everything was ready for opening time on her own.

Little did she know that Fuzz had not gone into the back shop to sulk, but to collect his plants, and had nipped a few doors along the lane to the taxi office to arrange a ride home…

By the time Marina opened the front door of the café for the early customers, he was well on his way back to the cabin with his present. She wanted to shout and swear when she finally discovered he'd gone, but refrained from doing so, as the colonial ladies had arrived, bang on their usual time. Marina knew they were loyal to Fuzz, and so for her sins, was she. However, she also knew that he had taken advantage of her, knowing that she would not walk away leaving the café unattended. But where had he gone? His scooter was still out back; then she noticed that the plants were missing…

*

The taxi dropped him off, and he rushed around to the back of the cabin, carefully carrying his tray of plants, and there she was, sat near to the back door under the shelter of her sunshade. "I've brought you some plants, Prue," he called to her excitedly. "I got them from a friend, because I know you wanted a flower garden."

"Oh, Fuzz thanks so much. That will fill it out nicely. Joel has already planted some seedlings, and I've scattered some wild flower seeds, but remember this is your garden not mine," she replied.

Her reply stopped him in his tracks! What he'd wanted her to say, was that the garden was for the two of them… but how could he have expected her to say such a thing, when she was still being towed along by the blessed Archangel? "Can I share these plants with Joel, as he's given you a selection of seedlings and seeds?"

"Of course... but choose the ones you like best first," he replied, "before you give any away."

"Thanks... listen... how come you're home at this time anyway, you must've just opened?" asked Prue.

I... just wanted to see you, and bring you the plants, was what he really wanted to reply, but instead he heard himself say, "Marina was on my back, so I left her to get on with it on her own. I've decided to spend the rest of the day here with you."

"And will she," asked Prue, "keep it ticking over sweetly, I mean?"

"I certainly hope so, I don't see why not," he replied. "Anyway, let's enjoy ourselves today, and forget about my business."

She nodded at him in agreement, and he felt pleased. Fuzz then remembered that he'd left his scooter in the yard at the café. He would have to blag someone to take him into town early tomorrow, but that would have to wait... he would arrange that later.

Prue by now had gone indoors to pour him a coffee, and to toast some of yesterday's leftovers. "Fuzz, can we plant these plants together, once we've finished our coffee? I'd like that," she called out.

"Of course, then we can watch them grow together," he replied. "Prue, sorry I've not brought anything fresh home, I left in a bit of a hurry." She nodded, and waved her hand to indicate that was no problem. She came out with the coffee and an assortment of toast on a tray, and slipped down beside him. Everything felt wonderful, but how could they make plans about gardens or anything else, while he was stood on the edge of this abyss, not knowing what was going to happen next?

*

A little later, after they'd planted their share, Prue took the remainder through to Joel and Marie, while Fuzz took some along to Bernice, as a thanks for her help.

"Get your butt in here," hissed Bernice, "I be wanting to talk to you."

Ominous, he thought? He didn't feel like talking to her, not at this particular moment, but respected her too much to refuse.

"Now boy, when you be tellin' Bernice the little lady's other name? I think someone's sure to be out looking for her by now. Give me the name, and I can put out some feelers, you know what I mean, Fuzz? We don't be wantin' no police inspectors out here, nosin' around, and diggin' up trouble, do we?" she asked.

Fuzz looked up to the ceiling thatch, and then down to the tiled floor, before looking her in the eye. "I know what you be thinkin', Fuzz… that the little lady

149

can just drop herself out of her other life, and nobody will follow, and it will all turn out cool. But I thinks with this little lady that they will follow, so, tell me her name." She then pushed a piece of paper towards him, along with a pen. "Write it down, Fuzz… it be for the best."

He stared at her, and she stared back, while her rough hands pushed the paper further towards him. Eventually, he lifted the pen, and wrote down the name…

"Thanks," she said. "I be gettin' on to this, as we speak."

Fuzz left her cabin, but didn't go straight back to his own. Instead, he turned, and taking his guilty conscience with him, sprinted through the trees to the beach, where he threw himself into the ocean. Christ… why had he done that, he wondered, spitting and spluttering? He'd done exactly what she had done previously! How was he going to explain the fact he was soaked? He perhaps could just say that he'd felt hot, albeit under his collar, and had gone for a dip, which was the truth or at least, in part.

CHAPTER TWENTY-THREE:

Bernice had now got hold of the Lambasto name. However, before she could proceed further, she needed more information, so that evening summoned Fuzz through to her cabin. His heart sank, knowing he was in for further interrogation. "Right, Fuzz, what be the guy's name?" she asked.

"Michael," he replied, "I don't know if he has any other names."

"How old be this… Michael?" she asked.

"I believe he's just a bit older than Prue, although I'm not sure," he replied.

"Which is…?" she asked.

"Well, she's twenty-eight," he replied.

She nodded in agreement. That was the same as Prudence had told her. She was just checking, as Missy didn't look her age. "What else do you know?" asked Bernice. "Come on Fuzz, I don't like this pullin' of the teeth."

"They went to Cambridge University, and got married a few weeks after she'd turned eighteen," he replied.

"Place of marriage would be... Cambridge, England... is that right?" she asked.

"I suppose... but I don't really know for sure," he replied.

"Prudence's folks... where do they live?" she asked.

"Somerset, England," he answered.

"What does her papa do for his cash?" asked Bernice. Fuzz, sat and looked about him. He hated this; he felt he was betraying Prue, although this was supposed to be helping her. "Come on Fuzz, think and tell me, for the Almighty's sake. You're startin' to piss me off."

"I'm sorry if I'm pissing you off, but I don't know much, just little snippets that I've picked up here and there," he replied. "Her folks are farmers, working the land... that I do know, but don't ask me about Michael, 'cause I know nothing about him or his side of the family."

"Okay, sorry, but I had to be askin' you them things," stated Bernice.

"It's okay, I understand. The whole affair's just a muddy mess of a path, and I don't know where to step," he replied.

Bernice put her strong washerwoman arms around him, and he felt as though he was being threaded through her hand-wringer. Eventually she released him, and he returned to his own cabin, crushed and exhausted.

Prue was already wrapped in her sheet fast asleep when he returned, and decided to join her. His lift into town in the morning was at four-thirty, just a trifle early for his café business...

*

He was there when Marina arrived, and had all of the routine chores in the café completed. After yesterday, she didn't know whether to ignore him, or try to make up? His back was towards her when she entered, and he didn't look around. She then went out into the corridor to hang up her *blouson*, and by the time she came back, her favourite drink and pastry was sitting waiting at her preferred table. "Thanks, Fuzz," she called over to him.

"You're welcome," he replied, "I'm so sorry about yesterday. Did you manage?"

"I had my helpers," she said.

"The ladies rallied round, did they?" he asked.

153

"Who else? The only problem was that a couple of them wanted to be top-cat," she replied, "but I showed them in no uncertain terms, that when the real top-cat was not here, who was the deputy."

A fantasy thought crossed Fuzz's mind… if they could manage so well without him, then perhaps he ought to retire, and leave Marina and her merry women to their own devices? These thoughts were all Prue based; based on his need to be with her, and to live in a world of simple pleasures. He could feel Marina watching, as he was having this Prue moment, and wished she didn't take such an interest. She was lippy too, some of that cheek she gave him yesterday was taking banter to a new and unacceptable level!

"How did you get into work this morning, with your scooter being in the yard yesterday?" she asked.

"I know where my scooter was… I left it there," he replied.

"You haven't answered my question," she stated.

"I don't intend to either," he replied. "Marina, as I've mentioned to you a few times before, can you butt out of my business?"

Marina was shocked! What's happened to him? This was not the man she knew, and liked, perhaps even loved? She didn't like this person, or the way he spoke. Stuff him, she thought, he'll get as little work out of me today as I can get away with, and tomorrow… and maybe the next day too…

Fuzz could see he'd upset her; but after Bernice and her inquisition last night, he'd had enough. The whole Michael Lambasto situation was distressing him. This island was too small, too full of money-grabbing, back-stabbing individuals for this to pass overhead and fly off on its own accord. Something was going to happen, of that he felt sure.

He should never have become involved with Prue, but he had, and now he couldn't conceive of her not being in his life.

*

Back at the cabin, she was feeling sick. It happened to her first thing in the morning. Imagine feeling ill again, and so quickly after the last time? Prue was glad Fuzz had long gone to work, or he would've been thinking what a sickly creature he had befriended? She'd have to hide this wobbly from the neighbours too, especially Bernice. "Michael, look what you've done to me now. All this worrying about you is running me down. Where the dickens are you?" she muttered.

*

Michael was far away in his luxury convalescent suite, awaiting his all clear to return to his real life. Prue was still uppermost on his mind however, and he couldn't move on until he was sure she was settled, thriving in her new life. He wondered why he'd the misfortune to be wounded so badly while far from home, and in such a shady part of the world? Of all the places for her to be left alone, that must rank pretty near the top of the undesirable list.

The Organisation were supposedly out looking for her, enquiries were being made, and Sir was insistent they were doing their utmost. What kind of numpties were on her case? Bloody hell, it was an island with a landmass which spanned only a few miles in all directions. How the hell could they not locate her? Surely a few palms amply greased, would come up trumps? Michael thumped the table with such force, that his cup of coffee spilled, and he watched as its contents spread across the table, and trickled onto the floor. This reminded him of one of his injuries... when blood had trickled down his leg, draining him almost dry, before they had thankfully located him...

*

Meanwhile, back in the café, the atmosphere appeared normal between Fuzz and Marina. They played their rolls so well, that the colonial ladies didn't notice anything amiss. Initially, Marina hadn't forgiven him for his outburst towards her, but on reflection, she came to the decision that this aggressive behaviour was not their fault. It was all down to his so-called cousin... that awful woman! Fuzz's construction of a garden, the sudden acquisition of plants, his taking time off, and the general neglect of his duties at the café, were all down to her bad influence.

Marina had not yet followed up on her plan to tail Fuzz to find out where he exactly lived; however, this now needed prioritised. She decided that it would be better if she didn't follow him herself, but used the services of her brother instead to track him down. Frankie had never been into Fuzz's café, as it was not cool enough for him to frequent, so would be ideal for the job. Yes, she was sure that little brother Frankie could be cajoled into a little jaunt along Green Plantation Road, following Fuzz's chug-a-long scooter...

Her plan however was put on hold, as an unfortunate event occurred in the café... the sudden and unexpected death of one of the Club members. Cécile passed away peacefully, while enjoying her favourite scone smothered with jam and butter. The ladies coped well, but to Marina, it was a tremendous shock! Once the body had been removed, Fuzz closed the shop, and took a shocked Marina home in a taxi. He'd never met her parents or been to her family home before, but they warmly welcomed him, insisting he come inside, while her *mama* took Marina upstairs to settle her in bed. Fuzz agreed, and chatted to her *papa* and her big little brother Frankie. The three men were comfortable in each other's company and soon became mates... with Frankie promising to look in at the café for a coffee or something stronger.

Marina, having been so upset over Cécile, was only too pleased to be taken home, and failed to realise that Fuzz and Frankie would inevitably meet. Frankie, in fact, offered Fuzz a lift home, once it dawned on him, that he and his sister had arrived by taxi. "Just a lift to the café will do, Frankie as I've my scooter there and need it for work tomorrow morning. Thanks for the offer," replied Fuzz.

"No problem, we can pick the scooter up on our way, and put it in the back of... *Papa,* can I borrow your truck?" asked Frankie. His *papa* agreed, as did Fuzz, who didn't relish scootering along the long Plantation

Road after the day he'd just had. He too, was now overcome with delayed shock, following the untimely passing of Cécile.

*

"I've never been here before, Fuzz, I didn't even know this place existed," exclaimed Frankie. "Talk about cool cabins, right in the middle of the forest... real nice man, this is the kind of bachelor pad I'd like."

"This isn't any bachelor pad," replied Fuzz, "it's mostly families around here; believe me it's not the kind of place you think... and I have my lady living here." If only she was, he thought.

"Nice," exclaimed Frankie," even better."

"Not nice, Frankie," clarified Fuzz, "she's beautiful."

After his shock at Cécile's passing, and his super early morning start, Fuzz had forgotten all about the relationship between Frankie and Marina. He had coped with the *Sérénité* police, the *docteur*, then the ambulance, to remove the body to the mortuary, whilst helping his ladies to deal with the shock at losing one of their own.

He had inadvertently told one sibling to keep her nose out of his affairs, but was now welcoming the other to his home... the whole scenario was just not registering with him!

The two men sauntered around to the back, where Frankie was surprised to see what looked like a small congregation gathered. They were drinking and singing with children playing around… all beneath an amazingly bright starry sky. "Who have we here, young Fuzz?" asked Bernice, her voice booming out. "My, he sure looks to be a strong boy."

"Hands off, Bernice," replied Fuzz, with a smile. "Where's Prue?"

"Our Prudence be restin'," she replied, which prompted whistles, wolf calls… the usual banter… "Let me repeat myself, she be restin', cause she be tired."

More calling out, and laughter ensued, and even Bernice herself couldn't contain herself. "Prue be tired 'cause she's sick. Shut your mouths you guys, Fuzz be just home from his daily toil."

More laughter and clapping, interspersed with wise cracks ensued. "Let me repeat myself, Fuzz be home, so let us be givin' him the peace he deserves, especially with him bein' a workin' man. Fuzz be our only man with a proper business… somethin' steady to get himself up for in the mornings!"

Cheers rang out, plus clapping, and then someone began to rap out a beat. "Hush there, boys. Showtime's gone to bed for tonight. Fuzz here needs time to spend with our dear Prudence," she called out. This time, before they could start again with their banging and banter, she motioned with her hands for them all to sling their hooks away from Fuzz's back door. Whatever Queen Bee Bernice said, went down like law in these parts. She was indeed a powerful woman… a giant in this small pond of little folks…

"Sorry Frankie, I need to go to Prue," said Fuzz. "Thanks for the lift once more... I'll come out front and help drag the scooter off the truck."

"I'll look into the café now that I've met you. I wasn't going to come in just to see our Marina," he replied, "but you're a sound guy." They unloaded the scooter, and Frankie headed off, hoping he would manage to find the main road; it couldn't be that difficult surely?

After the scooter was put to bed, Fuzz crept into his cabin to find Prue dozing. "Fuzz, I'm sorry... I've always been so healthy and just don't know what's wrong with me lately?" she said.

"Its fine... you can be as ill as you need to be. I'll be here for you," he replied.

"Thanks," she said, reaching out her hand to him.

He took it in his and gently caressed it. "Just go back to sleep. Sleep's the best thing for my lady," he replied. He'd taken a chance with these words, and she hadn't rebuked him, but had managed to smile. Fuzz realised that the more time he spent with her, the more bloody Saint Michael might pass into the annals of history or something not so pleasant!

As a mark of respect, the café remained closed the next day, which was the day of Cécile's funeral. When Fuzz told Prue, she was amazed with the funeral being held so soon. "Is it not a bit rushed?" she asked.

"It's the way they do things on this island. It's the heat, Prue… funerals are always speedy affairs here," replied Fuzz.

"Are you going?" she asked.

"Yes, it's first thing in the morning. I'll not be long, and then we can spend the rest of the day together," he replied.

"If I've recovered sufficiently, I'll look forward to that," she said. "Can we go into town afterwards, for a change?"

"Sure, if you're up for going," he said, more than just a little surprised.

*

He was back by ten the next morning to find Prue as bright as a newly hatched chick. He'd intended suggesting they give the town a miss, but as she was so excited to be going, he kept silent. It niggled all through Cécile's funeral service that it wasn't safe for her to go into town. Then again, things had quietened down recently, and with her hair in that unusual pixie style, it would be most unlikely anyone would recognise her. First, he thought one way and then the other, as to what to do, and decided to leave it to Prue. After all it was her decision and only hers to make.

They set off on the scooter, after running the gauntlet with Bernice, who disapproved. They would pay their fine to her when they returned, or try bribing her with a gift, to stop her booming on at them. With the wind in their hair, they turned off the track and onto the

161

Green Plantation Road, where the trees grew right to the edges of the road, and at places, the leaves and branches held hands forming an overhead canopy...

"Happy?" asked Fuzz, above the whine of the two-stroke engine.

"Very," she replied, as she held on to him tight, on what could often be a bumpy ride.

No mention of the 'M' word yet, he thought as he crossed his fingers and hoped it would long continue. They parked the scooter in the yard at the back of the café, and walked the short distance across the Square. At the far end lay the beach, and beyond that the small harbour.

"Fuzz, if we sit at that little milk bar over there, the one down by the beach, we can look back and see all the activity in the Square," suggested Prue. "I've sat there before to people watch."

"Good idea," he replied, as they headed in the direction of the milk bar.

"You grab a seat, and I'll fetch the drinks... what flavour do you fancy?" he asked.

"Whatever," she replied, "just get me the same as yourself. I'm just glad to be out and about."

She sat and gazed back up towards the Square. As always it was awash with folks, some going about their business, others laid back in leisurely pursuits, with a third, who made it difficult to identify just what they were doing?

Fuzz arrived back with two strawberry milkshakes and laid them carefully on the table, then slumped onto a seat. He could finally relax, happy in her company, with the ocean for background music. Their conversation and banter was light and humorous, as they slurped like a couple of contented kids playing hookey from school.

Prue recognised various people as they drifted past, folks she'd encountered when out and about with Michael. Fuzz and she giggled, as they all strolled past failing to recognise her. He reached across the table, and rested his hand lightly on top of hers. She smiled, and made no effort to resist his cautious advance. "I know this couple coming," she whispered, however they walked by, merely giving them a friendly nod with no sign of recognition.

They giggled once more, but when Prue turned her head, she was shocked to see Kate, arm in arm with her husband Bart, heading towards them. She nudged Fuzz, with her knee under the table, and as they walked past, Prue got the distinct feeling that something registered with Kate? She seemed perplexed, searching her brain for the answer… however, they continued on to the menu board, where they paused in discussion…

"What will we do if she places you?" asked Fuzz.

"We run… you take hold of my hand, and pull me to safety. I don't want to speak to her!" she whispered. He nodded in agreement… surely they could outrun them, especially that old geezer. Luckily, they moved on, and the impending emergency was over. "I'll fill you in about them later," she added.

Fuzz nodded. "Do you feel like taking a walk along the beach?" he asked. "We could always collect shells... I know Bernice likes shells."

"Ah, a gift for Bernice... at least she hasn't got expensive tastes," she replied.

Prue was in the process of standing, when she heard the monotonic tones of a familiar voice... "*Madame* Lambasto... *Madame* Lambasto, how you?" asked the voice.

She had her back to the voice, and gripped the table as she froze, looking at Fuzz, who responded to her panic... "Who are you?" he asked.

"I Marcel... *Madame* Lambasto's friend," replied the voice. Fuzz was unsure as what to say or do next? "*Madame* Lambasto, how *Monsieur* Lambasto? I no see him in places he go, and I not know where you go?"

Prue turned to face him, still trembling icily in the heat of the day, "Mar... cel," she replied slowly, her voice affected by her trembling. "How... are you?"

"I good, but miss you, *Madame*," he replied.

"Marcel, please sit with us," said Prue... then turning to Fuzz, "could you buy Marcel a drink, please?" He nodded and made his way over to the kiosk, still unsure of how to react? "Tell my friend what you'd like to drink, Marcel—— Oh no, they're coming back in our direction!" This last sentence was directed for Fuzz's benefit, as she didn't want to call out his name in front of Marcel.

"Oh, no… *Madame*, I no drink, but thank you with heart," he replied, patting his chest fervently. Fuzz by now could also see the couple walking back towards them. He kept a watch as he waited at the kiosk to see what she wanted him to do next?

He quickly considered if he would recognise her himself? Her face was more tanned, more vibrant and alive, despite the time recently spent tucked up in bed. She wore not one scrap of makeup, not even the waterproof mascara which, in the past, she never liked to be seen without, and the hair well… it bore no resemblance except for its colour, to the hairstyle she'd had when they'd first met.

"We need to go for a walk now," she said to Marcel, tugging him to his feet and then with her arm tightly tucked through his, they made their way across the hot sands towards the harbour, with Fuzz in hot pursuit.

"*Madame, Madame*… I no go… I no go," protested Marcel, quite unsure of what was happening.

"Oh, yes you do" she insisted, whilst Fuzz felt pity for the poor man, whoever he was!

He'd never seen Prue so animated or so focussed, "Hang on and wait for me," he called after her, "where in heaven's name are we going?"

165

"Never mind, just catch up Fuzz," she replied, and was instantly annoyed with herself for letting his name slip from her lips…

CHAPTER TWENTY-FOUR:

The little boats in the harbour bobbing on top of the sparkling waters, were akin to a throbbing dance floor illuminated by a disco glitter ball. The waves frothed high against the stone battlements of the harbour walls, as Prue, Fuzz and Marcel stood mesmerised by the sight... the ocean was definitely not in the best of moods today.

· "The power that is called Nature," stated Fuzz.

"It called ocean," replied Marcel.

"He knows it's called the ocean, Marcel," said Prue. "It's just that he uses different words to describe such things." She winked at Fuzz, who in turn wondered what her next party trick was going to be?

"I'm waiting for a sign as to my future," replied Fuzz, winking back at her.

"It's been very nice meeting you again Marcel, but we must say our goodbyes now," announced Prue, shaking his hand. Fuzz followed suit, whereupon they then took hands and slipped off deep into the mingling throngs which packed the narrow streets around the harbour... leaving a much confused and bemused Marcel.

Turning into a quiet narrow lane, they sought refuge in a bar, one which she recognised as one frequented by Michael. Fuzz found the bar far too dark in contrast to the bright sunlight outside. This was not where he wanted to be, and he felt more than a trifle annoyed. "What was that all about?" he asked, as they jostled for floor space.

"What do you mean?" she asked.

"Prue, that wasn't normal behaviour," he replied.

"It was all I could think of to do in the circumstances; Kate was on her way back, and if she'd got hold of me, the whole island would soon know," she answered.

"Would get to know what exactly?" asked a puzzled Fuzz.

"I don't know!" she snapped. "Heavens, I don't know what I'm doing on this godforsaken island anyway, living with you in a cabin in the middle of nowhere."

"Well, if that's how you feel, let me say I don't know why you're staying in my cabin either. I don't know from where you came, and I sure as hell don't know where you're going," he stated. "Why don't you find your husband… the Archangel Michael, as he's the cause of all your problems, not me?"

"I will then, I know when I'm not wanted," she snapped back, "and thank Bernice for all the kindness she and the others have shown me."

They looked at each other, each hurting so much from what had been said. The noise, the stench of stale seafood and spilled alcohol all wrapped together in a cloud of stale smoke, made them wonder why were they here at all? This place made all that had been spoken between them seem far worse!

Prue stared at him once more, and then hurriedly made her way towards the exit. He expected her to stop, turn and come back… but blinked and she was gone. He gathered himself and his thoughts, and headed for the door, but once outside found the lane empty, except for two young boys kicking a ball against the building.

"The lady… *la femme fatale*… which way did she go?" he asked."*De quelle maniere est-elle allee?*"

When they pointed in the direction of the main Square, he ran the twenty or so metres towards the end of the lane, but there was no sign… she'd disappeared and was lost to him in the throng. He climbed onto a bench, and then up onto a wall, trying desperately to catch a glimpse of her… but all to no avail.

"Prue," he shouted in desperation, "where are you?"

"Plenty more girlies down here on the ground; just say good riddance, and go fishin'," were the words of wisdom offered from an old codger who happened to be passing by.

"I don't need no lip from you," Fuzz snapped back.

"That boy's got that bug real bad," laughed the old guy, pointing at him standing on the wall. Fuzz could feel many eyes on him, and he despaired as he realised that he'd called out her name. Who knows who could be in the Square at that moment, and whose ears would pop at the very mention?

"Fuzz, Fuzz, what you doing up there?" he heard a very familiar voice call out. He jumped down from the wall, to find Marina barring his way. Bloody hell, not now Marina, not now, he thought. "Fuzz, what if some of your colonial ladies saw you creating a scene in the Square… what would they say?" she asked, grinning.

"Marina, at this moment, I couldn't give a toss what anybody said about anything anymore. I need to find someone, and that's all that matters to me," he replied.

"My God, what a state you've got yourself into, and over your cousin of all people," she spat out in return. He glared at her and pushed past, much to her displeasure. "Don't come running to me for help in the future," she yelled after him, as he disappeared into the crowd.

Where would Prue go... back to the café? Yes, he'd surely find her in the yard, waiting patiently beside his scooter ready to go back to their simple but idyllic life. He continued to push his way through the crowd, leaving in his wake a frustrated and angry Marina. "Damn you, Fuzz," she muttered under her breath.

*

Fuzz was in luck in one way; none of the colonial ladies were around, all having gone home after the funeral. His cogs turned... she had nothing, only her small backpack, but no phone, no money, and also no clothes. Prue had been making do with only two items of clothing, which Bernice laundered for her at the end of each day...

The café looked sad, dark and closed, which reflected his mood. He left it closed, and went straight around the back. There was no sign of her in the yard, and he noticed that she hadn't even collected her jacket, which was still slung on top of his panniers. Fuzz sat on an old wooden box to wait... she had to come... she had nowhere else to go, and when she did he would make up with her, apologise for the things he'd said, in the hope that matters would return to how they had been. A black cloud descended over him, and was his only companion, as he sat and waited in solitary isolation...

*

Prue had reached the Square, and scrambled through the crowds, her eyes smarting with hot tears. Once she'd reached the beach, the crowds thinned, and she found some much welcome shade under a tree. As she sat gazing and listening to the waves crashing, she realised she had nothing… only what she stood in at that very moment…

She had a purse in her backpack but no cash. In her purse were bankcards, but she hadn't used any of them for a while, and felt nervous about going into the bank. There was only one cash machine in the Square, and users were filmed with the best and latest of equipment, so she felt her cards were useless… "Michael, why aren't you here to help? I feel you've abandoned me, and after all we've gone through together," she whimpered to the breeze. Prue looked up, and through her misty, tearful eyes saw a familiar face coming towards her. She momentarily froze… what could she do to escape… she'd been noticed, and his tracks in the sand were steadily heading her way?

"*Madame* Lambasto, you still here? I no understand where you go," called Marcel. He came and sat beside her, and handed her a piece of fruit from a large basket he'd bought. She looked at her friend… she knew how much she needed one now.

"Where your friend, *Madame*?" he asked.

"I don't know… I appear to have lost him," she replied.

"Lost him? We go find, *Madame*," suggested Marcel.

"No, Marcel, he doesn't want to be my friend anymore," she replied.

"No friend? We go find *Monsieur* Lambasto?" then suggested a puzzled Marcel.

"I don't think he wants me either," she sighed.

"*Monsieur* no want?" he exclaimed.

"No, Marcel, I'm afraid not," she replied.

This time it was Marcel who stared out to the ocean. Prue joined him, and they sat with their eyes fixed on the rhythm of the mesmerising wave crests…

"What we do, *Madame*?" he eventually said, breaking the silence between them.

"I don't know what to do," she sighed.

"*Madame*," said Marcel, "I no leave my friend."

"Marcel, you must go. My problems are not yours… understand?" she replied.

"I know, but no leave. Come with me," he said. "I have my *femme fatale* Colette, and *deux enfants*."

"I never thought you had a wife and children, Marcel. You never told me," she replied.

"I tell Colette about *Madame*," he stated.

Prue had never imagined Marcel having a wife or family. How could he possibly manage on the little the Ocean Apartments paid? She'd given him generous tips, but she'd only been on the island for a relatively short time… perhaps three or four months. She recalled him fearing for his job security, which she now saw reason for… he needed a regular income to enable him to provide for his family.

"You come with me, *Madame*. We take fruit to *famille*," insisted Marcel, pulling on her arm.

"But Marcel, I don't have any money," replied Prue.

"I no have money," stated Marcel, with one of the first smiles she'd ever seen him produce. She smiled back, and accepted his hand to assist her up off the sand.

"I only have these clothes to wear," she said, pointing to them.

"I have these clothes only," replied Marcel, with another grin, as she walked with him along a dusty road towards another part of the island she'd never seen…

*

En route, she chatted the best she could with Marcel; sometimes he got things completely wrong, as did she, which made them laugh. They then approached, what was to Prue's eyes, a massive collection of makeshift buildings. It made her think of her parent's farm, with its run down outhouses, standing in a messy yard. It then dawned upon her that they were heading for the island's shanty town.

She followed Marcel into the jaws of the shacks, holding tightly onto his shirt, as he led her through a maze of rag-tag dwellings. He nodded and made comments to some of the men and woman he passed along the way, whilst also taking time to speak to the children, until they arrived at his… house!

"*Madame*, stand please, I tell Colette," he said.

God help me, thought Prue, why would Colette want to help me? This is ridiculous! She wanted to turn and run away, but realised she wouldn't be able to find her way back. Her only hope was that Marcel would at least take her to the edge of the settlement, back to the fringes of civilisation. Why had she come with him… she was not thinking straight? In fact, she was not thinking at all!

*

Fuzz waited for hours, but she failed to arrive. When the light faded, he reluctantly made the decision to head for home. He glanced at her jacket lying lonely and crumpled on one of his panniers; he lifted it and pressed it tightly against his chest, then folded it with care, and placed it where she was sure to find it… that was if she ever returned? When he was about to leave, he changed his mind about leaving her jacket, so picked it up and took it with him. If he had her jacket, then he still had part of her. What he was going to say to Bernice when he reached home… he had no idea!

The gloom had descended before he reached the track to the cabins. He cut the scooter's engine, and free-wheeled the last part, then parked at the front of his cabin, and entered by the front door. No one would expect him to do that. Once inside, the cabin's darkness encased him in an eerie silence; he didn't put on a lamp, preferring to fumble around in the gloom. From the kitchen, it was always possible to hear if there were folks out and about, and there were. He heard Bernice's hearty laugh, and cringed. If she knew he had lost Prue, all hell would undoubtedly be let loose. Fuzz splashed his face with copious amounts of cold water, before he slipped under the sheet on his side of the bed, and begun to howl, muffling the sound with his pillow…

With the arrival of dawn, he rose and silently left for the café. It had the makings of yet another beautiful day, and the island displayed what was the dawning of perfection. However, as Fuzz passed along the coast road on his trusty scooter, he couldn't give a damn about the beauty of Nature. It meant nothing to him, not today, as all beauty was missing from his life. "Prue, come back to me," he shouted to the trees. "Prue, I love you." The spitting, chugging noise of the scooter's engine, combined with the breeze in the branches of the trees, gobbled up the sound of his voice, spitting it out to be lost in the crashing of the waves…

*

There were raised voices coming from within Marcel's shack. Prue stepped back, not wanting to intrude. She was surrounded by crowded shacks and people, all speaking words she couldn't understand. The whole scene was so busy, and the heat so intense, she found herself drifting… when she opened her eyes, she was looking up at a strange ceiling. It was so low, she thought she could touch it, but before she had time to try, her attention was drawn to strange voices. Slowly, the voices came into focus… and she could see they belonged to an old woman, a young woman, and Marcel. "*Madame*, go down on ground… we give you to Dorothée. She has not the children… understand?" whispered Marcel. Prue nodded, although she didn't understand anything. Her eyes went back to the low ceiling, and then re-closed. She could hear them move away, muttering, then a loud unfamiliar noise, whereupon everything dissolved and was quiet once more…

Later, when she woke again, she forced herself to sit up. The ceiling seemed more distant this time, and there appeared to be more air. The old woman she'd seen before, was now sitting in a chair, her head supported by her chest, her eyes closed, and with heavy breathing spurting from her mouth and nose.

Prue lay back down and tried to think; but the ability to use her brain appeared to have deserted her. A noisy roar startled her, as someone else entered through the door. Then it fell quiet once more, and a young woman stood beside her. Prue pulled herself back up into a semi-sitting position and looked towards her... "*Je suis dur* Colette… my name Colette," she whispered, "you stay…" She then pointed to the old lady, "*avec* Dorothée," then left, and as she did so, Prue glimpsed the world beyond the makeshift door. It was a mixing bowl of noise and pungent smells or at least it seemed that way to her. She lay back down once more, and closed her eyes…

The next time she awoke, Marcel was in the room talking to Dorothée. He looked over, saw her stir, and shot over as a servant would to attend to his mistress's needs. "*Madame*, how you be? I have food for you," he said, "you want?"

She nodded and smiled a weak smile. Marcel, you are my hero, floated around in her head... "*Madame*, Colette say you carry *bébé*... *Monsieur* he happy man?" he said.

She looked at him, puzzled. Why do people keep talking about babies? "No," she snapped. "No, Marcel!"

"*Monsieur,* no happy?" he asked, rather shocked.

"I mean no, I'm not having a baby... Marcel, tell Colette that from me," she replied, annoyed for sounding so aggressive.

Marcel turned and spoke to Dorothée. The old lady rose, walked slowly over, and placed her hands on Prue's abdomen, and began to search all around that area. Prue couldn't believe what was happening, but didn't protest. She was frightened; this woman could be anyone, perhaps a *sorcier*!

Dorothée then turned and spoke to Marcel, who turned and spoke to Prue... "Dorothée, she say the *bébé* will soon... walk inside... I mean, legs and arms, you understand?" said Marcel, flapping his arms in the air.

"No, I don't understand, not one little bit," she replied.

He then announced he had to leave for work. "Marcel, you can't tell me what you've just said and then disappear," she exclaimed.

"*Madame*, I must work. You understand... you see my work, I go now," he replied, "but you stay."

178

He opened the door to the noise and then was gone. Prue found she was becoming used to her surroundings. It didn't seem quite as loud when the door was opened. Dorothée looked over, smiled, and rocked a pretend baby in her arms, which made Prue look away quickly. The old lady then moved around the shack going about her business... she was more agile than Prue had first thought. It was only she who remained in this room with its low ceiling, doing nothing, and being almost afraid to move a muscle. Tentatively she placed her hands on her abdomen... it did feel more rounded, perhaps a little swollen... her hands then strayed upwards to her breasts... there was something different about them too. If there was a baby on the way... only if... should she not have been sick in the mornings? Her sickness had only recently begun... she'd been tired, had fainted, and had spent time at Fuzz's place feeling under the weather...

Michael had announced only once that he did not want children, as his job meant they would continually be on the move. She had not queried his decision on that occasion. He'd been selfish; she could see that now. Something as important as children should have been a joint decision, not a dictatorial announcement. Fuzz would never have made such a pronouncement, she thought, but he didn't want her either, even as a friend. He'd made that perfectly clear, but she still didn't think he would have made such a selfish statement about children. Now she would never know for sure.

Prue lay back down on her makeshift bed, and fell back into a fevered, confused slumber...

CHAPTER TWENTY-FIVE:

The café usually began the day quietly, with trade building up over the course of the morning. Some folks always came in for breakfast, most still choosing the old colonial style comprising coffee, croissants and selected fruits. Then there was the scrambled egg and toast brigade, the preferred option of the lady members of the *Colonial Club*, which always made Fuzz smile as he had introduced them to this delicacy.

It was to be expected that the ladies would feel a bit raw and subdued after the funeral, thought Marina, so a more leading role was called for. Furthermore, she could see that Fuzz was going to be less than useless; at the moment he was behind the counter mechanically filling coffee cups and making toast, much in the same way a robot would.

"What's wrong with him, Marina?" asked Veronique, out of the corner of her mouth.

"Oh, I don't know… he's not saying. I believe it to be an illness of the heart," whispered Marina.

"His heart?" whispered one of the other concerned ladies who'd overheard. "Heaven's we've just buried poor Cécile, no more please."

"It's all right, Jeanette, it's not what you think," whispered Veronique. "No, we think it's a malaise… some kind of love sickness."

"Oh," whispered Jeanette, with a grin, "I do like a romance."

"But this is probably a romance which has gone wrong, wouldn't you agree, Marina?" asked Veronique, still mouthing from the corner of her mouth.

"Yes, I agree with you," she replied. "He should perhaps concentrate more on his business as he doesn't make good choices in affairs of the heart."

"Hmm, maybe he ought to look closer to home for his love interest," whispered Veronique, raising her eyebrows as she smiled to Marina. She smiled back… good, she's a handy person to have on-side…

Marina went back over to Fuzz with a proposition, "Fuzz, you're useless today. If there's anywhere else you'd be happier, then the ladies and I are prepared to manage the café without you," she suggested.

"Well, now that you've mentioned it, there is someone that I'd like to speak to," he answered, thoughtfully.

"Off you go then, don't linger, and we'll see you back in the morning. Don't make a fuss Fuzz, just slip away," replied Marina. He looked at her with a blank but thoughtful expression, then bent over and kissed her on the cheek. Some of the ladies were about to clap, when Veronique motioned for them to refrain... her hand reminiscent of a conductor's baton.

Fuzz knew how to shift when he needed, and he mounted his trusty scooter as a man on a mission. The strong winds coming off the ocean, gusted and played havoc with his fair fuzzy mop. He sped along the Green Plantation Road as fast as the winds would allow, and on arrival marched straight in to see Bernice, with the pain of his guilt bearing heavily down upon him.

Bernice was hard at work, when he knocked on her back door. "Where you been gone to, Fuzz, and what have you done with my Prudence girl? There be no sign of nobody at your cabin last night and it worried me," said an unusually subdued Bernice.

"Can I interrupt what you're doing? I need your full attention as I've something to confess," he replied.

Bernice knew this was serious, and laid down the laundry she was folding, "Sit over there, Fuzz, you know I be here for you," she said.

Hell was not let loose in the room as anticipated; instead Fuzz experienced a different side to Bernice. She listened to what he had to tell, and instead of recriminations, surprised him with empathy, and then gave him some startling, fresh information. She'd found out that a badly injured man had recently been discretely airlifted off the island in the private plane belonging to the island's all powerful dictator… Judge Maurice W. Stoker! The name recorded for that injured person in the airfield paperwork, was a Martin Lambert.

"What you be thinking, Fuzz?" she asked.

"What do you mean? I'm not thinking anything," he answered.

"I think he be Michael Lambasto. My man at the airfield says all the buttons were pushed for this guy's security clearance and comfort. Stoker was at the airfield to personally see him off. My informant thought this guy important, it being the first time he'd ever seen the Judge at the airfield, unless he was flying off or arriving back himself. He never even meets *Madame* Stoker when she arrives back from one of her dodgy trips."

"Why do you think it was the Dark Angel Michael?" asked Fuzz.

"Think about it… the initials M.L are the same," answered Bernice.

"So," said Fuzz, "I don't think that necessarily means anything?"

"Fuzz, I be a book reader, and I like the movie films. Folks in books and movie films who be changing names, often seem to keep the same initials," replied Bernice. "It's him Fuzz, I feel it in my bones."

"If that's right, then where does that leave Prue?" asked a now intrigued Fuzz.

"I don't know what will happen to Prudence and her baby," she answered.

"If there is a baby, then it's the Dark Angel's," said Fuzz.

"All I say to you my boy, is that I will be havin' everyone I knows and trusts on this island, looking for Prudence," replied Bernice.

What else could he say? He took himself down to the beach to think, but then quickly decided he should also be looking for her, instead of sitting listening to the roar of the ocean with sand between his toes…

*

The scooter chugged its weary way back into town. His trusty steed was in need of a rest, so when he reached the outskirts he patted the beast, and left it in a friend's garden under a shady tree. It would be much easier to get about on foot anyway, rather than run the gauntlet with the crazed traffic in the crowded town Square and labyrinth of surrounding streets.

Fuzz didn't know where to begin his search, so he retraced his steps to where he'd last seen her… at the bar which stank with all that was wrong with this place. There was no need to enter, so he re-traced his steps the short distance to the Square, and stood on the spot, where she must have stopped to ponder her next move. Where would she go next? Since it had been as busy, and as hot as it was today, she would no doubt have first tried to get out of the crowds, which meant crossing the Square to the beach and harbour. Once there, she would have sought shade. He followed his hunch and her imaginary footsteps, and looked around for a shady spot. On spying a small clump of trees that he'd never noticed before, he reckoned that was where she must have headed. He did likewise, and sat on a tree stump, under the convenient canopy... why had he not been thinking straight like this on that fateful morning, he wondered?

What next? This was where it began to get more problematic! What would she do next? Why had they headed to the bar in the first place... to escape from... what was his name? Marcel, that was it.

Wait a minute, he thought, the guy who'd spotted her was a native islander... while all the others she knew socially were not, and they had walked past her without recognition; but that one man had recognised her. He'd not only stopped to say hello... but had also asked about the welfare of *Monsieur* Lambasto! He then was virtually dragged along by her in her attempt to escape from this Kate woman and her old geezer of a husband. Fuzz was thankful for the shade from the trees, while he pondered these snippets of vital information. But what now? There was a slim chance that Marcel hadn't moved too far away from the harbour or beach area that day, and she may have met up with him, or more likely, he may have spotted her again...

Who was this Marcel? He was someone who'd served her, but not as a waiter in a restaurant... no, he seemed to know her better than that. She wanted to buy him a drink and wasn't surprised he recognised her. But how? Hardly anyone had seen her with her hair chopped, except for the folks back at the cabins. This guy had obviously known her with her long hair; he must have, as he'd asked her about Michael...

Where had she come from before arriving at the café looking for sanctuary? It was from the Blue Ocean Apartments. If Marcel worked there, that would explain how he knew her and her husband, and he must've recognised her when she'd left with her cropped hair. Prue also didn't seem surprised by the fact he recognised her. Indeed, Marcel might even have been a friend, perhaps the one who'd given her that ridiculous pineapple she'd brought into the café for him to slice, but never actually got around to doing? Fuzz reckoned that if he could locate this Marcel, he could be well on his way to finding Prue...

Michael had left the island; this seemed certain from the information Bernice had gleaned, which meant his lady was now on her own. With Judge Stoker in cahoots with Michael, Fuzz knew that he'd better watch his back... as should Prue!

*

She had slept right through, for it was morning when Colette sauntered into Dorothée's with a little girl by the hand and a little boy holding onto her skirts. They were beautiful children, with large dark eyes and wavy hair. Colette was pleasant to her, and the little ones handed her bread and fruit. Prue smiled and thanked them, then caught their mother's eye... "Colette, can you take me to the edge of the settlement where I can make my way back into town?" she asked.

"You want go?" she queried.

"Yes," answered Prue, "please."

"Marcel, he say you no place to go," stated Colette.

"I have, Colette… I have a friend," she lied.

"We go after you have eat, *avec moi*," she replied, pointing with her finger to her home next door. She then spoke to Dorothée in words which was beyond Prue's comprehension. The children ran over and sat by the old woman, and Prue got the impression that Colette would be relieved that she'd soon be gone.

She was right to want rid of her; she seemed nothing but trouble for everyone she came into contact with. At this moment, she didn't care she had nowhere to go, she just wanted away from this place.

"We go," said Colette, "*ne dites-vous pas a* Marcel, that I say you go."

"I think I understand," replied Prue. "You have not asked me to go; it is my choice." She had only her small backpack to gather up, not even her jackct, so she waved to the children and Dorothée, and followed Colette next door, relieved that she was not feeling sick, and was being fed before they left.

After they'd finished eating, Prue thanked her, and they got on their way. Soon they were weaving through the hotchpotch of makeshift structures. Colette walked so fast, that Prue had difficulty keeping up. She was buffeted as she tried to make her way through the throngs crammed into such narrow spaces. Colette continued apace, until Prue managed to grab on to her flowing skirts, "Please, Colette," she gasped, "wait, can't you walk any slower... please?"

Colette stopped, smiled, and then continued at a slower pace, "I say you have *bébé*," she announced, "you sure do have *bébé*, that's why you slow."

Prue didn't have either the energy nor the inclination to reply...

The dry landscape opened up ahead, as they passed the last few scattered structures. "Thanks Colette, and thank Marcel for his kindness," she puffed. Colette said nothing, but gave her a quick hug, and then vanished back into the bustling crowds, where she was lost to sight.

The enormity of what Prue had done suddenly hit home. Her feet moved slowly along the dusty track, where bicycles, motorbikes, old cars and vans, headed back and forth, each jostling with each other for space on the narrow sandy track. She felt unsafe, and found an alternative path, a short distance from the bustling traffic.

However, Colette had not abandoned her as Prue had thought, but had stopped to watch her go. It had been Prue's decision to leave... not hers. Nevertheless, she was unhappy at letting her go, particularly in her delicate situation.

Prue judged that it would only take her about fifteen minutes or so to reach the outskirts of town. What was she going to do then? What would Michael have told her to do? Why did she always wonder what he would have told her to do? Who was Michael anyway? At this moment in time, he was fading fast…

It was not Michael but Fuzz that caused the ache in her heart. He'd rejected her at a time when she needed him most. How had that come about? They'd been fine that morning; she would have sworn under oath that he was happy. What had changed that day? She replayed it over and over in her mind, and realised that she'd hurt him. Fuzz had only retaliated, and had probably said things he didn't mean. As sure as hell, she'd not meant to hurt him. If she'd not suggested they come into town, everything would still be fine…

She had to find him… he was the one she wanted to see, not Michael!

CHAPTER TWENTY-SIX:

Fuzz debated whether to collect his scooter or walk to the Blue Ocean Apartments, before deciding the latter would make a more discreet entrance. His scruffy old scooter would have had to sit cheek by jowl with the expensive vehicles on view there, a thought which made him smile.

Trust it to be one of the islands most upmarket locations, and he was not dressed in top notch style. His scooter ride into town battling the wind had also left his hair particularly wild. He quickly ran his hand through it, trying to tame his unkempt mane… why was he bothering about such things, this was no job interview, he was not applying for a position; he only wanted to enquire if Marcel worked there? "Strike now while the idea's fresh, and enjoy the walk along the beach," he muttered softly to himself, "the ocean, and the sand always make you smile."

All the best apartment blocks on the island faced the ocean, and were situated within one hundred metres of its fine powdery white beaches. Looking along the shoreline, he could see the Blue Ocean Apartments ahead, making an imposing impact on the otherwise unspoilt skyline. The fresh white building sparkled in the sunlight, and appeared to become more and more splendid the nearer he got.

Once there, he didn't hesitate, but brazenly negotiated the revolving door with his head held high. He briefly gazed at the glitz and glitter, then confidently strolled the short distance across the entrance hall to the Concierge's desk…

"*Monsieur,* can I help?" asked the Concierge somewhat disparagingly. Fuzz explained that he was trying to trace someone whom he believed worked within these premises, by the name of Marcel. "*Monsieur*, the family name of this man please?" he asked, haughtily.

"I'm afraid I don't know," answered Fuzz.

"Then I'm afraid I cannot help you, *Monsieur*," announced the Concierge, who then turned away on the pretence of tidying his empty desk… but Fuzz was not finished with him yet…

"*Monsieur Concierge*, a moment if you please. You must surely know if someone by the name of Marcel works here? It's not so vast an apartment block, that someone of your status would not know the names of all employees," he ventured.

"I beg your pardon, *Monsieur*? Please do not try to tell me what I ought or ought not to know," he answered. "It would be better if you left now, otherwise—,"

"Otherwise what, *Monsieur?*" asked Fuzz, unfazed by this officious attitude.

"You would not want to know, *Monsieur*," he answered.

Fuzz heard a shrill ringing sound, and a muscular young man suddenly appeared from nowhere. The two men exchanged a brief conversation, which Fuzz failed to follow, but understood well enough what was coming next. The young man stepped in front of him, and directed Fuzz to the door with an authoritative sweep of his hand. Fuzz complied; he could see which way the odds were stacked. He wanted to say that he was a friend of *Madame* Lambasto, but knew that would only stir the soup to boiling point. In any case, he was relieved to be back outside in the hot dry air, out of that artificially cooled atmosphere. At least he'd progressed his idea, however weak his attempt had been.

Wondering what to do next, Fuzz noticed a path in the grounds that led to the beach, and was about to follow it, when he heard someone call out... "*Monsieur*," a soft voice spoke. "It is Marcel... *le Bar a Lait, a six heures.*"

"Where are you?" asked Fuzz, looking around.

"*Aller, Monsieur*," whispered Marcel.

Fuzz continued on his way, and was relieved when he reached the beach without further incident. He decided to go to the milk bar at six as suggested, and wait to see what transpired.

*

When she eventually reached the outskirts of town, Prue made the decision to go to Fuzz's café. She had no other choice, as she had nowhere else to go. He might agree to have a coffee with her, which was more than she deserved, after being such an ungrateful wench. This was all her fault, she'd started all of this, and had no one but herself to blame.

It looked busy through the café's window, but she brazened it and entered regardless. Marina was waiting tables, with three or four women crammed behind the serving counter. Prue tried to avoid her, by weaving through the tables towards the women. "It's waitress service only, unless you're sitting at the counter on a high stool," stated a woman, whom Prue only vaguely recognised.

"Can you tell me where Fuzz is plea—?" she asked.

"He's not here today," interrupted another woman, looking at her with disdain.

Prue ran her fingers through her cropped mop. It must look a mess, as would her clothes, which were sweat stained and clinging to her as if she'd lain in them all night. What a sight she must look, as she had lain in them all night!

"What can I get you," asked the first lady, "as I've already told you, you'll have to sit on a stool if you want to stay at the counter, otherwise find a seat and Marina will attend to you?"

"I don't want anything thanks, I don't have any money," replied Prue. "I just came in to speak to Fuzz."

Marina heard her words, looked over, and realised who it was, "It's all right Amabel, she's Fuzz's cousin, or at least he says she's his cousin. What does she want?" she asked.

"She says she's come to see him, and doesn't have any money," answered Amabel.

"She came in for a freebie the last time too," replied Marina. "I'd show her the door, if I were you Amabel; she looks mighty scruffy to me, and not the type you ladies would wish to associate with."

Prue was so embarrassed that she turned and left without another word. Once outside, she walked on a little before her tears arrived. At that same moment, she was surprised to feel a small flutter within her abdomen, which made for even more tears…

Inside the café, Jeanette, who was one of the colonial ladies, looked at her watch and announced she had to leave. "I'm sorry ladies, but time has overtaken me," she announced, hurrying towards the door. Once outside, her eyes scanned the street… I hope I'm not too late, she thought.

Prue next felt someone tap her on her shoulder, "Excuse me, I was in the café just now, and also that day

194

when you came in before. You looked beautiful that day, with your hair as your crowning glory, and I remember Fuzz telling Marina that you were family," said the lady ."He appeared smitten, and given the circumstances, I think they've all behaved rather badly to you just now."

"Marina's right," replied Prue, "I'm not Fuzz's cousin... he was a friend, but I don't think he is anymore."

"What's your name," asked the lady, "mine's Jeanette?"

"Prudence, but everyone calls me Prue," she whispered.

"Prue, please don't be offended, but are you expecting a baby?" she asked.

"I don't know, everyone keeps telling me I am, but I just don't know," she replied. "Something has just moved inside of me."

The tears then began to flow, and Jeanette felt at a terrible loss as what to do next. "Look, I didn't like the way you were treated back there, and you look rather the worse for wear. If I grab us a taxi, will you come back to my apartment, and tell me what's been happening to you? Will you come... I think Fuzz would want you to?"

Prue looked directly at Jeanette for the first time. She had a warm kindly smile, and honest eyes. She nodded in agreement, and gave her a watery-eyed smile of appreciation.

*

At five minutes to six, Fuzz arrived at the milk-bar by the beach, and ordered *au chocolat*. He didn't expect Marcel to appear, but decided to give him the benefit of the doubt. Suddenly he heard the familiar voice behind him, "*Monsieur*, it is Marcel."

Fuzz spun around in his seat, to find Marcel had already slipped into an adjacent seat at his table. "Can I get you something to drink?" he asked... God the man can move like a lizard, he thought...

"*Non, non, Monsieur,* I okay," replied Marcel.

"Why would they not tell me that you worked at the Apartments?" asked Fuzz.

"They no tell," replied Marcel.

"But why?" he asked.

"I no know why... they not do," he replied. "*Monsieur... Madame* Lambasto, she stay with me."

"What?" said Fuzz, bewildered. "Why?"

"She no more place to stay. She on beach, so I take to my wife," he explained. "*Madame* say you no want her... my Colette say *Madame* Lambasto has *bébé*."

"Marcel, will you take me to her please, I need to find her?" pleaded Fuzz.

"We can go now," he replied.

196

Marcel rose, and Fuzz wiped the foam from his mouth, and followed. The little guy could definitely shift like a lizard, he thought, as he chased after him along the South Road out of town. He soon realised where they were headed. Oh, Prue, this is not what you've been used to; his own cabin was basic, but this would have been a culture shock!

He eventually caught up on Marcel, but there was little effort given to conversation, as both remained deep within their own thoughts. He followed him into a place he'd only been once before, a few years previously. It had not improved but had grown much larger, much dirtier and noisier than he remembered.

When they reached Marcel's shack, he told Fuzz to wait outside. He did as instructed, feeling somewhat lost and conspicuous, but fortunately Marcel was not long before he re-emerged. "She no here… Colette say she want go," he explained.

Colette then appeared at the door with her children, "She nice lady, why she need come here," she asked Fuzz, "what you do to her?" She glared at him, which made him feel extremely uncomfortable. "You make *bébé*, and then you no want," she continued, then spat on the ground near to his feet, before disappearing back indoors. Marcel made no attempt to apologise, and also made to leave.

How were either Colette or Marcel expected to know the truth? Fuzz decided to tell him, "Marcel, wait… it's *Monsieur* Lambasto's baby, not mine… do you understand?" he began. Marcel nodded, but followed Colette indoors.

Fuzz then hurriedly left, trying to visualise the way they'd come. After a few wrong turns, he managed to somehow find his way back into the fresh open air. What a place..., thank the Lord for his Plantation Road home.

His mind buzzed as he thought of Prue, and what she must be going through. For the first time, he considered the reality that she was pregnant. However, he'd have to leave thoughts of that until later, as his first task was to find her, wherever she was.

He clambered down the rocks onto the beach, and walked along the foreshore, until he reached the harbour. By now, it was almost seven, and his own café would be closed. He decided to first check she wasn't in the yard, then collect his scooter from under his friend's tree and hit the road home. If she'd somehow gone to the café, Marina would surely have looked after her. He decided to phone her once he'd checked the yard or that she'd not by any quirk of fate managed to reach his cabin.

It was dark in the rear yard of the café, so he called out her name. There was no reply. *The Coffee Palace* across the way was open until midnight, so he checked inside just in case, but she was not there either. He then made his way to pick up his scooter, thanked his friend for the use of his shady tree, and set off for home.

Tonight he didn't creep in through the front door, but went straight around the back and discussed Prue with the folks who were sitting outdoors, including

Bernice. "I've no more news about Prudence, but my troops are onto her case," she said, "mighty strange."

"Anyone doing your bidding on the South Road, Bernice? That's where she was last night, but she moved on this morning," enquired Fuzz.

"The South Road, you say... Lordy be, surely Prudence is not in Shanty Town? Fuzz, what be going on?" she exclaimed. "Come here, boy."

She hugged him, and he gasped for breath, until she let him go. They were his family... he was far from his homeland, but so lucky to have these folks around him as friends. He'd arrived on this island with a wife and top job, but both had abandoned him. He now had to find Prue... he was determined not to abandon her.

"Go sleep, Fuzz, and get yourself up fresh tomorrow. You have the café to open?" ordered Bernice.

"Yeah, thanks for reminding me. I need to go now... I've also a call to make," he replied. It was to Marina... he'd meant to phone earlier.

*

Time had slipped by as he'd meant to phone Marina earlier... "Hi, Frankie, how's it going?" asked Fuzz. "Is your sister around, I need a quick word?"

"I'll fetch her... and I'll look in to see you soon," he replied.

"You do that," answered Fuzz.

199

"Fuzz, what is it… is everything okay?" asked Marina, taking hold of the phone.

"No, Marina, it's not. Have you seen Prue, the girl I told you was my cousin?" he asked.

"Do you mean the girl with the long hair? No, I would've remembered her by the length of her hair," she lied.

"She's had her hair cut short… it's kind of cropped now," he stated.

"Well, I wouldn't recognise her without her long hair, even if she had been in today," she replied.

"So, are you telling me that she hasn't been in today," he asked again, "think Marina, it's important?"

"Look Fuzz, we were very busy. The Colonials and I have done our best, and that's all I can tell you," she replied.

"Okay, I'll see you tomorrow morning," he said.

Marina came off the phone and re-thought the scenario. She hadn't let on to him that she had recognised her, which was fine until she remembered that she'd told the ladies who she was; she would need to have a word with them first thing tomorrow morning!

*

Jeanette made Prue feel welcome, but first, asked her a very obvious question… "Would you care to take a shower and freshen up?"

"Oh, yes please… I feel absolutely—," she replied.

"No need to explain, I fully understand," interrupted Jeanette, who produced a selection of clothes her daughter kept in the spare room for when she visited. In the bathroom, she also laid out a toothbrush, comb, and a brush. "Help yourself to anything else," she called after her, as Prue disappeared inside.

The hot water caressed her, as she soaped her body and rubbed shampoo into her messy black mop. The suds felt and smelled divine. She lingered in the shower, not wanting to leave, but as they say all good things must come to an end sometime. Whilst drying her body and hair, she looked at the clothes Jeanette had laid out for her. There was a modern pale blue, scooped-neck dress and a pair of rope sandals, that looked a shade large, but she couldn't be too fussy…

*

Jeanette sat in her lounge window-seat, which offered her a marvellous overview of the old town… wondering if she'd done the right thing? What else could she have done in the circumstances as the girl was in desperate trouble? It was in her nature to help needy people, unlike most of her friends and definitely all her relations. She didn't understand the behaviour being shown, especially from Marina, who had most definitely recognised her? She must've noticed Fuzz's reaction when the girl had called into the café previously? It was obvious that he'd been smitten…

She then rose, and walked through to her spare bedroom. Her hand reached for the switch to the ceiling fan… this underused room needed some cooler air to circulate. She checked the bed, pulled back the sheets, and laid out her daughter's cotton nightdress… Jeanette presumed her visitor would stay the night, but first, she would cook a little food, and seek some kind of explanation…

*

The explanation came amid tears and watery smiles… it took a lot of words to recount all that had happened… she started at the very beginning and stopped when there was nothing more to say.

"My, that's been some adventure you've been on Mrs Lambasto," announced Jeanette, once Prue had brought her right up to date. "What do you want to do now? I think the first thing you and I should do tomorrow, is to call in and see my *docteur*. Do you agree?"

Prue nodded with emotion, her hand gently clasped on her now rounded stomach.

The two women spent the rest of the evening listening to music, with Jeanette taking two phone calls both in Prue's presence. She never mentioned that she had a visitor, although she put someone off, who wanted to visit the following afternoon.

"After our visit to my *docteur*, I believe you have a phone call to make," suggested Jeanette. Prue nodded. So much for her looking after herself, she thought. She had now let Jeanette take control. Tomorrow, after the *docteur* had confirmed her pregnancy or otherwise, she knew she had to make the phone call Jeanette suggested. To say she was dreading making it, was not a sufficiently expressive phrase to show how she felt.

*

Fuzz didn't sleep much that night, and rose at the first sign of light. Work is the answer, he concluded… try to focus on the café today. A thought suddenly struck him; should he report Prue as a missing person to the police? He could imagine what the gallant *garçons* of the *gendarmerie* would make of his account! It was messy; what with Michael, this angel of a man having gone missing, and now Prue. He would hate to become embroiled with the Authorities; they were a law unto themselves, albeit under the iron fist of Judge Maurice Wiseman Stoker.

The folks out at the Green Plantation Road cabins would not take it kindly if they even had a whiff that the police were coming their way. He then remembered that the police had searched the Lambasto place at the Blue Ocean Apartment complex, not to mention those other tough guys, who'd been sniffing around asking for her…

Just go to work Fuzz, and try to push it to the back of your mind, he decided… which was nigh on impossible, as he was so desperate to trace her.

*

Prue remained in bed at Jeanette's until dawn, then rose and sat for a couple of hours on the front facing guest bedroom's window-seat. From there, she watched as the morning was born... nodding in time to the sound of the waves. Fuzz must have scooted beneath her window when he reached the outskirts of town on his way to the cafè, but he had no reason to look up, and she had no reason to look down...

*

Jeanette hadn't slept too well either, and had read in bed for several hours. But come morning, she was up and on the phone to her *docteur's* surgery, and rewarded with a ten-thirty appointment for Prue. "That's not too early, and not too late," she announced. "We can have breakfast whenever you're ready... and then, take our coffee on the *terrasse*."

As Jeanette prepared a light breakfast, Prue assessed her... she was probably around sixty, maybe slightly younger, and had a pleasant, honest face. From the photos scattered around the lounge, and from what she had gleaned, she was the widowed mother of two boys and a girl. There were grandchildren, and other family members in the photos, but none appeared to be here on the island judging by the backgrounds. Why did she live here then, she wondered?

During coffee, Prue asked her that very question, "Are none of your family here with you on the island, Jeanette?" she asked.

Jeanette looked at her and smiled, "I have some relatives on the island, my brother being one of them," she replied. "Have you heard of Judge Stoker?"

"Yes, I have," exclaimed Prue, with a gulp. "Are you telling me that he's your brother?"

"I am indeed. What have you heard about Maurice?" she asked. Prue didn't answer, and looked away embarrassed. "It's okay, I know what you mean, and I happen to agree with you," continued Jeanette. "Why do I stay? The answer is that I feel safe here. This is the place where I have lived all my married life. When my dear Jacques died, I stayed on. I think I'd be lost anywhere else, as nowhere else is home to me anymore. There are quite a few of us island widows who've stayed on here; we've all been here for so long that it would be very hard for any of us to relocate elsewhere. Some have taken to congregating at Fuzz's café most days, it's sort of our Club. He's even put a sign up calling the café the *Colonial Club*, would you believe? We just took to him, and he made us very welcome. Nice and homely, you understand, not like the more up market cafés where we used to meet in the past."

Prue nodded, she knew all about the *Colonial Club*, and its ladies… after all, she had named the place.

"Now to return to my brother… having Maurice more or less in total charge of this island is a comfort to me, although I'm content to rarely have any dealings with the man," she continued. "In fact, being related to him is a double-edged sword… it cuts both ways, good and bad."

Prue was thinking what a pickle she'd now got herself into. She didn't want to say anymore, and felt she'd already said more than enough. For one thing, she had mentioned to her the Lambasto name... but what was done was done! "Have I time to take a shower, before we go to see your *docteur*?" asked Prue.

"Plenty... he's actually coming here to see you. I thought that would be for the best," answered Jeanette.

Prue was surprised at the *docteur's* home visit, but pleased about having time for another deliciously hot invigorating shower. Once in the shower, her hand caressed her body. It did seem different, and just as she finished and reached for a towel, she felt another flutter deep inside... Prue stood in shock, there it was again, faint but clear, sending out a message that things would never be the same for her ever again. The *docteur* would no doubt think her silly to have reached this stage without realising the significance of her bodily changes...

"How was your shower," asked Jeanette, "nice and refreshing, I hope?" Prue sat in the lounge, and told her what she had just experienced, and what a fool she felt.

"No, you're not," replied Jeanette." Sometimes life doesn't always go to plan, as you have found out lately. Let's see what *Docteur Charbonneau* has to say. I'm afraid he's around my age or even older, not one of these smart young medics most people seem to have these days. I think diagnosing a pregnancy should still be within his capabilities though."

He was as Jeanette had described, his old school language and ways limiting his communication skills. Prue had never been examined in such an intimate manner before, and it stored up feelings of embarrassment and discomfort that she never knew existed. Just let it be over, and let him leave…she prayed.

Humiliation then spread through her, as she was left lying atop the bed, while he went to find Jeanette to discuss his findings. She hated this island and its ways… Michael, damn you, damn you, damn you! Where are you… you selfish pig, leaving me in this godforsaken backwater, all alone with my forbidden fruit?

Once she had learned from Jeanette of the *docteur's* diagnosis, she decided to make that phone call they'd discussed the previous evening… the call she was dreading. This was causing ructions within the pit of her stomach, along with the now stronger little flutterings…

*

"Sorry about that," said Jeanette. "I'm used to the old fart, but you clearly are not."

"Oh, don't worry… he was fine," lied Prue.

"No, he wasn't, but at least he still knows his stuff," said Jeanette. "You're about halfway, four and a half months, he said, or perhaps a little more? Why he told me and not you, I have no idea, but the old fool insisted."

"Thanks for that, Jeanette. I have no money here, but I do have in the bank," replied Prue. "I need to pay you for his services."

"Not at all… it's my gift to you. I heard you say you didn't have any money in the café remember. You don't need any at the moment, and in any case, I think it's best if you stay here," she suggested. "Anyway, he wants you to rest. He does know the basic stuff, so rest is what you ought to do."

"Thank you so very much. I'm going to make that phone call now… the one I promised I'd make," replied Prue, "then I'll rest, just as the good *docteur* ordered."

Jeanette gave her a hug. "Please trust me Prue, I'm on your side. We'll get through this together," she stated, as Prue left her to make the call.

CHAPTER TWENTY-SEVEN:

Most of the routine chores were done when Marina arrived for work. He must have been up with the birds again, she thought? Her conscience felt clear as to what she'd said last night on the phone, regarding his so-called cousin. It had been for his own good! That woman was not for him, as there was someone far more suitable… and much closer to home. However, she would need to get hold of the ladies as soon as they arrived, to brief them on what to say, or rather what not to say.

"How did it go yesterday? Did you get done what you needed to do?" she asked.

"No," he replied curtly.

God, it's going to be yet another teeth-pulling day… he's in that kind of mood. "Are you okay for working today, Fuzz?" she asked.

"I'll just have to be; nothing else for it, Marina," he replied. He'd called her by her name... that was progress. She had noticed in the past that he usually avoided calling her by her name whenever his mood was sour.

She hastily made two coffees and slipped a few slices of bread into the toast machine... "Who's the toast for?" he asked, looking around the closed café.

"For you of course, and just a little for me," she replied.

"Thanks," he said, "that smell's del—,"

"Oh, damn... I've burnt it! That machine makes the toast so fast," she suddenly yelled, interrupting him mid-sentence.

"That's good isn't it? We don't want our customers hanging around for their toast. Pass me a slice over here," he replied. He sat opposite her caressing the burnt offering as he munched.

This was just like old times, she thought... before that blooming cousin bird of his arrived on the scene!

"I spoke briefly to Frankie," he stated. "He answered when I phoned. Can you remind him to look in. I like him, despite him being a certain person's brother."

"And what certain person is that?" she asked.

"Hmm… I wonder?" he replied, as they both laughed.

What about his sister, Fuzz? Do you not like his sister better than that dirty wench who waltzed in here yesterday? What's wrong with me, I'd do anything for you, well most things, she thought!

This moment between them disappeared as opening time arrived, and the first few eaters of the day, began to sleepwalk their way inside. Marina would be on tenterhooks until she had briefed her ladies to not mention yesterday's unsavoury visitor. She was having second thoughts about what she'd told him, and black thoughts about what he would say or do if he ever found out. She offered up a silent prayer that he never would.

*

At their Somerset farm, Mr and Mrs Dibble received an unexpected phone call from their only daughter, from whom they'd been estranged for several years…

The funny thing was that a few days earlier, they had received another surprise; a visitation from two dark-suited men from a certain hush-hush Government Department, who had brandished IDs and informed them of the tragic news that their son-in-law, Michael Lambasto, had been reported missing, presumed dead! They had also mentioned that their daughter, Mrs Prudence Lambasto, was proving extremely difficult to locate, although gave assurances that no stones would be left unturned in their continued search for her. Her Majesty's Government would also continue to make the equivalent remuneration to their daughter, as her husband had received when in service. When his status was confirmed, she would then receive full entitlement to her husband's pension rights.

Jim and Elizabeth Dibble were left in no doubt, that should their daughter contact them, they were duty bound to inform them on the secure number provided.

And then it happened... the call out of the blue from Prue. So it now fell to them to relay the tragic news of Michael's fate to her, which was callously thrust in her direction by none other than her mother!

It stung hard down the phone line, and made Prue gasp, and then cry out. At first, she couldn't absorb the actual meaning of the words she'd heard. "Prue, listen to me, we all get bad news! You need to learn to deal with it, and pull yourself together. Stop all that hysterical hee-hawing at once," her mother commanded, with astonishing dispassion.

Once recovered enough to speak, Prue countered with her own news, which she overheard being recounted to her dad, with language that shocked. Her dad then came on the line, and spoke to her with genuine concern, "Prue, I'm really pleased with the news of the baby, but so very upset about dear Michael."

All the while in the background, she could hear her mother ranting and raving, and whilst he was in the throes of asking her to keep in touch, her mother came back on the line, having control of the handset. She immediately went into a tirade... making out it was

212

all Prue's fault she'd been left on her own with the additional complication of pregnancy.

"How can you say or think that, Mother?" gasped Prue. The temperature in Somerset clearly hadn't changed for the better over the years, there being a distinct lack of forgiveness or mellowness, as old grudges continued to hang in the air like a poisonous cloud.

"At least you'll not be beholding to us for your keep," her mother spat out. "I wish someone would leave me a nice fat pension, but no such luck... as some of us are born to labour all our lives."

"Mum, I've just had shocking news about Michael; have you nothing nice to say to me on that score?" asked Prue.

There was a pregnant pause, followed by an icy blast, "You know fine well Prudence, that I never took to that man you married. But, I'll say no more about him, because I refuse to speak ill of the dead," she replied.

"Mum, you said he was missing... only presumed dead; yet you already seem to have him six feet under," she exclaimed.

"That's because he will be. The Government doesn't give out that kind of money and pension, unless someone is proper dead," she answered. "Believe you me Prudence, he's snuffed it good and proper."

Prue broke down in hysterical tears at her end of the phone, but there was no such reaction at the other.

"For goodness sake, Prudence, stop making that wailing noise," her mother yelled. "You've gone and got yourself in the family way, so you'd better pull yourself together my girl, because nobody else is going to do that for you."

Her dad managed to take back control once more, "Prue, I'm so sorry my girl. Listen, I'm so very proud of you, and want you to know that I'll always be here for you. Michael struck me as being a fine young man on the few occasions we met."

"Thanks, Dad," she sobbed...

When Prue came off the phone, she was gutted, and wished she hadn't let Jeanette talk her into making the call. However, Jeanette couldn't have anticipated the news about Michael, and probably thought her mum would welcome her home with open arms on hearing about a grandchild...

Later, Prue recalled that her folks had never asked from where she was calling. These men from the Government must've mentioned that they believed she was still on *Sérénité*, but its name or location probably wouldn't have registered.

*

The colonial ladies began to arrive at the café, and Marina made a beeline for them, as soon as they entered. She racked her brains as she tried to remember who'd been present. It was difficult to remember who exactly had been present as it had been busy, and she hadn't been paying too much attention...

214

Nevertheless, she followed each into the cloakroom, where most were happy to oblige in order to save Fuzz's distress, as she put it. A few queried this as they remembered the girl helping in the café, but Marina's perseverance eventually won out…

*

Jeanette was waiting for Prue in the lounge, ready to hear all about her phone call, but when she didn't arrive she headed for her bedroom and knocked on the door, "Can I come in or is it inconvenient?" she called out. Prue opened the door and Jeanette could see at once, from her tear-stained face and forced smile, that everything was far from right. "Come through into the lounge, where I've a pot of fresh coffee. Join me and tell me what's happened."

"It was a disaster, Jeanette. My mother told me that Michael was dead," sobbed Prue, the words spurting forth like boiling water from the spout of an overfilled kettle. "My parents were seemingly told he was missing, presumed dead, but she was adamant he was gone."

Jeanette gave her a hug, took her through to the lounge, and poured her a coffee. "Now tell me again," she asked, "but this time, a little slower."

"I'm ashamed to tell you about my mother's behaviour… and I just can't believe I'll never see Michael again," cried Prue.

"You've nothing to be ashamed of; it's your mother who ought to be ashamed," exclaimed Jeanette.

"Now let it all out, I'm here all day, so take your time. I know that 'presumed' means precisely that, and nothing more. What did they say about the baby?"

"My dad was interested, but she only ranted on, and blamed me. For goodness sake, she even blamed me for being left on my own, and in the family way," she sobbed.

"I see," said Jeanette, but in truth, she didn't. She hadn't expected any of this, when she'd encouraged her to phone home. After it had all spilled out, she encouraged Prue to take a rest, while she sat and worked out what was the best way forward? First, she would have to involve her *docteur* to deal with Prue's shock in the light of her pregnancy. She also realised that she couldn't handle this entirely by herself... it was growing into a lot more than she had ever bargained for when she'd brought her home.

Jeanette cancelled another friend who was due over later that afternoon, then sat and thought everything over. She would have to make a decision soon, on how big a part in all of this she wanted to play. But first of all, she made a call to the *chirurgie du docteur*...

Dr Charbonneau arrived promptly, and brought with him the medication he considered most suitable for Prue in her current condition. "What's going on, Jeanette?" he asked.

"Just do your job," she replied, "and don't get involved, Gilles."

After he'd left, Jeanette cracked open Prue's door, and was met by the steady rise and fall of her body, along with light breathing as she slept. She gently pulled it closed, and headed for the study, where she made a certain call... "Maurice, I need some information from you," she quietly asked.

"Nice to hear from you too, dear sister. You would think we would come into contact more often, given the size of this island. Do I detect an urgency in your voice, Jeanette?" asked Maurice Stoker.

"Perhaps and on the other-hand perhaps not... I'm in a bit of a quandary, and I've made you my first port of call. Have you ever heard the name Lambasto?" she enquired. "Michael Lambasto to be precise?"

There was a delay in her brother's usual quick-witted reply. She detected it, while others perhaps would not have. "I'll tell you what's going to happen. You will be picked up and brought here, where you and I can discuss this in more detail," he snapped.

"I only asked you a simple straightforward question, Maurice. I don't know why I need to be brought there? Anyway, I can't manage to come," she protested, her anger being difficult to defuse.

"A car will come for you in fifteen minutes. Make sure you are ready," came the curt answer, as Maurice hung up, leaving her looking at the receiver in disbelief.

"Damn and blast that man, what have I gone and done?" she wailed.

217

On her way back from the toilet, a startled Prue looked towards the study door, alarmed at what she'd inadvertently overheard. What in heaven's name was that about? It was Jeanette whom she'd heard shouting, of that she was sure. She slipped back into her room, and closed the door without making a sound. This sudden development had given her yet another shock, albeit a minor one, given the circumstances in her life at present. She sat on the edge of her bed, rigid with fear and trepidation…

Not long after there was a gentle tap on her door, and Jeanette entered. Her demeanour seemed the same as usual, but Prue sensed a change… "I took it upon myself to ask Gilles, you know my old *docteur*, to drop off some medication to help deal with the shock to your system. He's taken account of your pregnancy. I thought you'd rather not have direct dealings with him at the moment. It took me years to get used his quirky ways," she stated, feeling awkward having just delivered what seemed to her to have been an eerie monologue.

"Thanks," said Prue, "I think I'd like to sit out and get some fresh air on the *terrasse*, if I may?"

"Of course… I have to go out, as I've a few things I need to do. Will you be okay on your own?" she asked.

"Oh yes, I'll be fine, I could do with some time on my own," replied Prue.

Jeanette felt a trifle uneasy at her reply, but there was nothing she could do as she had been

218

summoned! "Remember to take your medication, he's very good at prescribing... it's only his manner and technique that's flawed," she stated, giving a reassuring laugh, which was not reciprocated.

Before leaving, Jeanette briefly stepped out onto the *terrasse* to say she only hoped to be an hour or so, to which Prue nodded by way of acknowledgement. However, as soon as the outer apartment door closed, she sped through to one of the rooms which overlooked the front of the building, and watched her leave the apartment block and climb into an ominously awaiting limousine. She recognised it as being one of Stoker's cars, as Michael had often pointed them out to her when they'd been in town together... they all flew distinctive personalised flags, which had caused them both to laugh, as they thought it tacky and tasteless.

As she watched, it entered her head that Stoker was a dangerous, bumptious individual. The fact that Jeanette was being taken somewhere in one of her brother's cars, rang alarm bells. Coupled with the phone call she'd overheard earlier, she concluded that she was no longer safe in this place...

Michael was suddenly in her mind telling her that everything would be all right, and to stay; but it was not him she wanted to see and tell about the baby. Perhaps she was not processing information properly, but now only had her own instincts to trust? She gathered up her few belongings, stuffed them into her small back-pack, then left the apartment, wearing her borrowed dress and sandals.

Once outside, she crossed the road towards the beach, then headed northwards… away from town.

CHAPTER TWENTY-EIGHT:

Michael couldn't believe that nobody could locate Prue. He'd told them the deal was off if they couldn't reassure him about the whereabouts of his wife.

Sir was more than angry with his men on the ground. "For God's sake, she's a well-heeled, good looking woman, not a bloody needle in a haystack. Bloody incompetents," he shouted at one of his lieutenants. "Michael's threatening to go back himself, and I don't want that happening. If we can't reassure him as to her welfare, and he does attempt to find her, he'll take himself out of service for good. I can see that happening. Christ, the man's too useful to retire... crack the whip for fucks sake, or heads will be for the chop over this damned fiasco."

"Sir, we're stepping up the search as we speak, and a positive result must be imminent, unless... she's already left the island," he offered hopefully.

"And how the hell could she have done that, let me ask you?" demanded Sir. "It would have to have been in a bloody rowing boat! Stoker has control of all boats leaving the island, even the small motorised fishing boats. There is nowhere to go, don't you understand? That place is in the middle of nowhere… there are no neighbours to drop in for a visit… so there's no bloody chance she's left by rowing boat."

His lieutenant merely nodded by way of response…

"I need answers… not just a fuckin' nodding donkey," commanded Sir. "Now get out!"

"Yes, Sir," replied the stunned lieutenant.

*

Her body was sore, and the sand felt uneven under foot, then the strap of one of her borrowed sandals suddenly burst as she ploughed through the soft sand. There was nothing to do but feed them both to the ocean, as she'd left her own worn footwear at Jeanette's. Prue's body didn't feel like her own; its balance seemed all wrong. She felt around the curvature of her stomach, which appeared to have become ever more pronounced with the passage of each hour. She didn't think she looked pregnant, perhaps just a shade plump. "Pretty Prudence Dibble," she sang to her travelling companion and friend, Miss Ocean, as they meandered along together. Then she remembered Michael… and returned to being Mrs Prudence Lambasto, plump and pregnant… there would be no more pretty Prue Dibble for her.

222

It seemed so much further than she had initially thought. The beach stopped in places where the sand petered out, giving way to clumps of impassible rocky outcrops. There was usually a path around such promontories which led to the next bay, but these were mostly punctuated with sharp protruding stones. Her feet were cut, sore, and bloody, and her naked shoulders scarlet from the fierce, relentless rays of the overhead sun. She paused and sat on a rock beside a slimy seaweed covered pool, while she bathed her aching feet. There were cliffs that overhung the beach at this point, providing welcome shade for her wretched body. She was parched, surrounded by water, but with not a drop she could drink. Surely she would reach their cove soon? The distance had seemed to fly when a passenger on Fuzz's scooter on the Green Plantation Road...

She struggled up once more, and stumbled on, with strands of seaweed now strewn over her feet and ankles. She tried to kick them free, but they clung on obstinately. By now, she felt hopelessly alone and began to cry, "Please let the next cove be our cove," she cried out in anguish.

It had been a while since Prue had noticed any other people on the beach, but now she spotted a young couple walking hand in hand towards her. "Do you be needing help?" asked the girl, when they'd come close enough to notice her distressed demeanour and tear-stained face.

"The Plantation cabins... are they nearby?" gasped Prue.

"The cabins in the woods you be meaning?" she asked. "Bernice's?"

"Yes," replied Prue, nodding hard.

"Just 'round there," answered the girl, pointing to the next headland.

"I think I know my way from the beach," replied Prue, "thanks." She then plodded onward, as the young couple watched her with concern. "Just one more path, and then I'm there," she mumbled to herself.

Finally, her spirits surged, as she began to make her way up the track towards the cabins. Yes, they were there, and their very sight was exhilarating and far more than welcome... but what now? Prue's spirits suddenly nose-dived, as coming towards her were three silhouettes. She couldn't make them out as the sun shone directly into her eyes, blinding her... the last thing she wanted was to meet any more people; then she heard a voice... a familiar and most welcoming voice. "What you be doing girl? Look at the state you be in; praise the Lord that Bernice has gotten hold of you. I'll soon have you clean and beautiful again."

A deliriously confused Prue peered closely, and saw that it was the young couple she'd met earlier, with Bernice...

"Let me be thankin' you two. That be good of you to come and fetch Bernice. I can deal with her from now on... my friend has been so worried about her daughter."

The young couple left, and Bernice watched them go before she helped Prue towards the cabins. "Thanks, Bernice," she whispered, through dried, parched lips. "Why did you say I was your friend's daughter?"

"Cause my dear Prudence, we need to get you hidden. That be why I didn't let them see where I be takin' you," she replied. "I'm needin' to hide you."

Prue didn't query things anymore, she was beyond that. She waited to see where she was being taken. It turned out to be Bernice's own cabin, which was a bitter disappointment. "He loves you, Prudence, but he can't know you be here. They will track him down soon I be thinkin', and it's better that our Fuzz does not have to lie," stated Bernice. "You understand?"

Prue nodded… she understood, but was still disappointed. "Bernice, you need to know that I'm four or five months with child. It's moving about… I can feel my baby," she said.

Bernice looked at her thoughtfully, then laughed. "I knew you had a *bébé* on the way, but I didn't think you be that far down the track. However, I can see that for myself now," she replied. "I will fill me my big wash-tub, and make you proper pretty. You be havin' to stay in my linen-room, where I keeps my laundry when they be dried. You can help with the foldin' and other things, Prudence."

"Bernice, what about Fuzz," she asked, "can't I see him?"

"No, you ain't seein' nobody, not now, not till we hear what be happenin'," she answered. "This is not Fuzz's *bébé*, it's Lambasto's, and there be something that don't smell too good with him."

Prue didn't understand what she meant by that, but decided to let her take control, as there was nothing else she could do. Bernice heated water in a big tank, from which she filled her wash-tub. Prue undressed and then let her wash her aching body. It felt so good, and when finished, her body and hair felt clean once more. She was then wrapped in a large towelling sheet, since she couldn't go outside to dry off in the sunshine.

Suddenly, there was a knock on Bernice's door, "Get lost," she shouted with such force, that Prue felt sorry for whoever was there. Bernice was a larger-than-life character, but one that Prue felt so grateful and privileged to know…

*

Long before she stepped into her brother's limo, Jeanette wished she hadn't contacted him. She didn't want any part of Maurice's world, yet here she was up to her neck in his boiling pot of intrigue and suspicion. On arrival at his mansion, he spent precious little time on social niceties. Instead, he went straight for her jugular… Michael Lambasto was seemingly not dead, but his wife was to be informed that he was…

What kind of people were they, and what kind of lives did they lead, to behave in such a cold and callous manner? Jeanette had never heard of anything as stupid as this hushed up UK Government operation... and to compound matters further, her dumb brother was a compliant accomplice!

"Where is he, if he's not dead, Maurice?" she asked.

"For your ears only, and I mean that. Sister or no sister, if you breathe one word, I will lock you up, and throw the key into the deepest ocean," he replied, "or worse."

She laughed, until his icy stare told her that he was deadly serious. "He was injured, and I arranged for his initial rescue and care, followed by an air-lift off this island, as a favour to my friends in the UK."

"And just where did this plane of yours take him?" she asked.

"Back to good old Blighty, as they call it... well not all the way in my plane, but that was the final destination. He's apparently one of their top guys, Jeanette. The Government there, together with top politicians from various other countries, are exceedingly grateful to me for my assistance... and I intend to milk their gratitude at a later date for all its worth, which you must agree is only fair," he informed her, with unqualified smugness on his face.

Maurice then lifted a cigar from his desk humidor, lit it, and drew on it until it was properly aglow. He then exhaled the sweet plume of smoke in her direction... "Lambasto was on a mission to track down certain people who have infiltrated this island, with the intention of threatening its stability. These people… terrorists, are wanted by many governments, and I was grateful for his help. Lambasto, together with his wife, had been undercover here for three months and I'm told, making sound inroads when it all kicked off and backfired," he continued. "You may not believe this Jeanette, but there are people on this island who would think nothing of doing your precious brother harm, and he was smoking them out for me, if you excuse the pun. Sometimes, even I need help with certain undesirables. Now it's your turn to tell me how you, my dear, came to know the name Michael Lambasto?"

Jeanette didn't know what to do or say about Prue? He would ultimately squeeze it out of her, one way or another, and she was no longer a young woman. So, she decided to tell him what she knew…

"They only want to find the stupid woman, to tell her she will be well looked after financially. That's all they want, but she's been leading everyone a merry dance," added Maurice.

"If that's all, then why is it so important they find her?" asked Jeanette.

"Cause Lambasto has now recovered enough to demand proof that she's fine and has been made aware she will be well looked after in the future. If they cannot satisfy him on this, he's threatened to return and look for her himself. If he does as he's threatened, they reckon he would quit the service, and reunite with his wife. The Service however is not ready to let him go," he replied. "Still, thanks to you, we have the little minx now, so I suggest that you stay here while we go and pick her up from your apartment."

He then made to leave, "I'll have lunch brought up, but don't move out of this room until I return... and... well done, big sister."

Well done her? Not from where she was sitting. She had been a traitor to Prue. The Judas bug had bitten her, and this messy affair was making her ill. The whole sorry scenario seemed like something out of a bad B-movie she'd been caught up in. Although Maurice had stated that nothing nasty was going to happen, she was not entirely convinced. Was it not nasty, to allow someone to think their husband was dead, when he was not? To her that was far more than nasty.

Jeanette already knew that Prue's delightful sounding mother had already delivered the news about Michael's demise. She then thought about Prue's unborn baby, her relationship with Fuzz, and all the things she hadn't disclosed...

She sat in her brother's house, trembling and extremely ill at ease with herself, and when her lunch tray arrived, she thanked the girl who brought it, waited until she had left the room, and then accidentally dropped it with all her might.

CHAPTER TWENTY-NINE:

They searched every inch of Jeanette's apartment, but there was no sign of the elusive *Madame* Lambasto. In the spare bedroom, they however did find a pair of dirty worn sandals and some prescription tablets…

When a raging Maurice received the news that *Madame* Lambasto was gone, he returned and turned upon his sister, "Why did she need prescribed tablets?" he snarled, thrusting the packet into her face. "Tell me or I'll get the truth out of that old fool *docteur* of yours. Now woman, what are these fuckin' tablets for, and don't miss anything out? You're going to stay here until the bitch is found, and there will be no more food trays for you my dear!"

Jeanette told him they were prescribed to Prue for the shock she'd experienced on hearing the news about Michael's death from her mother back in Somerset. She left it at that. She was a kind decent enough person to keep the baby a secret, and enough of a romantic not to involve Fuzz.

"Where did you meet her? I know you mumbled something about the Square, but where exactly... tell me Jeanette, I know when you're holding something back," shouted Maurice. "I have more than an idea that it would have been at that café you widow women from the old country have been using as some kind of Club. I know all about your stupid little activities, as I run a tight ship on this island."

He laughed at his own half joke, but she did not, to which he did not take kindly. "Is that where you met this *Madame* Lambasto... at that café?" he asked. "What I don't understand is why she's gone on the run? And I don't understand, why was a guy like that married? He could have the world on a plate, so why bother with a wife?"

"Because he loved her, I expect," she replied.

"Grow up, Jeanette!" shouted Maurice. "I've changed my mind. You can go back to your apartment, but I'm sending one of my own people with you. He will stay in the apartment in case our friend *Madame* Lambasto returns. I want you to continue as normal, by going to your cafè Club place, chatting with your fuddy-duddy friends, but not one word to them or the owner about what you know. Sister or not, you will be in massive trouble if you open your mouth!"

"I'm not staying in my apartment with a man," replied Jeanette, in disgust.

"Very well, I'll send a woman," he replied, with a laugh, "but once you meet who I have in mind... you'll wish you had accepted a man."

*

Jeanette was in shock when she returned home. Where had Prue gone, and why? Had she heard her on the phone to Maurice... or perhaps had seen his car? What had she done to the poor girl?

Her brother's threat about her female jailer however, turned out to be an empty threat. The next day, when she went out, Jeanette left her apartment in the capable hands of her new friend Francine. Her live-in minder was actually not as half as bad as expected, not the *Rosa Klebb* type at all, and the two women formed an instant bond of... compatibility.

"Off you go now, and amuse yourself *Madame* Jeanette," announced Francine. "I'll be here if she returns, and make sure she doesn't run off again. Judge Stoker knows he can depend upon me."

"That's nice to know Francine, very reassuring," replied Jeanette. "I'll bring you some pastries for tea, if you like?"

"*Merci, Madame* Jeanette, let me say it must be wonderful having Judge Stoker as a brother," she replied.

"Yes, it does have its moments of wonder," she agreed, then left the apartment, feeling quite upbeat and amused by Francine.

She walked the short distance to Fuzz's café, to join her lady friends for coffee, and restore a little normality into her life. She had only just seated herself, when Marina hurried over to her side. "Jeanette, were you here the day Fuzz's so called cousin called in? She was in a mess so you'd remember her if you saw her?" she whispered.

"No, I don't think so, I've had quite a bit on recently, and not been in much," she replied.

"That's fine then, not to worry," whispered Marina, who then left to attend to another waiting customer. She managed a slight smile... Jeanette had been the last on her list. Job well done, she thought.

"You were here, Jeanette," whispered her friend Marguerite.

"I know, but I'm not telling her that," she whispered in reply. "Why did she want to know anyway?"

"Marina told us not to tell Fuzz about that girl being here," whispered her friend. "You know the one who came in that day... all dirty and messy?"

"I thought as much," whispered Jeanette. "My memory sometimes comes and goes, Marguerite."

"Good for you, Jeanette, I wish you had been here when Marina asked me. Then I would have said the same as you," she whispered.

"That's fine Marguerite, we're a team… you and I," she replied to her dear friend. "But leave me to deal with Marina."

*

Bernice made Prue as comfortable as she could in her box-room. There was no window, just a tiny fan to circulate the constant warm air. Prue found that life there added to her tiredness. She did have past experience of this kind of confined living recently… during the time when she'd been encamped in the café back-shop, but that was nothing compared to this. The hot arid air dried her skin, and made her permanently thirsty.

In the late evening, she could go into the room next door and sit with Bernice, but not until the last rays had departed and all the folks had gone indoors for the night. She sometimes stole time to sit on the back step and breath some real air, whilst Bernice kept a watchful eye… just in case. They had to sit in silence, as conversation would have carried on the breeze around the cabins. By the time they returned inside, Bernice was usually too tired for much conversation, and went to bed. Prue therefore spent much of her time experiencing a solitary confinement.

Tonight's snippet of news was that Fuzz had been visited by Judge Stoker's men at the café, and asked about the whereabouts of a certain *Madame* Lambasto. They'd supposedly had an anonymous tip that he knew the lady well.

*

On arrival home that evening, Fuzz rushed to visit Bernice, whilst Prue sat with her ear against the paper thin wall, listening to his lovely voice. It was more than she could bear, for her not to let him know she was there.

"Bernice, I told them the truth," he stated.

"And what be that?" she asked.

"That I didn't know where she was," he answered.

"That be the way to go, my boy," replied Bernice. "You just keep tellin' them the truth."

"They also told me her husband was dead, and that they wanted to tell her that on behalf of the UK Government," announced Fuzz. "Do you think that's true, Bernice? Is the Dark Angel Michael dead?"

Prue, gulped and nearly gave out a yell, at Fuzz's description of Michael.

"I don't know, Fuzz. This island be full of bad guys. There are folks who knows nothin', folks who knows a little… and then there be them who knows everythin'," she replied.

Fuzz looked at her unsure of what she'd meant. She was being very philosophical, he thought, instead of her usual bluntness.

Prue could hear his voice as they talked, and wanted to run into his arms and tell him she was sorry… but she couldn't and didn't. She was surprised to hear

235

Michael being referred to as the Dark Angel, but that was typical of the way Fuzz talked, and on reflection she didn't feel offended. Probably just him showing that he had affection for her... she hoped?

She had all but forgotten the reason she was in this crazy position; it was no longer clear to her, from whom she was hiding, or indeed why? She no longer trusted anyone, except the two people in the other room. Her mother, and latterly Jeanette had all let her down, but she was most disappointed in Michael, as she'd supported him all the way for a decade. This latest escapade of his was the cruellest thing he'd done yet, taking her to this island and then dying! Why did he do that to her?

On the other hand, there was Fuzz... she didn't want Judge Stoker getting his hands on him. Fuzz was so close, and yet so far from her at this moment. She knew her fate partly lay in his hands, but mainly in those big rough hands of Bernice.

"Do they know you brought her here, to the cabins, I mean?" continued Bernice.

"Not from me," he replied. "Will everyone here close ranks to protect me?"

"I hope so, they be good folks," replied Bernice, "as you already know."

Fuzz gave her a hug and left; then Bernice came in to tell Prue it was safe to come into the salon. "Bernice, will Fuzz get into big trouble over me?" she asked.

"I don't know, what be happenin' next, Prudence. I need to hear what the word from town be. It must have been that bitch who tipped them off, she be scum like her brother," she replied.

Prue nodded, but couldn't quite think of Jeanette as being a bad person, perhaps frightened or maybe intimidated… she didn't know. "It was so hard for me not to tell him I was here," she said.

"You did good girl. I be proud of you," answered Bernice. "Is *bébé* movin'?"

Prue nodded, as Bernice's rough hands reached to touch.

*

Things were running smoothly at the café. Marina was attending to Fuzz's every need, or to most of them. Jeanette watched her at work, trying to wriggle into his affections… laughing, nudging him, standing up close to him; she was a true mistress of these tricks of seduction. And the clothes she was wearing… all had an edge to them that she hadn't seen before… short skirts and dresses, all made from skimpy, almost whimsical materials. The low-necked tops, that were cut much lower than had been her norm, revealing to one and all soft mounds of tempting flesh. Her whole demeanour had changed, and she'd become more pleasant, more smiley, more chatty.

The ladies of the *Colonial Club* all watched with interest. They thought of it as a free show of titillation, mixed with coffee and cake… a heady

237

mixture for some who were of the more advanced years to swallow! They were all in favour of this union and why not, thought Jeanette? Then, Prue tugged at her heartstrings, and she began to concentrate on Fuzz, watching to see where his heart lay.

*

The time has come to ask him, thought Marina. She'd waited patiently all day until now. It had just gone six, and they were clearing away the remains of the day, making the place fresh and clean for tomorrow's repeat session…

They'd bumped into each other as they worked, and he'd steadied her with his strong hands. She'd told him not to worry about the spilt milk that lay on their clean floor, and he found that amusing… so she pounced. "Fuzz, tomorrow after work, would you like to come to my house for… a barbecue? My parents have asked me to invite you. Frankie will be there, he's always asking after you," she ventured.

"I don't think so, Marina. I need to get home," he replied.

"Why, what's so important at home?" she asked, pushing him for an answer.

"It's just that I—," answered Fuzz.

"Frankie's offered to collect you; to save you having to come on your scooter," interrupted Marina, making him a tempting offer.

My scooter! He suddenly pictured it in the back of the truck that night when he'd taken Frankie along Plantation Road into the woods and shown him where the cabins lay. This was worrying enough, without the fact that Frankie had also heard Prue's name bantered about while there. He returned to the present, and could hear Marina talking again… it was evident, she wasn't going to let go easily. "Come on Fuzz, let your hair down, or let it be more fuzzed in your case," she encouraged, with twinkling eyes.

He smiled at her reference to his unruly mop, "Marina, I know you're just being kind," he replied.

"No, I'm not; we really do want you to come." Her eyes gazed into his, and he had to look away. She had made him feel he was being petty, and unappreciative of people who were trying to show him kindness, and so finally agreed... "That's great, Fuzz," she announced, as she gave him a more than generous hug. She could feel he wasn't wholly comfortable, and released him gently. Oops… take your time Marina, just wear him down, little by little, she thought, and whatever you do, make him think he's in charge.

*

The next evening, not long after Fuzz had arrived home from the café, a truck stopped outside his cabin. Bernice recognised the driver as the young guy who'd brought Fuzz home not that long ago. She remembered him when Prue's name was being bantered around. Who was he, and why was Fuzz all washed and dressed up neat like? She felt uneasy… she had hoped

239

to have a private word, regarding some news she'd received. What should she do?

"Fuzz, you come in and sees me when you comes back from wherever you be goin'. I be needing us to have ourselves a chat," she hollered, as he clambered into the guy's truck.

"I'll try Bernice, can't promise though," he replied.

"Don't you can't promise me... you be sure to come and see me when you gets back," she insisted, before slamming her door shut.

Prue sank to the floor not knowing the reason for the sudden discord. The baby fluttered its little parts, and she shielded her stomach in an act of maternal protection.

"Sorry," said Bernice, popping her head into the darkened box-room. "You doin' okay?"

"Okay... just resting as usual. Give me a call when it's all clear, as I need to stretch my legs... and the rest," she replied. As Prue lay on her makeshift bed, she considered taking flight to some other place... she was not okay... none of this was okay. Bernice was now somewhere outside, and so, in this her latest prison, Prue afforded herself the luxury of letting her tears flow...

Outside, Bernice joined a group of neighbours, but tonight she was noticeably quiet. She'd obviously something bearing down on her, something which was noticeable to the others, so they left her well alone. Bernice remained lost in her own thoughts, as she

240

pondered the news that Michael Lambasto had arrived back on the island that very day. It was no rumour either, but verified by her trusted confidents, who had their ears firmly to the ground… and what was most troubling was that the Judge himself had welcomed him.

Prudence was showing signs of losing the plot, so Bernice decided she wasn't going to keep her a virtual prisoner any longer. Fuzz had brought her to this place, so her welfare and state of mind was not hers to bear alone. But what the hell was he up to, and with whom, she thought? "I should have grabbed him and stopped *le crapaud*, from hopping out in his going-out clothes," she muttered to herself.

In truth, she couldn't have reached him as the advancing years were catching up on her fast. An unusual sensation flowed over her… the eerie sensation of her own vulnerability…

CHAPTER THIRTY:

The rings from Judge Stoker's cigar smoke floated upwards, flavouring the air in his study. Michael was inwardly disgusted, and quickly made an excuse to leave. He headed for his suite in the Judge's mansion, where he splashed his face with cold water, and sprayed his clothes. He'd just arrived, but decided he wasn't going to stay longer than necessary.

"I'm out of here," he muttered under his breath, "that man's just a jumped up bully-boy crook, with a pumped up belly and smoky breath." Why the hell the powers that be have anything to do with the little shit, he failed to understand?

He gathered his belongings and told a passing servant to apologise for his hasty departure. He then scrawled his apology into letter form, and explained his leaving was due to new orders he'd unexpectedly received. He was going to add that he needed to borrow a car to get around, but changed his mind, not wanting to look a jackass. He clearly remembered watching the Judge's limos drift around town with their tinpot flags fluttering in the ocean's on-shore breezes. He remembered once pointing them out to Prue, while they enjoyed a drink together in the Square. She'd made him laugh when she told him they looked like some spiv company trying to break into the taxi market.

Michael headed out and was about to hire a car, when he remembered he'd a vehicle parked within their apartment garage. He jumped into a passing taxi, and within a few minutes was dropped off at the revolving entrance to The Blue Ocean Apartments. When he alighted, he stood and drew sustenance from the view. The endless noise of the roaring ocean was still music to his ears, and he allowed himself the luxury of a few moments reminiscence…

He then turned, looked upwards towards their apartment, and paused as he recalled the last time he'd seen Prue… it was that brief exchange by the pool, when he had behaved so badly towards her. He'd been annoyed at events, but that was no excuse and nothing to do with her. If it had to end, he wished it had not ended like that…

He tried to make an excuse for himself, by thinking that he was only trying to play down the danger he was in, but that was feeble. He hated himself for being the man he had become, and for the way his relationship with her had developed… but the truth was that he could no longer cope with living simultaneously in two vastly different worlds…

She would've watched him that day from her poolside *terrasse* vantage point; he knew exactly where she would've stood to watch him depart. He wanted to turn and wave, but had not done so out of some sort of ill-founded pride and bloody mindedness. From then on everything was sketchy. He'd seen her from a distance the next day as he tried to warn her about Bart. He'd known from her diary entries, she was meeting his wife Kate in *The Coffee Palace*. However, he hadn't had time to stay, and consequently had missed his chance to tell her that he'd always love her. Whatever had happened afterwards was a complete mystery…

His eyes momentarily glimpsed their magnificent *terrasse* far above. It was their private Garden of Eden… their green paradise. Why had she left the apartment that belonged to them? He had been so pleased when it had become available to purchase, so why not stay? She had a car in the garage, money in the bank, the apartment staff at her every beck and call, a pool, and not least their beautiful *terrasse*… he could go on and on, but what was the point… the fact remained she had left!

He had two days to find her, or at least to find out where she was, after that he had a difficult choice to make. He could either carry on searching, or continue in the Service under a new identity. Michael was a danger junkie, and his addiction was pulling him ever closer into danger. It was like opium forcing its way through his drugged veins, dragging him further and further from the normality that was Prue…

*

His appearance had changed along with his name. He might have a car in the garage and an apartment full of possessions upstairs, but he could hardly access any of it without drawing unwanted attention. That would create such a messy situation, and wipe out his covert disguise. He decided he shouldn't have ventured back here, there was nothing for him now anyway, but would've still loved to have once more visited their apartment… and their *terrasse*.

As he sat on a wall facing the ocean, he phoned for a taxi. It had been as stupid a mistake to come here, as it had been for him to walk out on Judge Stoker's hospitality. He would return there tonight, but would leave the island tomorrow or whenever the Judge's jet was available. This whole visit had been a bad idea… a damned fiasco!

Michael then spotted a man looking at him, his eyes penetrating, and drilling deep within. As he slowly walked towards him and sat on the wall close by, he realised who it was. "*Monsieur*, is it you?" the man whispered.

Michael did not reply.

"*Monsieur*, is it you? *Madame* she need you … *Monsieur*, *Monsieur*," pleaded Marcel.

Michael still did not reply, but continued to stare at the ocean until his taxi arrived. He took out a large bill, and tossed it in Marcel's direction. Marcel picked it up while watching the taxi depart; *Monsieur* did not look back…

245

At Marina's house, the barbecue was already spitting and sizzling by the time Frankie and Fuzz arrived. Marina rushed over and linked arms with both men. "I had no idea there would be all these people here," remarked Fuzz, who'd been under the impression he was coming to a small family affair.

"They're mostly neighbours, plus a few relatives," replied Marina. "Our barbies are always popular."

"How's it all going?" asked Frankie.

"Fine, but I think Dad could do with your help," she replied.

"Okay... Marina will look after you, while I give my old man a hand," agreed Frankie.

Marina tightened her grip on Fuzz's arm. "Don't worry, I'll not let go... there are some dodgy folks around," she stated, with a giggle.

"Really?" replied Fuzz.

"Could well be," she giggled. She brought over her free arm and clamped her other hand onto her left. Fuzz was still looking around, checking for faces he recognised, and didn't realise he'd been locked in a vice-like hold.

"My, my, Marina, that's some mop of hair your young man has," commented an elderly man.

"Uncle George, nice to see you… this is my boss, Fuzz," she replied.

"That's the way to do it, marry the boss," stated Uncle George.

"We're not getting married," replied a shocked Fuzz.

"You will eventually; men always succumb in the end, you'll see. I only hope I'm spared long enough to come to the wedding," answered Uncle George.

Marina laughed, but didn't reply. Fuzz was bursting to tell him how it really was, but the old man had moved away, and the moment had passed. Now he found himself in the midst of a throng of younger folks... "Very nice, darling," said one young guy, giving Fuzz the once over…

"Eyes off Ben, can't you see he's taken," answered another young man, placing his arms around him, "and you're taken yourself. Hi, how's tricks, Marina?"

"Hi, guys, this is my boss… Fuzz, this is my cousin Tony, and his partner Ben," she announced.

Fuzz nodded to the guys, but felt like a cut of meat ready for the chop. He then looked down and noticed Marina had clamped his arm. He wanted to pull it free, but to do that he'd need an excuse. He couldn't think of one quickly enough, and found himself being slowly escorted to where Marina's parents were seated... "Here he is, I've managed to get him here, albeit with our Frankie's help," announced Marina.

247

How could he manage to escape now? He would be expected to make small talk with them... they appeared nice enough folks, but he was being slowly smothered...

"Fuzz, you're not driving, so help yourself to a proper drink," said Marina's dad. "My Frankie has taken over and has given me a break from barbie duties."

Fuzz had the thought that he'd have to be set free to help himself... but Marina's mum speedily offered to get drinks for both him and Marina. He decided that there was nothing else for it, but to use the oldest excuse in the book, and asked where the little boy's room was?

"I'll take you, it's easier than trying to explain," replied Marina.

"Yeah, that's a good idea, darling, I think most of the others know how to find it by themselves," replied Marina's mum, with a giggle. "They've all been often enough."

Heavens, surely she's going to let me go into the toilet on my own, thought Fuzz? This was turning into a nightmare... and Marina was acting as his gaoler. "I'll be outside waiting," she announced, with a grin.

"That's stupid, don't waste your time waiting on me," he replied.

"No problem, unless you're going to be a long time," she answered. "You're quick enough in the café... it's usually just a quick in and out job."

"But I do take more time when at home," he replied.

"Ah, but you're not at home, you're here, so just pretend you're at the café," she purred.

Once inside the toilet, he didn't know whether to lock the door or not? She would hear it being locked, and might think he didn't trust her... which was actually true... so he locked the door. Fuzz hadn't really needed to relieve himself, so spent his time making sure that all his hatches were securely battened down, and that everything else was in order. He then flushed the toilet to fool her, then followed up with the ceremonial running of taps at full force. Finally, he checked everything over, before he unlocked the door...

"I heard you washing your hands. That's good, as I often have to remind Frankie to do that at times," stated Marina. Fuzz then made a break for the staircase.

"What's the rush?" she cried, but before he had time to answer, she was by his side once more. He wriggled his body in an attempt to keep himself free from her clam-like grasp.

Music began to blare from the loud-speakers, and a passing girl glided by, "Would you like to dance?" he called out to her. She smiled a surprised smile, but held out a hand in acceptance; Fuzz stumbled his way towards her and made a grab for her outstretched hand. "I'll see you later, Marina," he mumbled...

*

249

Bernice sat up late and waited for him, but he didn't come home. She thumped the table, and had to apologise to Prue. First thing the following morning, she went to his cabin to check but could tell he hadn't been home. "Damn and blast you, fuzzy boy; you ain't goin' to treat Bernice like that," she muttered, then took herself off to see some folks she'd been thinkin' bout durin' the night who she knew would help her.

And so it was arranged… later that morning, a van arrived and Prue was speedily removed to a place of safety. Bernice hugged her and promised she would visit, as a confused Prue was driven off. "Lord help our Prudence, and keep her safe," she silently prayed when she was once more alone in her cabin…

*

Next morning, Fuzz was up early for work. Marina was ready early too, and her dad gave them a lift as promised. However, relations were icy between them, due to the fact that Fuzz had kept hold of his new dance partner for the remainder of the evening, and then had slept in Frankie's room. She was livid at him for taking up with another girl in her parents' house. If the girl had been gorgeous, she may not have forgiven him, but perhaps would have understood why… but it had been Harriet, a plain and homely neighbour…

*

Never again would Fuzz do something he knew he didn't want to do. That had been one of the worst nights of his life. He had thanked Harriet for keeping him company, but told her he'd a regular girlfriend. She told him she was sorry about that, but had nevertheless enjoyed his company.

He wished he could sack Marina, and never have to see her again... but how could he do that? He decided he would tell her for the last time that his relationship with her was purely business... in fact he decided that he'd tell her that today, or at least try...

CHAPTER THIRTY-ONE:

Michael was on his way to see Jeanette. Maurice had been all set to have his sister brought to his mansion for interrogation, as he had called it, but Michael had shown a preference to see her in her own home. He had returned to his suite of rooms in the Stoker mansion for the duration, stating another change of orders, but couldn't wait to get off this godforsaken island. If Prue was intent on playing hide and seek, he didn't have time to participate in her game.

Jeanette received instructions to stay in her apartment, and to expect a visitor. When he arrived, Jeanette found Michael to be more refined than expected. He was tall, broad shouldered, and good looking in the extreme. His eyes were bright and shone with intelligence; they certainly did not look like the eyes of a dead man to her! They looked at each other, neither wanting to be the first to show their cards.

Jeanette however, because of Prue, felt annoyed and could not contain herself. "She's been told you're missing, presumed dead, which was communicated to her through her dreadful mother. Can you tell me why?" she spouted forth.

"Jeanette, I hope you don't mind me calling you by your first name; first, can I ask you to please forget that you've ever met me? I realise now that I should never have come back to this place. However, my intentions were well meaning, as I wanted to be sure she was in a good place… well you can surely understand what I was getting at? Words don't always convey an accurate meaning," he replied. If he was looking for absolution, he did not receive any. "I do love her," he continued.

"I have only your word for that. When I met Prue she was in a very distressed state… I took pity on her, and she stayed here and now she has left. I'm going to be absolutely honest with you, I believe she heard me making an ill-judged call to Maurice, and that's the reason she left. I bitterly regret making that call, but what's done is done and there is nothing else I can or wish to tell you," stated Jeanette.

"Fair enough… I still don't understand why she had to leave our apartment? There was no reason for her to do so. Right, I'll leave it to the professionals to find her then, I need to get back to base," he replied. He then left as he'd come, in one of the Judge's cars.

Jeanette watched him leave from her bedroom window, unimpressed, "I do love her,"… his words rung hollow in her head. What a pompous prick, she thought.

She'd felt angry when he was with her, but nothing like as angry as she felt now that he'd gone; she was incensed by his throw away love remark, not to mention his altogether callous attitude. She was thankful he hadn't enquired where she'd met Prue, which was the one thing she expected to have been asked. One thing he would never have heard from her lips, was the fact that Prue was pregnant; that man did not deserve to be a father… and the one thing Prue would never hear from her, was the fact that he was not dead!

*

A short time later one of her brother's cars drew up once more outside her apartment, with Michael on-board. After some pleasantries, which she found hard to bear, he told her why he had returned, "Jeanette, I can't go without trying a little harder to find her. Where did you meet Prue… your brother told me that it was at some café you frequent?" he stated. "Can you tell me please?"

He would find out anyway, she knew that to be true, so she decided to tell him its location, and with a slight variation, on how they'd met. When he asked the owner's name of this *Colonial Club* place, he detected a reluctance on her part to answer...

"Fuzz," she finally replied.

"Fuzz?" he repeated with a smile. "That's an interesting sounding name."

"That's the only name I have for him," she replied.

"You've been very helpful, thank you very much," said Michael.

"Francine... Francine, will you show this gentleman out please," asked Jeanette.

She nodded and obliged, then came back and asked what that had all been about? She sat on the sofa sipping her coffee, while Jeanette made up a story that would satisfy her curiosity. The two women then relaxed and chatted about other things.

Jeanette smiled as she looked at her; she'd previously complained to Maurice that she didn't feel safe in her house, and he'd told her that Francine, who was seemingly getting a bit long in the tooth for his purposes... could remain there for as long as she felt she was needed.

The two ladies were delighted at this turn of events, as Jeanette now had friendly, lively live-in company, and conversely, Francine was free from serving a bully, and could cast off her badge and bullets.

Jeanette's mind then strayed to *Monsieur* Michael Lambasto. She had recognised him as the man in the photograph Prue had produced from her purse, but only just... he looked as though he was going through a metamorphosis!

*

Bells were ringing in the distance, and their resonance filled Prue's head. She was in shock; Bernice had suddenly hugged her, before handing her over to who knows who, whereupon she was bundled into a

255

van. After a very short journey, she found herself being whisked in a wheelchair along corridors of a building, whose walls were adorned with statues, cruciforms, and other such artefacts.

The confusing journey suddenly came to an abrupt halt outside an old oak door, which was too narrow for the wheelchair to pass, so she was instructed to enter the room on foot. Next she was directed to a chair on one side of a file laden desk... "Hello my dear... Bernice did not want us to know your name, so please do not tell me," stated a nun with an endearing smile.

Prue blankly nodded... "Can I ask where I am, and what I'm doing here?"

"You may, but, just one moment," replied the nun, closing a weighty ledger, and slipping it into one of the desk's drawers. "Right my dear, you are in the *Couvent de Notre-Dame des Pauvres*, of which I'm one of the Sisters. You can call me Sister Monique or just Monique, it's entirely up to you. We are a Religious Order, but also run a refuge for girls and women who's pregnancies are almost full term ... and who have no, or little means of support. If circumstances are... difficult when the *bébé* is born, we can also make... how shall I say... appropriate arrangements. Our friend Bernice has asked us to look after you, and during your stay your name will need to be changed. This was something she made very clear to us... do you understand?"

Prue nodded, although she did not! "Bernice has also asked me to tell you not to worry, and that she will visit soon. Now, what name would you wish to be called during the remainder of your confinement?" Prue was silent, traumatised... "I do not wish to rush you, but I have much to do, and prayers are beckoning," she continued, "so, please give me a name that we can introduce you as—"

"Elizabeth," blurted out Prue.

"A shorter name would be preferable," stated Sister Monique.

"Liz," she replied.

Why in heaven's name had she picked her mother's name of all names? Her mother had always called herself Elizabeth with no shortening and no twists, but Prue had often thought when she'd been a young girl, that Liza or Liz would've been a friendlier version. She never dreamt that she would become a Liz herself.

"Then you will have to remember at all times whilst here, that Liz is your name. Can you manage that?" asked Sister Monique. "I will mention it to Our Lord at prayers, and ask Him to help you."

Prue blankly nodded, still in a state of confusion... she was to become someone called Liz? When she left the office, instead of bells, she could hear the sound of babies crying, and that was when the reality of her situation hit home...

*

The icy atmosphere in the café did not melt, until the issue was raised by the ladies of the *Colonial Club*. "We're not coming back until this dispute or whatever it is, has been resolved," stated Amabel. "We are your customers, and you would do well to remember that, Fuzz. Marina, you would also do well to remember who your employer is, and if it was up to me, I would have you dismissed. We don't come here to get grief from you Madam!"

Fuzz and Marina looked at her, and then at each other, "I understand," he replied.

"Fuzz, please... I'll try, I'm very sorry," said Marina.

"Right, let that be an end to it. From now on we want fixed smiles, professionalism, and personal battles kept out of café business hours. You know Fuzz, that without our patronage, it would be mighty hard for you to survive let alone thrive," Amabel pronounced.

After closing time, Fuzz asked Marina to stay behind, as he wanted a word with her. She doubted it was a marriage proposal or a declaration of his undying love, and as it transpired she had doubted correctly. She was put on her final warning. He told her he had no problem working alongside her, but had no romantic notions or intentions.

"These might develop given time," she tried to counter...

"No, they will not, and that's final," he replied.

*

By the time Fuzz arrived home, he was ready for an early night. But instead, all hell was suddenly let loose outside. Bernice appeared at his door like a banshee coming in from a storm. She proceeded to read him the riot act for not returning home the previous night, with a force rarely seen or heard in these parts. The neighbours sat out in the balmy evening air listening, as Bernice bellowed inside Fuzz's cabin, whilst all the time swigging from their choice of comforters.

After a while it went quiet, and the notion that she'd perhaps killed him, wafted around in the warm evening air. In reality, Bernice's tirade stopped when she'd just run out of words, and had seen how upset and repentant he was. Enough was enough... just let him have your news... that Michael, the Dark Angel, had returned to the island in disguise, and that he would soon trace him to the café. He thanked her, and equilibrium was again restored between them.

Once back in her own cabin, Bernice's thoughts turned to Prue. She decided she would visit her the next day, and hoped she had settled and accepted what had been done? The Convent would be yet another shock to her already overloaded system, but it was the best and safest place she could find. Within these hallowed walls, the Sisters could make Prue disappear...

*

Liz quickly worked out that she was in the island's equivalent of a Mother and Baby Home. She knew that in Somerset, nuns used to manage such facilities, and perhaps they still did? Stuck on this island in this place, with her name changed, would the outside world ever see her again? She very much doubted it at

259

this moment in time. Michael was dead, and Fuzz must've gone off her, for he'd not even tried to find her. Her folks were ashamed of her, or at least her mother was, and people were hunting for her, for what reason she did not understand? Strangers she'd once trusted, like Jeanette, had betrayed her. Marcel had tried so very hard, and she had to give him credit. Kate... well, she wouldn't trust her with the custody of a toffee apple. Even Bernice had shut her in the dark, and then sold her off to the nuns, or at least that's how it felt!

The little one inside moved... that upset her, but gave her joy at the same time. "What's to become of us little one?" she said, silently to herself, as she gently caressed her swollen belly...

"In here," said a young nun, who had walked with her to a room in creepy silence. The corridors in this place seemed like decorated tunnels, dragging her ever further into a labyrinth of utter hopelessness. "Ladies, this is Liz... be welcoming to her please," continued the nun, who had shown her a level of indifference that was not entirely welcoming.

There were four beds in an otherwise empty room, with two girl occupants. They looked at her, making their first assumptions and absorbing their first impressions. "Who cut your hair, girl?" asked one, who looked younger.

"Me... I did it myself," she replied.

"I not be seeing me a haircut like that before," commented the other female, who was around Liz's age, or perhaps a little older.

"Suppose it looks good enough though," replied the first girl, "you be lucky you've the right kind of face for that style of cut."

Necessity makes us perform what is needed most, thought Liz.

"You don't look like you be near your time, Liz," continued the first girl.

"I'm five months, I think," she replied... the sound of that name left her cold. It was not who she was...

"Well, Liz, we both be nearly ready to drop. They don't usually let our kind stay here so early. Your guy... he been knockin' you about?" asked the second female. "I'm Lucy, and she be Gracie... has he... your guy, I mean?"

"Something like that," answered Liz.

The women noticed her looking at the other beds. "She delivered this morning... a girl," announced Gracie. "It was her first... poor child, and she only fourteen. So scared she was, like a frightened animal in the forest. She be moved into the nursery ward now, so won't be back. Just thank the Lord we won't have to put up with her cryin' and wailin' when the *bébé* be taken."

Prue's innards turned to ice at the thought of what they'd just said. Both Gracie and Lucy looked ready to give birth, she thought, judging by their size. She instinctively placed her hand on her own stomach once more, and was in time to feel another little flutter, then lay down on one of the empty beds. They'll not ask me any more questions tonight, if I can manage to keep my eyes closed, she thought. What had they meant when they said the baby is taken... taken where, she wondered?

*

Next morning, Gracie gave Liz a gentle shake, "Breakfast time, Liz, you don't want to miss it or you'll go hungry. They expect you to gobble up whatever trash they dish out," she announced. Liz then dragged herself up to face the day.

In the Refectory she didn't eat much, as she couldn't face a plate of food, not here, not now. "For God's sake, at least eat some fruit girl, if you ain't touchin' nothin' else. Eat it if you be able to as it fills your belly up for the mornin'," whispered Gracie. "Remember, there be no break-time, unless you need to pee."

"Drink the water and eat somethin'. Think about your *bébé*," urged Lucy. Liz could hear bells once again in the distance, as she sipped on the lukewarm water from an earthenware cup. "Them bells ain't ding-dongin' for us. I would be likin' a nice rest, sat with my feet up in that Chapel of theirs. I would just love to be sittin' with my Lord beside me, makin' me strong, and makin' me understand what the hell's happened to me to end up in here?" continued Lucy.

Liz's eyes travelled around the refectory table. There were around twenty women and girls, all heavily pregnant. Where did they all come from, with this being such a small island, and what were their sad stories?

At eight o'clock, Liz was escorted along to the main office. "Bernice told us you wouldn't be any trouble, so we've agreed to take you, even at such an early stage. As you are capable of work, you can help out in the laundry. Work hard and things will be okay for you, do you understand?" asked a stern faced nun, who's tone terrified her into submission.

CHAPTER THIRTY-TWO:

He longed to see her, but understood it was no longer possible. He now walked in dead man's shoes. Michael only had a few hours left before he needed to leave, and was desperate for her to be traced. Prue had now become an official missing person, who when located, would be informed officially that she was now widowed. His wish was to leave this island knowing she was safe, and with her future well provided.

Where could she be? On this size of island where could someone hide? He puzzled again over why she'd fled their apartment? What the devil had happened that had made her leave and go into hiding... someone must be aiding her?

Michael didn't want to be recognised. The only person, apart from the Judge, to whom he'd identified himself to, was Stoker's sister, Jeanette. Maurice Stoker had guaranteed his sister's integrity and that she would never disclose his identity. No one else had seen him in his new guise and recognised him, except for… Marcel. That little runt would now need to be dealt with…

*

Within the hour, Marcel found himself being forcibly dragged to the *Sérénité* Police Headquarters, where under extreme pressure, revealed that *Madame* Lambasto had a friend, a man with fair fuzzy hair. That was all he disclosed, and as a result was unceremoniously dropped off at the entrance to the island hospital… unlikely to work again for some considerable time.

*

There were not many men on the island with fair fuzzy hair, and as a consequence, Fuzz was quickly rounded up and brought to Police Headquarters. In his absence, the café was searched, and Marina confirmed to the police officers, that Fuzz knew the woman for whom they were searching. She also mentioned that they could acquire her whereabouts from her brother Frankie.

Frankie, being terrified of the police's reputation, quickly coughed up the location of Fuzz's cabin…

Three police cars later stole quietly through the woods, and stopped well short of the Green Plantation Road cabins. With strict instruction, they quickly pounced like hungry scavengers, and Bernice, together

265

with other neighbours, watched as they ransacked the contents of their friend's cabin…

They then turned their attention to the onlookers, who quickly closed ranks. Bernice being loudest in her protests was singled out, and the neighbours watched as they made an example of her by turning over the contents of her cabin. She protested but was physically slapped down for her trouble. This last action was akin to a red rag, and the signal for the residents to turn on the hapless police officers. This was their cue to leave… as the Judge would not want a bloody riot on his hands which could easily spread like wildfire across the island, where there already existed a tinderbox of discontentment and defiance bubbling under its surface.

A fruitless sweep was then carried out across the island for Prue, but she was burrowed too deep to be so easily unearthed…

That evening, Michael Lambasto, thanked Judge Stoker for the concerted efforts of his officers, and with a high degree of regret, left the island of *Sérénité*… for pastures new.

*

Devastation and all that accompanied it, was how Fuzz felt when eventually released. He had to make his own way back to his café… seemingly no cars were available, although he'd passed a number idly parked outside Police Headquarters. As he walked, his mind churned over the answers he'd given during his interrogation. He'd answered them as truthfully as he could, as he had no reason not to do so. Moreover, he also wanted her found, and quickly.

The level of noise hit him as soon as he entered the café. His customer's heightened voices were a result of them having experienced their most exciting day in a long time. They fussed over him and sympathised with his treatment at the hands of the establishment. Fuzz cast his eye in Marina's direction, and noticed she wore a blank detached expression, which convinced him that she'd played a central role in this debacle, and was up to her pretty neck in something dark and messy...

*

At this point, Fuzz didn't realise what was awaiting him at home, namely Bernice having been assaulted... his and her cabin contents trashed... and his neighbours up in arms at the heavy-handed actions of the police. In the midst of all this negativity, was however the positive reality that they'd stuck by him by closing ranks...

Next morning, a tired and aching Bernice, managed to drag her weary legs along the path through the woods to the Convent, where she told her friend Sister Monique, what had happened the previous night at Plantation Road.

"I can't believe they raised their hands to you, well I can, but not in front of your own people, Bernice," stated Sister Monique. She turned her head to show the extent of her head injuries... comprising of an open wound on the left side of her head, caused by the butt of

267

a hand gun, together with numerous bruises on her abdomen, arms and legs.

"The Judge, he ain't goin' to be pleased," she replied. "He likes his violence to take place within his own private spaces... I be knowin' that for a fact. I had worse done to me before Sister Monique. There be big trouble brewin', and if I be you, I'd keep everyone inside them Convent walls... this here island be about to erupt from its very core. Previously, we always crawled back into our holes, but I don't think that's about to be happenin' this time. The feelin's they be too strong against Stoker and his band of thugs."

"They came here yesterday too, Bernice, and asked if we were harbouring any women who were not pregnant? I was able to reply in all honestly that we were not," revealed Sister Monique.

"I be wantin' to see my girl right now," stated Bernice.

"Liz, is working in the laundry. There's nobody with her at the moment, so I'll take you there," replied the Sister.

"Liz? That name be suitin' her," smiled Bernice, "Monique, take care of her please, if anything happens—"

"Bernice, I promise, but nothing's going to happen to you," she interrupted her friend. They then walked the short distance to the laundry area in companionable silence. The holy pictures on the walls, the statues and crucifixes, gave Bernice a strange deep spiritual feeling; one which, until now, had been alien to her. Sister Monique opened the laundry door, allowing Bernice access and whispered, "May good fortune go with you, my dear friend."

Liz saw her arrive out of the corner of her eye, and at first tried to ignore her. However, Bernice was not someone who could easily be ignored. "Please believe me, my girl, this be the safest place for you on this here godforsaken island. It's gettin' nasty beyond these walls" she warned.

"Why? What's been happening?" she turned and asked.

"There's been trouble, even out at the Green Plantation cabins," answered Bernice, turning to show her wound.

"My God, what happened to you? Is this all because of me? I can't have this, I must turn myself into the police," she cried.

"Listen, this ain't over you. It could be over anythin'… it just be somethin' that's been waitin' to happen for a long time. Enough is enough… do you understand?" replied Bernice.

"No, not really… enough is enough of what? What's going to happen?" she asked.

"An eruption child, a mighty big uprisin'," replied Bernice.

Liz wondered where this had all come from… eruptions… uprisings, none of this made any sense? The island to her had appeared stable and controlled. She didn't ask about Fuzz, although Bernice could see from her eyes, that he was uppermost in her head and in that heart of hers.

"Just stay safe… you and the *bébé*," continued Bernice, who then laid her hands on Liz's belly, just in time to experience a strong movement, ironically a kick or a fist punch… it did not matter which, it was the *bébé* saying hello.

Liz laid her hands over hers, and they both shared a nervous laugh, "Bernice, promise you'll come back for me," she pleaded.

"I promise, of course I'll come back for you, my girl," she replied.

*

A woman's body was washed up on some rough waterside shingle in the vicinity of the *Sérénité* town beach the following morning. It had supposedly been brought in by the tide, and was speedily mopped up and taken to the *mortuarie de police*. Later, the body was identified as being that of well-known island dissident… Bernice Duval!

When the news filtered through to Jeanette, she took fright. Her brother had gone too far this time. Bernice Duval was a heroine, a leader… a legend in her own time. The dissident islanders would surely unite; all factions would come together, and Maurice and his army of cohorts would be in deep shit or worse.

She then pondered over Prue. Where was she and her unborn baby? Michael had left, never to be seen again, leaving behind a police force ordered to find his widowed wife. It had been her stupid mistake, which had prompted Prue to leave her apartment, and go to where she knew not. Her ill-timed phone call to Maurice must have been overhead, as there was no other reason for her to have left. Did that make her responsible for the mayhem that was about to unfold? If she'd not made that call, then none of this would have happened, or would it? She decided to desperately cling to that slender hope.

Jeanette did not know how Fuzz was coping over his loss, as she'd stopped patronising his café. She wasn't sure what had made her stay away, just a feeling that she should. She decided that she'd lie low in the hope she survived the coming trauma. Luckily, she still had Francine to run errands and shop for her, so she could bury herself deep inside the fabric of her apartment…

*

Fuzz was in the café when news filtered through to him of a woman's body having been washed up on the town beach. The haste in which it had been removed by the authorities, added to the already rising public speculation…

This finding of a body affected the atmosphere in the café, with tension contaminating the air. The grim news added to the ladies anxiety… they knew the underclasses were restless, and the ugly sounds of dissent were becoming evermore audible…

It had been a terrible shock to Fuzz when two evenings previously, he'd gone home to find the police had trashed his cabin... but far worse, was the fact that Bernice had been assaulted. Yesterday, he couldn't wait for closing time, so he could escape home. However, when he arrived he'd found the Green Plantation Road to be a hive of bubbling hostile activity. The surrounding roads were jammed full of old cars, rusty vans, scooters and bikes, and he could not help but hear the overpowering noise of ranting, excited voices coming from the back yards. He'd made his way through his cabin and opened his back door, only to be confronted by bedlam...

Being an outsider and a relative newcomer, he'd never realised the depth of resentment, frustration and fear, that Judge Stoker's regime had brought to bear upon the islanders of *Sérénité*. Their voices were tempered with mind-blowing anger, their prime aim to over-throw and wreak revenge on the corrupt establishment.

Bernice noticed his state of bewilderment, and had made her way over. "Fuzz, now listen my boy, you be keepin' yourself out of this," she'd warned, waving her hands and pointing her finger at him. "This ain't your battle... you're not belongin' here, you're not one of us," she had added, with a passion exceeding anything she'd ever shown him before.

He could have taken umbrage at her last remark, but hadn't. It was not meant to be unkind, which he recognised. He knew she was only trying her best by looking out for him. Later that night, she'd sat on her backdoor step, and beckoned him to join her. She'd told him not to worry, as all he desired would be his in the end.

"Bernice, you can't just say that without further explanation," he'd said.

"Bernice can… and just has," had been her reply… "Bernice has fixed it for you."

"Come on, are you saying you know where she's gone?" he'd asked.

"You be needin' a lesson in trustin' young man. I hear the wind say that a certain person is well, that be all," and that was the last thing she'd ever said to him.

*

There had been shouts for her to rejoin the buzzing throng, so she'd left and headed back to the waiting mob. It consisted mainly of people he didn't know, some had rifles slung over their shoulders, and who knows what else concealed on their bodies? Fuzz felt saddcncd to scc women whose beauty was being extinguished, by twisted faces and angry minds. Nevertheless, he decided to take her advice, and remained seated on his doorstep to watch the scenario unfold. Suddenly, the mob dispersed… it was seemingly not the moment to implement their plan… but something big was going to kick off, and soon!

*

The next morning, the news filtered out that the woman found dead on the beach, had been identified as Bernice Duval, the well-known dissident. Fuzz could not comprehend what he was being told... Bernice dead... how? He'd only been talking with her the evening before? "I was with her last night. I was sitting beside her talking to her, just her and me, and it was her who was concerned for my safety," he announced, in a distressed state.

"You know... you knew... Bernice Duval? How did you know her, Fuzz?" asked the choir of ladies of the *Colonial Club*.

"She's my neighbour, and a very good friend," he replied.

"She was your neighbour, and good—," corrected Marina.

What a callous bitch, he thought. He glared at her, and she answered him with a forced smile, which added insult to his upset. The ladies by now had perked up in their seats, interested in the fact that Fuzz knew, or had known the infamous Bernice Duval. They were also interested in the minor spat fast developing between Marina and Fuzz.

"That one's flying too close to the sun," whispered Pamela to Amabel.

Amabel nodded back to her friend, but it was not Marina's romantic intentions or her and Fuzz's spat that were of interest to her. There's more to Fuzz than meets the eye, she thought... a friend of Bernice Duval, now that fact was interesting. Bernice had been a dangerous dissident trying to spoil their way of life on this beautiful island. Amabel's eyes like many others, were blind to the hardship that faced the majority of the indigenous population.

Fuzz then announced to his customers, predominately the ladies of the *Colonial Club*, that he was closing the café for the foreseeable future. They understood why, and Amabel gave Fuzz her phone number, so he could reach her with a re-opening date. They then each gave him a hug before they left. Marina joined at the end of the queue, but he managed to body swerve her. "Fuzz, call me, and let me know when to come back to work," she said.

"Let's see what happens first. At the moment I've no plans to re-open," he replied, and left it at that.

They locked up, and Marina watched him chug off on his scooter, until he was no more than a speck of dust as he disappeared into an uncertain future…

CHAPTER THIRTY-THREE:

When Jeanette phoned her brother to ascertain what was happening, no one answered. That in itself was alarming, as he had quite a number of staff. Surely someone would have picked up an annoying ringing phone?

She had heard the sounds of gunshots earlier, along with the echoing of explosions, and in the street below there was a great deal of confusion… cars, vans, and scooters, some of which were heading into town, with others heading out. Jeanette and Francine could only speculate!

*

At the Green Road Plantation cabins, Fuzz sat on his back doorstep, looking out over the deserted plots. It was like a ghost town, as the women, children, and the elderly were holed up indoors; but he didn't really notice that... he was still in a state of shock over Bernice. Not only her death, but also the knowledge that had died with her... especially the knowledge of where Prue was. He recalled how she had been so up-beat about his future, and like a fool, he had believed what she'd told him. He then rose and went inside before he began to cry.

Indoors, Prue's solitary change of clothing hung forlornly in the bedroom. He hugged it placing his arms around its empty shell. He'd never felt so free with her body when she had been with him... the inhibiting ghost of Michael having always been an unseen barrier.

Letting go of her was difficult, but he slowly released his grip on her dress, then sat on his side of the bed, and cried for Bernice. She had been a true friend and one he would never see again. He then cried for Prue and the hurt he'd caused her, and then finally he cried for himself...

Paradise found and paradise lost, summed up what had happened to him...

CHAPTER THIRTY-FOUR:

In the *Couvent de Notre-Dame des Pauvres*, Liz worked tirelessly. There had been an occasion when she hadn't felt well enough, but that had only happened once. Her days were spent hanging laundry out in the yard, or ironing and folding it into seemingly never ending batches. She'd started off being inept and rather awkward at her tasks, but now had become skilled, even managing to gain a level of satisfaction from performing these menial duties.

The Convent bell pealed, announcing time for evening prayers, which in turn was her cue to finish work for the day. She'd taken to attending, and found it prompted within her an inner calmness which greatly helped to cope with her new life. The nuns had gradually accepted her into their midst, and was no longer looked upon as the woman who had once stood out in this place like the proverbial sore thumb. Sister Monique secretly prayed for some divine advice as to what to do, now that dear Bernice would no longer be coming to collect her.

She now looked different, spoke differently, and indeed was different, and nobody appeared to know from where she'd come or was going. Moreover, her room companions changed every few days, or at least weekly, most of which were girls or women who only arrived when they were due, or if there were unforeseen complications. No monetary charges were made for the delivery of their newborns as the Sisters managed a successful adoption service, a fact duly recognised and utilised by many of these unfortunate individuals. Nevertheless, Liz talked to her ever changing room-mates, and learned the true reason why many left without their babies. She felt great pity for most, but a total lack of understanding for a few.

Life now proceeded on a day by day, hour by hour basis. Her bag containing her private possessions, remained safely locked within the Convent's safe on the advice of the Sisters, who considered some of the visiting women to be somewhat light-fingered.

Liz had no real name, no past, no future... all she had was the uncertainty of her wretched present...

*

In the distance, the sound of the Convent bells could be clearly heard on the balmy air currents. This was Fuzz's cue to put his tears behind him, and think about the living, especially his neighbours. The children, along with their mothers and most grandparents were still here, and it was his duty to help

279

them deal with whatever was happening elsewhere on the island.

*

Meanwhile, back on his Somerset farm, Jim Dibble was now living with what seemed to him to be a nightmare. His wife Elizabeth refused to talk about their only child's situation. He could not understand her reasoning, as he'd always thought that even the hardest of women would soften if a baby was involved? He didn't understand why she was taking such a position… and if the truth were told, he'd never really understood her or her hard stances. What had Prue done? It appeared to him that her only fault was to become a widow, while pregnant…hardly her fault, and most certainly not a crime… at least not in his book.

Jim hated himself for being a sham of a man, and this thought gnawed away in his mind as he worked his fields and tended his animals. This situation could not go on any longer, and he decided that he'd tackle Elizabeth head on after supper. As he drove his tractor up and down the fields, his mind wandered… all his married life he had endured Elizabeth, with her strange moods and attitudes towards all and sundry. Poor Prue had suffered so much from her mother's treatment, and what a wimp he'd been to stand back and let it happen. How Prue had managed to survive and grow up to be the clever, beautiful, and sweet natured woman she was, he would never know. He'd failed as a father… but that was going to change as he wanted this grandchild more than anything, and vowed that he would try to find her and bring her home himself. If his wife couldn't change her ways and forgive, then she could move out. The farm was his; his through his father and his grandfather before him.

*

The battle for *Sérénité* was over in no time. Judge Stoker had upped and left with his wife, son and daughter in their private jet, as soon as the crowds showed the strength of their collective anger. The staff from his mansion and administration, scattered in all directions in an effort to distance themselves from their previous associations. The police, on hearing of Stoker's departure, surrendered en-masse, and were rounded up for questioning, most of whom would probably don their uniforms once again, when things had settled.

A dictatorship cannot survive if there is no dictator, and so Judge Stoker's empire crumbled, with the pieces turning eventually into inconsequential particles of historical dust.

Fuzz was not impressed when he heard the news of Judge Stoker's departure. Bernice's death had been such a waste, a waste of a life of one of the island's genuine characters, and a cruel ending for a much loved friend. Worst of all, was that no one would be called upon to take responsibility for the horrendous crimes that had been committed, now that the main culprit had fled.

"Suicide my arse," he shouted at the walls of his cabin... and heard it echo back on himself. The official line that Bernice had committed suicide, had hurt and

281

made him so angry every time he heard it repeated. Bernice would never have committed suicide!

"Where are you, Prue?" he wailed once more... Bernice had known where she was, but that knowledge had escaped to a better place along with her. How had Prue's disappearance come about? Who had caused it to happen? Michael Lambasto, was definitely involved, perhaps with the help of the strange unknown men in suits? Marcel, maybe... but himself, definitely. Whilst Michael must shoulder most of the blame, he must share it with him, as it had been his responsibility to look after her and he'd failed miserably.

He had at last found the one with whom he wanted to share his life, and had let her slip through his fingers. Fuzz slipped to his knees and began to pray, not to God, but to Bernice... "Guide me, Bernice, please, I love her," he prayed out loud.

*

Very little news from the outside world trickled into the thick walled cloisters of the cosseted Convent. Its bell tolled as normal... a distant sound that all islanders were familiar with, but paid scant regard. It was taken for granted, in the same way as the sweet song of the birds high in the tree tops, or the incessant crashing of the waves upon the islands rugged shoreline.

To Liz, the sound of the bell now meant many different things. It could indicate the time she must rise or go to bed... the start or the finish of her working day... the time she must eat or drink... or her time to pray...

Every evening, she joined the good Sisters in the Chapel. They'd never had an expectant mother do that before, or at least not on a daily basis. Surprisingly, Liz now looked forward to that time of day, and to hearing the nuns chant their prayers in the quiet serenity of the Chapel cloisters. It helped her through the tedium of her monotonous day.

Now heavily laden, she sat while she ironed, folded and sorted the laundry. One day she felt strangely faint, and Sister Monique arrived to find her doubled over with pain, "Liz, that's enough of this work for you. You must rest from now until you deliver," she announced. "Come with me… can you manage to walk?"

Liz nodded and the Sister took her arm, "I will move you to a small room on your own, and get our *docteur* to visit. Let's get you to bed. Have you felt like this before?" she asked. Liz shook her head. "Thanks be to God. I hope all is good with you, Liz. So much has happened outwith this place since you came to us."

The Sister's tone was sad enough for Liz to notice, and it added to the confusion already circling around in her head. In her relatively short time living in the Convent, she'd become institutionalised, and had lost all notion of time, except for that directed by the pealing of the Holy bell.

Sister Monique realised this was the case from the glazed look in Liz's eyes, she wished she'd spent more time with her. What was she going to do after the *bébé* arrived? She did not even know Liz's personal story, or if it was now safe for her to venture outside these walls?

Bernice, God rest her soul, had left her with a real big problem... "I have not done a good job here, Lord," she whispered, "please guide me, as to what to do with our dear Liz."

*

Sister Monique hated having to call that man. He was an enigma, for whilst he offered his services freely, he made sure the girls knew they were charity cases. He always let that show in the way he treated and addressed them. The Sisters had no choice but to use him as they had no one else to call upon, or at least no one who wouldn't charge them the earth.

*

Dr Charbonneau duly arrived, and was met by Sister Monique. After their usual curt pleasantries, they got down to business... "I have a young woman that I need you to examine, *Docteur*," she told him.

"You have far too many young women, Sister Monique, but I like to help the Sisters as you know, so I do what I can. Let me have a look at this fallen women," he replied.

She did not answer him; she was ashamed of this man's attitude, but required his help. Followed by the *docteur*, Sister Monique entered Liz's dingy cell like room. Liz tried to raise her head to see who'd entered, but her acute dizziness forced her head back down onto her threadbare pillow.

284

"Liz, I have brought the *docteur* to make sure all is well with you. He will need to examine you... will that be all right?" she asked.

Liż indicated with her eyes that it was okay. That was before she turned her head and saw that it was him... *Docteur Charbonneau.* She froze! It was the pig from before... the horrible beast from Jeanette's. He showed no interest in her frozen expression, as he began to prod and poke...

"*Docteur,* please be gentle, the girl seems very nervous," cautioned Sister Monique.

"My dear, Sister Monique, I will examine her my way or I will leave... the choice is yours," he curtly replied.

"I'm sorry, I was just... it is fine, *Docteur.* I am sure we both have Liz's welfare at heart," she answered.

"Help me turn her a little, Sister Monique, and some refreshment would be appreciated... some wine perhaps, to steady my hand," he replied, with a hollow laugh.

Monique left to do his bidding, and in that moment, Liz felt all sense of dignity leave her. A side of meat would have received more careful handling, than that afforded her. When his hands had finished their crude examination, he looked at her with recognition, and surprise, "*On se revoit...*we meet again," he announced, then deep in thought, turned and left.

He met Sister Monique in the corridor, and they retired to her office, where he helped himself from the carafe she had laid in front of him, "She is fine for the moment, although will probably need a caesarian section when she goes into labour… which will be soon. So, be prepared to involve *l'hôpital*," he announced, in between gulps from his glass.

"Are you saying we ought to allow her go into labour here, although she will probably need to go to hospital? Should we not make the necessary arrangements to take her there now?" asked Sister Monique.

"These poor souls deserve to experience a difficult labour," he replied.

"Why is that?" she asked.

"For goodness sake Sister Monique, surely even someone like you can see that if it is too easy or too comfortable, then they will be back in nine months time to further abuse your kindness," he replied. "Nice drop of stuff, Sister, I'll have some more of the same the next time I call."

Sister Monique could only look at him in disbelief…

CHAPTER THIRTY-FIVE:

The *Colonial Club* re-opened for business; Fuzz, encouraged by the ladies, finally agreed it was time. The **Free Island Security Council (FISC)**, had set themselves up in power, and taken over from the deposed Stoker regime. Although they seemingly had been preparing themselves for this moment for some time, Fuzz did not expect there to be much in the way of visible change in *Sérénité* life, except for the personnel. This was a society engrained in corruption. However, for the present anyway, it did seem to be a fairer and more caring group of people in charge. Long may that last...

There had been no news of Prue... and the loss of Bernice had left a permanent gap in the lives of the Green Plantation residents. Bernice's cabin lay empty, with no one inclined or having the heart to touch it... or to communicate with its ghosts.

287

Fuzz hadn't needed to make the dreaded call to tell Marina that he no longer required her services. Her brother Frankie had unexpectedly arrived at the cabin before he'd re-opened the café, to tell him that she had a new job with one of their suppliers. She had also started to date the owner's son... "Bet that's a relief to you, mate," he'd announced. "She had the hots for you, but I knew your heart was already taken."

"My heart was... and still is taken, but I don't know where she is, or even if she's still alive," Fuzz replied.

"But you surely haven't given up looking for her?" he'd exclaimed.

"I don't know, Frankie... it's like living in a dead-end city, where every road is sealed off with a brick wall," replied Fuzz. "I feel her flame's burning low, and I keep thinking her candle is not far from being snuffed out... permanently."

"Come on Fuzz, chin up boy," said Frankie. "Don't let go now... she must be somewhere on this island, frightened and alone."

Fuzz couldn't bear to think of her that way, alone and scared, and if she was having a baby, then her isolation was an even worse scenario to contemplate.

Frankie and Fuzz parted friends, and agreed to stay that way, despite Marina.

CHAPTER THIRTY-SIX:

Dr Charbonneau was intrigued. Liz was not the name of the woman he had examined at Jeanette's, and yet they were one and the same? He had enquired from Jeanette of the health of the woman he'd treated at her home, and was informed that the girl had left suddenly, and that her whereabouts were unknown.

Well, he knew now where she was, and that was what intrigued him. Why had this woman left the comfort of Jeanette's apartment for the island's whore sanctuary? The nuns would be shocked if they knew that was how he looked upon their services, but that was what it was. He even believed that its existence as a refuge, encouraged promiscuity. The only good thing stemming from it was that it provided a ready source of *bébés* for the unfortunate souls who could not produce their own.

The *docteur* could not wait to inform Jeanette of his discovery…

*

Life was almost back to normal for Jeanette. She had kept herself concealed in her apartment for some time, with Francine bringing her reports of the happenings outside. Maurice had upped and left, without a thought about her or her welfare, and that had been a rude awakening. She was now well and truly on her own.

Businesses were once again open for trade, and the commercial life of *Sérénité* continued as before. The social side of the island had also been rekindled, and she came to the conclusion that nobody was interested in her or the other colonial ladies. They were just looked on as harmless relics from a bygone age.

That was what she was, a relic from a past that was gone forever. Jeanette decided there was no point in her or any of her lady friends not embracing the new regime… it would certainly be in their best interests to just accept what had happened. She had heard that the ladies were now helping Fuzz run the café, and she couldn't wait to get involved once more herself. Marina was seemingly no more… but as far as she was aware, he had not yet found Prue.

Prue, what's happened to you since you left here that day? You and your born or unborn baby are out there somewhere? She didn't have long to wait until she got her answer.

He'd made a special journey to her apartment to tell her in person what he had uncovered. "She's now calling herself Liz, but it's her, Jeanette. I would stay well clear though, if I were you," the *docteur* informed her, "you don't know where she's been."

She gave nothing away to him, and kept her composure until he'd left, then let the floodgates open. Prue in that place and with these women? She'd never been inside herself, but she could well imagine. She then became angry with herself for thinking like that… where was her new approach to things? Seemingly gone before it had even begun.

Jeanette decided to pay a visit to the Convent and Sister Monique was somewhat surprised when she asked about a woman named Liz? How can she know? The only outsider who's seen her was *Charbonneau*… they must have some connection. "Do you know *Docteur Charbonneau*?" she casually asked.

"Yes, I do, and I also know the girl's name is not Liz but Prue… Prudence Lambasto to be precise, and she's a married woman… well, actually a widow," replied Jeanette, unsure if any of what she had said had been appropriate in the circumstances? She felt a bond with Prue, because of the secret she would have to carry to protect her from the sad truth.

"I'm afraid I do not know if what you're telling me is correct or not. I am also not at liberty to proceed any further with your enquiry," stated Sister Monique. "This is a refuge, and as such, all information regarding the women who come here is confidential."

"*Docteur Charbonneau* examined Prue at my apartment and confirmed her pregnancy there," announced Jeanette, "so I'm not just some passer-by who's called in on some spurious whim."

"You will need to let me consider what you've told me," Sister Monique replied, "I am finding this an extremely difficult and delicate situation."

"I respect that Sister… of course you need time," agreed Jeanette. "Will you call me? I'm very keen to know how Prue is faring."

"If I decide to speak with Liz about your visit, would that bother you?" asked Sister Monique.

"If that's the case, I'd like her to know that I'm truly sorry for my stupidity in seeking my brother's advice about her. Please tell her that I genuinely wanted to help, and that— no, I will leave it at that," replied Jeanette. "Has Prue had her baby?"

"I am not at liberty to answer your query… but this refuge is for women in-waiting," she answered.

Sister Monique showed Jeanette out, then went and relayed to Liz what had transpired. Liz's eyes looked at her, and she could see genuine fear… "I don't want to see her, and please don't get back in touch. I just want to have my baby in peace. Can I go to the hospital when it is time, Sister Monique? I don't want to see that *docteur* again," she pleaded.

"I understand," replied the Sister. "How are you feeling now?"

"Fine, but very tired," confessed Liz.

*

Jeanette left the Convent, and drove home. She had a feeling that Sister Monique would not get back in touch, so once inside her apartment she re-ran the events of Prue's short stay in her mind. Was there something she'd perhaps overlooked?

Whilst she had respected Prue's wishes, and had never told Fuzz about her brief stay, Jeanette was now in a quandary... she had to get Prue someone she loved and trusted by her side, before her baby is delivered...

That evening, she told Francine of her visit to the Convent. "Christ, we never thought of looking for her there! It makes sense when you think about it," she replied.

"It makes me feel like a right fool... living on this island, baby on way, destitution... she had all the correct qualifications," said Jeanette, "but she just was not that type."

"The whore house type, you mean?" replied Francine.

"Don't ever say anything like that again Francine or our arrangement for you to live here will be terminated," snapped Jeanette.

Francine shook her head, and made a face. Jeanette hadn't meant what she'd said about their arrangements, and in reality, had been thinking along the same lines, she just wasn't as expressive. She also liked having her about the place, so backed off. "Francine, is there anything in the room she may have left?" asked Jeanette.

"Well, if there is, it must be mighty small. I was a member of your brother's Special Forces remember… the eyes, ears, and nose of *Sérénité*, so not much gets past me," she answered.

"Anything… a scribbled phone number perhaps, or a name… that sort of thing?" pressed Jeanette.

"Did she make any phone calls that you know of?" asked Francine.

"She made one to her parents, that's the only one I'm certain of," she replied.

"Now that you mention it, I remember tossing the top page from the pad that lay beside the phone in my bedroom. I'll have a look to see if there are any imprints on the page underneath," stated Francine. She went through to the bedroom, pulled the pad from the top drawer. "There could be a phone number," she shouted, "but it's definitely not a local one… why would she need to write down her folks number, I would've thought she'd have known that one off by heart?"

"Not if you hardly ever phoned them, and never from *Sérénité*," replied Jeanette, as she rushed through to examine the pad. "It could be a number to a UK phone… it looks as if it has the correct country code? Thanks Francine, you are a star," she continued excitedly. "I'll have to think what I'm going to do next.

It's the only lead I've got to finding someone who cares, and who could be responsible for her. She's such a lovely person and doesn't deserve to be abandoned."

"Perhaps... but she did take off without saying as much as goodbye to you," replied Francine, with a shrug, "and she left dressed in your daughter's clothes for goodness sake!"

"We all do strange things whilst under pressure," defended Jeanette.

"You're such a soft touch," replied Francine, "soft as fudge."

Jeanette drew breath and reached for the phone. This new technology thing amazed her, and it being available in *Sérénité*, blew her senses away. Not that long ago it had been booked calls, and lousy, unreliable connections, via a dubious switch-board operator...

A woman answered so speedily, that Jeanette was glad she was seated, "Hello, my name's Jeanette," she stuttered, "I'm a friend of your daughter... well, not exactly a friend, we had a strange relationship..."

There was an explosion of sound at the other end of the line, and Jeanette got the impression that the hand-set had been walloped against something hard, as if in temper... then a male voice floated towards her, soft and respectful. He introduced himself whereupon she repeated her tale and gave him her contact number, without daring to ask what had happened at his end, and was most surprised by his attitude and words. He appeared caring and interested, and his words flowed with sympathy and compassion. "I'm coming over as soon as I can arrange care for my animals and flights. Will you meet me at the airport... I presume there is one?" he asked.

"Yes, there is a small one, and of course I will meet you if you want. Is there anything I can do for you in the meantime?" asked Jeanette.

"If you could arrange accommodation, I'd be more than grateful," replied Jim.

"I'm sure I could manage that too. Just tell me as soon as you have a flight arranged... which could take some time, as there's not many Carriers in or out of here," said Jeanette. "You've heard of our troubles, I presume?"

"Afraid not, are they serious?" he asked.

"It all depended upon who you are or were, that sort of thing. It seems to have settled down now," she replied.

There was a pregnant pause, after which Jim asked about Prue. Jeanette filled in the missing gaps with her imagination. Then, she could hear the tirade starting up again in the background. He announced that he had to go, adding that he'd be in touch very soon...

"How did it go?" asked Francine, arriving in the room with two mugs of coffee.

Jeanette related her tale, and Francine beamed as she listened. "He's left his accommodation up to you...

who's he going to be sharing with… you or me?" she half joked.

"Francine, what a thing to say," she replied, "I haven't decided yet." The two ladies laughed at this turn of events…

*

Back in Somerset, the hostile diatribe continued until an exhausted Elizabeth Dibble fell silent. "Right, is that you finished?" he asked her. "If you have… I'll make us a cup of tea, and then I'll tell you what I'm proposing to do."

"You do whatever you like, I want no part of it," she replied.

"You think on lass, before you cut your own throat," cautioned Jim.

CHAPTER THIRTY-SEVEN:

Amabel was seriously concerned about Fuzz... the guy was a shell of his former self. She called a meeting of her ladies and asked for their support, and as usual, they agreed. "Fuzz, I've had a word with the other girls, and we're willing to go the extra mile and let you take a break while we hold the fort," she announced. "What do you think?"

He looked at her with disbelief. It was for him to tell her what was happening, not the other way around. "Leave it out, Amabel," he replied. "I sometimes wonder where you dredge your ideas up from."

"God, you are one ungrateful wretch these days, Fuzz," scolded Amabel, in a way that made him realise he'd hurt her feelings. She made to leave, but he stopped her and apologised.

"Accepted, now when are you off?" she asked.

"Off where?" he replied.

"In search of your fair lady and perhaps her child," she answered.

He was pleased by the gesture, but embarrassed by the mention of a child. Did Amabel know the whole story? Did she know that the baby was not his? She could sense what he was thinking. "The answer to your unspoken questions are, no and yes," she replied, with a wry smile.

What a strange woman he thought, but it was enough for him to capitulate. He knew she meant well.

And so it was arranged for Fuzz to make one last push along a hitherto unknown trail, that could perhaps lead him to Prue…

CHAPTER THIRTY-EIGHT:

With her head bowed, and her arm entwined with Sister Monique's, she entered the Chapel. They walked slowly down the aisle, and sat for a few minutes in a front pew, in prayer and contemplation. "It is time for me to have my baby, and Bernice hasn't come for me," whispered Liz.

Sister Monique felt squashed... like a tomato when it's inners are exposed.

"Will you send someone to tell her for me please? I can't go on hiding. I don't know what or who I'm hiding from, and my days have blurred into nights. I need Bernice to come with me to the hospital, if I can't have Fuzz," she continued.

"Is Fuzz the baby's father?" asked Sister Monique. She'd broken her own rule, and asked a question… Oh, Bernice, what do I do? Do I act on any information she gives me, she thought?

"No, my husband is the baby's father," she whispered.

Her husband? She had just confirmed she has a husband, so what's this all about, and why is she in hiding?

"I need to go," whispered Liz, with uncharacteristic urgency. "Now!"

"Sorry, I forgot for a moment… it was the hospital you meant, is it?" she whispered back.

"Yes," stated Liz, her teeth gritted so tightly, her reply made a whistling sound through her pursed lips. She slowly eased her way towards the Chapel door, with a certain urgency exuding from her every pore. "I can't go any further," she suddenly screamed, as she grabbed hold of a pew to steady herself.

"Liz, Sister Juliette's waiting to take you to hospital," replied a shocked and confused Sister Monique.

"Tell her I can't manage… I'm staying here," announced Liz, as she laid herself out on a pew.

Christ, please tell me how I'm going to get her out of that pew, there's no room to move, thought Sister Monique? She quickly glanced at Our Lord's statue and speedily crossed herself and genuflected, "Forgive me, Lord," she muttered. "Liz, you need to get up and come with me, you can't stay here, it's not allowed."

Her suggestion was met by a growling noise, which not only took her by surprise but also struck a note of fear. Why is she making such noises in the Chapel, has she forgotten where she is? "Please Liz, you can't growl here," continued Sister Monique. "I can't allow you to growl in the Chapel."

The noise continued unabated, so Sister Monique took action, and pushed open the heavy Chapel door which led onto a long dark hallway, "Help, someone help me, I'm in the Chapel... help me... please, someone help me!" she yelled at the top of her voice. She then rushed back inside to find that the growling had now changed to intermittent screeching and desperate moaning.

She had no way of telling if any of the other Sisters had heard her cries for help, so she pulled off her coif and wimple, and then poured holy water over her hands before filling a dish. The next layer of her clothing was also removed, as she began to improvise...

"Liz, I'll have to get you and the baby out of here. First, you're in the Chapel, which is not the best place, and second, I can't reach you, the pew is far too narrow. I need you on the floor," she yelled.

"Tough... I'm going nowhere. God won't mind me being here, so why should you?" Liz forced her reply through clenched teeth. This type of talk was out of character for both Liz or Prudence for that matter.

"Prue, I know that's your real name, so let's have no more of this Liz nonsense. I want you to try and pull or push yourself off that pew," directed a now desperate Sister.

"Blast you… for wanting me to lie on that damn hard floor," yelled a now sobbing Prue.

"The ruddy pew's just as hard as the damn floor, and there's no room to move in there," announced Sister Monique. The realisation of where she was, and what she'd just uttered, shocked her. Prue however was unfazed, and reached out her desperate hand towards her… Sister Monique took it gently, and then bathed Prue's face whilst loosening her clothes. "Just stay where you are, Prue; this is for me to manage, not you. Here, this will do for a pillow," she said, placing her discarded habit under Prue's head.

Prue suddenly screamed, and this time grabbed Sister Monique's hand with all her might… "Monique… Sister… it's coming… it's bearing down on me. I need something for the pain… I can't… do this…" she sobbed.

Sister Monique was now sobbing herself… something for the pain? She wants something for the pain? She looked across to the altar where the chalice stood, and thought about giving her a cup full of their best, but luckily at that moment the door opened and in came Sister Juliette… "What's the delay, I can't wait all day—?" she began, before her eyes took in the scene which presented itself. "What are you doing, Sister Monique? You've delivered enough *bébés* in your day, so why are you in such a state?" she asked. "This administrative job of yours is making you soft. Out of the way… I'm coming, Liz dear."

"I know I've delivered plenty of *bébés* Sister Juliette, but not on a pew in our Chapel," she replied. "Don't use the name Liz anymore, her name's Prue or Prudence. I'll explain later."

Juliette made a face, that said to her that at this moment in time it didn't really matter what her name was... "Thank you, Juliette, now please take over... just tell me what you want me to do," continued Sister Monique.

Necessity makes us perform what is needed most...

"Just pray Sister, pray," ordered Juliette, "come on Prue, let's get this *bébé* born."

*

Juliette Monique Lambasto was born in the Chapel of Our Lady of the Poor, *Sérénité,* within ten minutes of Sister Juliette's arrival. A healthy daughter for Prudence and her late husband, Michael...

Prue and her daughter were then taken to the island's only hospital by ambulance, leaving the Sisters to look after their other dependents. Her parting words to Sister Monique was to send for Bernice...

Monique wondered why she'd not told her during the time she'd been at the Convent about dear Bernice? She had made such a mess of this whole business, and would have to face Prudence and confess her sins as soon as possible. But not just now, she would give her a couple of hours to recover first.

CHAPTER THIRTY-NINE:

Jim Dibble scrubbed up well and was a transformed man when he swapped his overalls for a lounge suit. He'd been lucky with his travel arrangements, and would manage to make his way to *Sérénité* within a few days of having received Jeanette's phone call.

In the meantime, Jeanette had been undecided about whether to go to the airport herself or to take Francine with her? She was feeling flustered, as she was not in the habit of arranging to meet strange men, or booking their accommodation.

With regard to the accommodation, she had foolishly allowed Francine to talk her into giving him her own spare room, whilst Francine and her would double up together. She had protested that this arrangement was far from ideal, and that he would be far happier in one of the local hotels…

"Would you want to stay in one of those seedy watering holes that masquerade as a hotel on this island?" Francine argued. "Remember Jeanette, this is *Sérénité* we're talking about, not the wide boulevards of Paris, lined with its classy establishments."

Francine had a point... she herself had led a privileged and sheltered existence on this island, and had not shared Francine's experience of life. She had therefore succumbed to her pressure, and agreed. In the end she decided to travel to the airport on her own, leaving Francine in charge of the accommodation.

*

As she stood in the small space that served as the airport's Terminal building, it all appeared very informal. At least when Maurice had been in power, there had been a military presence, a certain sense of order... but she swallowed such thoughts, and decided that this felt better... nicer, and far more welcoming.

Six passengers arrived off the small plane, and after crossing the tarmac, they filed through the swing doors, followed by a couple of trolleys, one carrying their luggage and another stacked with miscellaneous parcels, boxes, and other items of mail.

Jeanette did not want to stare, but couldn't resist a quick glance in the direction of the emerging passengers. As she peeped, she counted four men and two women... and wished in that moment, she had brought Francine with her. She wouldn't be fazed by anything or anyone, unlike her...

When she looked up again, she watched as the passengers queued at a desk, waiting to have their papers checked and stamped. She noticed they were using the same big clumsy stamps that Maurice's men had used. Her eyes strayed from the desk, and followed a line upwards to the wall behind the desk… it was gone, thank heavens, that official picture of her supercilious brother, which had always made her cringe…

There were now only two men left at the desk, the two others and the women having moved on. Jeanette found herself inching forward, her mouth trying to speak… "Are either of you gentlemen, Jim Dibble?" she asked tentatively, in a voice far too low for them to either understand or hear above the noise of the airport.

"Jeanette, nice of you to meet me… unexpected, but extremely welcome," said a man partially bent over the desk, scooping up his papers. Jeanette's world suddenly crashed… it was Paul of all people, Amabel's loud mouthed brother, arriving for yet another freebee holiday on the back of his long suffering sister…

"Paul, I'm sorry, I'm not here to meet you, in fact I had no idea you were coming. I haven't been out and about too much recently," she stammered her reply.

"Keeping your head beneath the parapet no doubt. I understand, awkward for you with all the goings on around here, and you being such a close relation of the old dictator," stated Paul, partially lowering his voice as he mentioned the dictator word, whilst glancing to where Maurice's picture had once hung. "I was concerned about Amabel when it all blew up, but she

307

says most folks knew it had to come, and that it's all pretty much back to normal now. In any case, Paul's back to see how all his ladies are bearing up, so everything's well ——."

"Excuse me, Jeanette… I'm Jim Dibble. I was telling Paul on the plane that you're a friend of my daughter," interrupted the other man, "and that you were arranging things for me, with her being out of action, so to speak."

They shook hands and Jeanette gave him a thankful smile for coming to her rescue. He looked like Prue, but in a manly sort of way; kind eyes, nice hair, a healthy outdoor type… Jeanette then became aware that Paul was observing them… that man was such a sweetie wife, always looking for an angle…

"Where have you booked our friend into, Jeanette," asked Paul, "pulled out all the stops, I hope?"

"My friend Francine has arranged the accommodation, and I forgot to ask her where she had finally decided," lied an embarrassed Jeanette. "I'll take Jim back to my apartment to meet her and then she can take over."

"My God woman, there's not exactly that much choice! This place is not much bigger than a clutch of football pitches," laughed Paul.

"Have you collected all your luggage, Jim? Oh, I see you're travelling light," said Jeanette, quickly changing the subject.

"Best way old chap. I always bring far too much, but you look to me as though you've gone too far in the opposite direction... only some socks and underwear I fancy, judging by the size of your bag," replied Paul.

"I had to leave in a hurry. I can surely pick up a selection of shorts and tee-shirts here... there are shops, aren't there?" asked Jim.

"Yes, of course we have shops. Don't pay any attention to him," replied Jeanette. "Now, I'd like to get on our way. Are you in need of a lift, Paul?" Oh, God I hope not, I really hope not, she thought.

"No, you're all right, Jeanette. Amabel's sending a friend to pick me up, some young chappie. You'll know him... he owns this *Colonial Club* joint... the place you all seemingly frequent and help run, from what I can make out," he replied.

"Yes, I know him. Don't worry Paul, Fuzz won't let you down," replied Jeanette. "Now let's go, Jim."

"I'll see you later, Jeanette... you too Jim. I can see she's taken you to her bosom," called Paul as they moved off...

Why in heaven's name had she not brought Francine with her? She would've crushed Paul where it hurt. Perhaps she ought not to leave the house without her in future? How embarrassing was that? And imagine Amabel sending Fuzz in her car to pick him up. Thank goodness he was late or that would have really been complicated...

Jim was smiling, aware of the anguish that Paul had dished out. "I take it our mutual friend Paul is... a tosser?" he ventured.

"I don't know what you mean by a tosser?" she replied, feeling her face flush.

"Good, I prefer it that way. You'll just have to take my word for it that he is a tosser," he added with a smile. He then reached forward and opened the car door for her in a gentlemanly way, and she thanked him. Her bosom, as Paul had called it in such an undignified way, was heaving, as she still had to explain about the accommodation... how embarrassing!

They drove out of the airport and continued for a short distance, before she pulled over, causing him to look at her quizzically. "Mr Dibble... Jim... I've something I have to tell you—," she began. She suddenly stopped mid-sentence to take breath, and to watch Fuzz drive past towards the airport, before she launched into her confession...

*

Fuzz now had the use of Amabel's car. She had decided it would make it easier and quicker, than using his scooter for moving around the island whilst looking for Prue. Whether that was true or not, he'd accepted her offer, as it was a top notch machine. He was determined he was going to smoke Prue out from wherever she was...

However he'd first had to pick up Amabel's brother from the airport as part of the car deal... what a pain that man was! Still, that job hadn't taken him too long, and now he had four trendy wheels at his disposal.

Later, he sat with the most detailed map he could find, and divided the island into segments. As he'd walked around the town on so many occasions, he was sure she was not there, but somewhere else... she was somewhere... hidden away on this island.

CHAPTER FORTY:

The residents of the Green Plantation Road had begun to deal with the task of clearing out Bernice's cabin with the help of a few of her relatives. It was hard to believe she had now been gone for almost three months. Her death had never been investigated, nor had anyone paid the price. On the island of *Sérénité*, her death remained listed as one of suicide…

     She would never be forgotten by her friends and neighbours, especially Fuzz who would never forget her kindness to him and Prue. He then considered the message she had given him with her beaming smile, the night before she died. She implied that Prue was safe and that everything would work out in the end. That had been around three months ago, and her smile along with her message was fading fast. "Pull yourself together Fuzz," as Amabel would say to him… "do not give up on others if you don't want them to give up on you…"

*

Sister Monique's stride grew shorter with every step she took on the hard flagstone floor. She was a Sister of the cloth, guilty of a mammoth deception. As she stood in the doorway of the hospital's Maternity unit, she could see Prue sitting up in bed staring lovingly at her daughter with a glassy-eyed smile. As she watched, a nurse arrived at her bedside and drew the curtains around her bed. Good, she thought, that might hide some of my shame and embarrassment from the other patients and staff?

"Can I come in," she called, "it is Sister Monique?"

"In you come," answered the nurse. "Prue's going to try to feed her *bébé*."

"Yes, in you come, Sister," insisted Prue. "Look at Juliette Monique, isn't she gorgeous lying there asleep?"

"Yes, I agree… she's absolutely gorgeous Prue. I'll come back later," she replied, "and let you feed the little one in peace."

"No… stay Sister, the little one's sleepy, so can wait for half-an-hour or so for her feed. We just want to give her practise at suckling," said the nurse. "I'll leave the curtains drawn."

"Well, if you're sure?" replied Sister Monique. Half-an-hour? She had half-an-hour, which was not much time in which to cleanse herself of the terrible secret she was carrying…

The reaction she received from Prue, was not what she had expected. "Sister Monique, thanks for telling me. I will have to let it sink in slowly," was all she said, before turning her attention back to her baby daughter.

There was no anger, no distress, which was worrying, even when told about the demise of Bernice. She had not anticipated this reaction. Sister Monique continued by telling Prue that the Judge had also gone... deposed, and that there appeared to be no one who wished to do her any harm on the island. There actually appeared to have been no reason why her name had been changed.

"Bernice said it needed done, and she was looking after me," answered Prue in response.

"Can you tell me where you stayed, or where you lived before?" asked the Sister. Prue looked at her then glanced away, her eyes ever drifting towards Juliette's crib... "Do you want to bring Juliette back to the Convent?" continued Monique.

"No, I most certainly don't," stated Prue, in horror.

"Then tell me where you stayed, or I am afraid you will have no choice but to come back to the Convent," stated Sister Monique.

The underlying meaning of what she meant, slowly filtered through. "We have an apartment, a lovely apartment... I should say, that I have an apartment... Michael is dead," she replied.

"Was Michael... your husband?" asked Sister Monique. Prue nodded, whilst fixing her eyes firmly on her new born. "That's good that you have an apartment, but if it was rented, you may have lost it by not keeping up with the payments," she announced. "You were at the Convent for three months."

"It's our own apartment. Michael always bought wherever we went. He usually made money when we resold," replied Prue. "It was a game he liked to play."

"That's good news then," said Sister Monique. "Can I ask you who Fuzz is? You asked for him when we were delivering the baby."

"He was a friend... no, he was more than a friend, he was my best friend, but he doesn't want to know me anymore," she replied.

"Are you sure?" asked Sister Monique.

"He said that to me... but only after I had said—," replied Prue.

"What had you said?" interrupted Sister Monique.

"Nothing, I said nothing," she snapped. "Could you go now, and ask the nurse to come. I want to try to feed my baby."

Sister Monique did as asked, stepped out from behind the curtains, and thanked the nurse for her help, before leaving. What should she do now? She would take a step back, for the moment anyway…

*

On reaching the Blue Ocean Apartments, Fuzz entered for the second time, the glitzy reception hall. He did not recognise the Concierge on duty, and for that he was glad. This guy turned out to be far more amenable than the last one.

Madame Lambasto does have an apartment here, but has been away for some considerable time. Yes, he was positive that the apartment was empty, and no, it was not possible to go up there. He then suggested that Fuzz telephone her.

Fuzz thanked him for his help, and left through the revolving door…

"Monsieur, monsieur… you see *Madame*?" asked a voice, the owner of which he recognised, but could not see.

Fuzz looked around… there was no one? "Marcel, I have unlocked my car doors. Get yourself inside," he hissed through his teeth, "understand?" Marcel was inside as quick as Fuzz, who then drove off at speed down the drive. Once outside the grounds, he found a convenient spot and stopped the car. "Is there any good reason for your secrecy, Marcel?" he asked. "You behave mighty strangely."

"I no understand?" he replied.

"Why do you hide," he asked, "understand?" Marcel nodded, raising his palms upwards and shrugging his slight shoulders, in a gesture that communicated that he did not know why. "Now that the Judge is no more... do you continue just out of habit," asked Fuzz, "understand?"

Marcel nodded once more, but obviously didn't understand. "You see *Madame* Lambasto, you see *bébé*?" he asked. "My Colette... she say *bébé* come now."

"How does she know that?" asked Fuzz. Marcel counted up to nine on his fingers, and showed them to Fuzz, who nodded in return, with a wry smile. "Well, Marcel, nice seeing you again," he said, handing him as large a tip as he could muster. Marcel slipped out of the car, and gave a slight bow, before he disappeared. Fuzz could not help but smile, this time a proper smile. He was convinced now, that she wasn't staying at the apartment. Marcel would have known if she was in residence.

Where to next? He turned onto the road to Shanty Town for no special reason. Once there, he continued beyond the various shacks, along a track leading further south. He just knew that she wasn't there, not in Shanty Town. He next headed on towards a mainly uninhabited part of the island, an area he'd never been to before, and it looked like few others had been there either. It was as barren, as the rest of the island was lush. Why was he looking in this place, there was nothing here, certainly not her and her baby?

Fuzz stopped, and let the tears flow in response to Marcel's words about her having had her baby. He should have been with her when she had given birth! His job was to look after her… but it was not his job to bawl like a baby himself. He wiped his eyes and turned the car around in the direction of the town and the *Colonial Club*.

"This is where I need to be… here, in the café," he later announced to the ladies. "There is no point in me looking for her out there. She will come back, if it is to be, at least… that is what I believe."

CHAPTER FORTY-ONE:

Francine found Jim Dibble to be like a bar of gold bullion... "He's wonderful, Jeanette, and what a delicious looking man... I could eat him," she announced.

Jim had no problem with Jeanette's accommodation arrangements, and said he would be delighted to stay with the ladies. As usual, she had worried needlessly... perhaps she should always listen to Francine in future?

First thing the following morning, she decided she must take him to the Convent, but tonight he'd insisted on taking them both out for a meal. Jeanette would have liked time to talk to him privately, but Francine had taken over, and was flirting outrageously.
Jeanette found herself wishing she could shove her inside the coffee pot and firmly close down the lid. What a childish way to think, and her a

grandmother too! She allowed herself a small smile… Jim smiled back which caused her to blush…

"Jim, you don't look like a farmer to me," observed Francine.

"I can assure you I do once I don my overalls; just ask the wife," he answered.

Jeanette had forgotten all about his wife… she was that horrible woman who had upset poor Prue. How could a lovely man like Jim have such a nightmare of a wife?

That night Jeanette couldn't get to sleep for thinking about the man sleeping through the wall from her. She listened, by putting her ear to the wall to hear if he snored? He didn't as all was quiet, but Madam Francine did… she was snorting and grunting as usual as if her life depended upon making these dreadful noises…

A little later, Jeanette rose and quietly headed for the kitchen. The light was on which surprised her, and when she peered around the door, sitting at the table with a mug of tea, was Jim. Once inside, she pushed the kitchen door closed, and as she did, realised that she was only wearing her skimpy nightdress. Jeanette imagined steam rising from her blush, however if he noticed he didn't let on, but sprang to his feet and poured her a mug of tea; what could she do but join him at the table and brazen it out?

"This is very nice," he said, "I'd been hoping all evening to get a chance to talk to you in private... about Prue that is."

"But you didn't, thanks to Francine. I know she's loud, but she's been a great companion. I went through a bad patch not that long ago, and she pulled me through," flustered Jeanette.

"She's lovely I agree, but I'm afraid I've had enough of the loud-mouthed variety of women. Give me the quiet life every time," he replied. Being unaccustomed to the heat, he had discarded his pyjama top, and was bare chested. Jeanette didn't know where to look, but he didn't seem in any way embarrassed.

"Jeanette, tomorrow... I mean today, I hope to meet up with Prue. You are going to come with me, aren't you?" he asked.

"If you would like me to, I will," she replied, in a hushed voice.

"Just you, no offence meant to Francine, but I'd just like you to accompany me," he stressed.

"As you wish... that can be arranged," she agreed.

*

Baby Lambasto was fit and well, as was her mother; and so, as was the custom, Prue was asked about arrangements for her daughter? The hospital had a very quick turnaround time, as spaces within the Maternity unit were extremely limited.

Prue confirmed she had her own apartment, and with that information, was speedily discharged. A nurse did her a favour and called a taxi, whereupon mother and baby left a short time later, with baby still wearing its hospital gown and wrap...

Once in the taxi, it dawned on her that she had nothing prepared. If she went back to the Convent, they would probably kit the baby out from donations, but that was not for her. She asked the driver to stop at the bank, and for the first time in many months, used the card that she had safely stowed in her rucksack. Much to her surprise and relief, it worked normally, so at least she had cash. In fact there was a considerable amount of money in her account, which was comforting.

They then carried on until they reached the Blue Ocean Apartments... Prue paid the driver and went inside the building. It seemed bright and surreal to her, after the dim lights of the Convent corridors. She had no key, and didn't recognise the Concierge on duty. Just as panic was about to set in, her good friend appeared as if by magic, and explained who she was to the Concierge.
A little later, when Marcel opened the door to her apartment, Prue began to cry... "*Madame* Lambasto, I can come inside... Judge gone and new people good," offered Marcel.

"I am so glad to hear that, Marcel. Could you help me, please?" she asked.

He smiled, and for the first time saw his face take on the hue of a happy man. Prue passed Juliette to him, and he held her with pride. "*Madame*, you need things? I say to Colette, and she bring things for *bébé*?" he asked.

"Could you… would Colette not mind?" asked Prue. "I have money to pay for what we need."

"*Non*, my Colette for a *bébé*, she will do," he replied. "Tonight I cut up towels for the *bébé*. There are many things we can do. You have *bébé* milk in your—?"

"I don't know, I have tried… they say it will come soon," interrupted Prue.

Marcel did not look convinced, but Prue thought the hospital seemed pleased enough with her. As he left, he told her that what the *bébé* needed most of all, was love. Prue offered him cash, but he declined, saying that what they would bring was a present for the *bébé*…

When Marcel had gone, a loneliness spread through her like a wave crashing across a bleak sandy shore. She opened the door to her beloved *terrasse*, and took Juliette out into the sweet air… this time, the sounds of the waves crashing in the distance had a soothing influence. She had forgotten how beautiful her *terrasse* was… the plants had been looked after… who had done this, it must have been Marcel? She then went inside and phoned the Concierge to send out for a few essentials. Surprisingly, this new Concierge seemed genuine and only too pleased to help.

Returning to the *terrasse*, she thought about the people, especially the girls she had met recently. How hard their lives were compared to hers… she felt so lucky. But how could she feel lucky? She'd lost Michael… her little girl would have no daddy's knee to sit upon. When she tried to picture it in her mind however, it was Fuzz she saw… not Michael! Fuzz was alive, but gone, and his loss seemed to hurt more than that of her husband.

Bernice, dear Bernice, it had just sunk in about her. It was too upsetting to think about and a tiredness swept over her. She quickly changed a still sleepy Juliette, and temporarily laid her down in Marcel's makeshift drawer-crib. She then lifted the baby out again, and took her into bed beside her. She was the most precious little bundle in the whole wide world.

CHAPTER FORTY-TWO:

The phone rang in Jeanette's apartment, which Francine chanced to answer. It was Paul, wishing to know in which hotel Jim Dibble was staying? "He's staying here... with Jeanette and me... who are you anyway?" she asked.

"I'm Jeanette's friend... Amabel's brother. I arrived over on the plane with Jim and we got friendly, so I wanted to show him the sights," explained Paul.

"Well, he's going out with Jeanette this morning, on some secret mission to which I'm not invited," revealed a somewhat peeved Francine.

"You sound nice, I certainly wouldn't mind some of your company. I'd like to spend time with someone who's not part of my sister's clique, so if you're game, that would suit me just fine," he replied.

"Are you… asking me out?" she queried.

"Well, put like that, I suppose I am," replied a confident Paul.

"Well, I could show you the real sights on this island. In fact, I could take you to places you've never seen or imagined," she laughed.

"Mmm, that sounds like an excellent invitation," he purred.

*

"You've what? You've arranged to go out with Paul?" gasped Jeanette, when told later of her arrangements.

"Yes, what's wrong with that?" replied Francine.

"What's wrong with that? Nothing but everything! The man makes me squirm. Why did he phone anyway?" asked Jeanette.

"He wanted to know where Jim was staying… as he thought he would show him the sights," she replied, "however, as he's going out with you on some hush-hush mission, I agreed to show him around instead."

"I suppose you told him that Jim was staying here too? I'll never hear the end of it from the girls or him. This will take years to evaporate. I do hope you realise what you've done?" groaned Jeanette, most upset.

"What did you expect me to do, lie to the man? For God's sake, Jeanette, you can be such a prune at times," answered Francine.

"The word is prude Francine, please think about your words before you spit them out," corrected Jeanette.

"You're the only one spitting here; you should hear yourself. You're behaving like a stuck up cow," she replied, "and I also think that you're a little jealous, because I'm going out with Paul."

"Don't be so stupid, I absolutely detest the man," she protested.

"Why can't you just use the word hate, the same as most normal people? But, oh no, Jeanette can't do that, she has to detest," replied Francine, sarcastically.

"What's going on here, ladies?" asked a bemused Jim, on entering the room.

"She's jealous because I'm going out with Paul, that's all," huffed Francine.

"Pay no attention to her, she's talking utter rubbish," replied Jeanette.

"Who is this… Paul? Surely he's not the Paul I met on the plane?" he enquired.

"Yes, the very same… so you can perhaps appreciate how absurd she's being," replied Jeanette. "She hasn't even met the man, but after a few cheap words of banter over the phone, she's anybody's."

"I don't believe what I'm hearing—," exclaimed Francine.

"I think that was a little too strong, Jeanette. I don't think you meant to say she would be anybody's," interrupted Jim, the lilt in his voice giving off a soothing tone.

"Yes, you see Jeanette, you could learn something from Jim," agreed Francine.

They all looked at each other after that remark, trying to work out its exact meaning... Smiles then began to gather on the two previously stormy dispositions.

"Right you two, give each other a hug, and then we have to be off. I need to find my daughter," suggested Jim. "I think Francine could be the one Paul needs to educate him on how to behave. In fact, I think she could be the one to bring out the best in him."

Francine grinned at this statement, whilst Jeanette merely raised her eyebrows. Jim, on the other hand, silently congratulated himself at his much underused mediatory skills.

*

The darkness of the night lingered long and heavy with Prue. If she dozed, people came to join her, people alive and people dead, all mixed together like some uneasy cocktail... but when she was awake, all she saw was Juliette's beautiful little face. When dawn finally arrived, her body ached. How was she going to look after Juliette when she felt too weak to even look after herself?

She was about to drag herself to the toilet, when there was a knock on the door. Instead, she wearily dragged herself over to see who was there. Prue opened the door on seeing it was Marcel and Colette, and they helped her back into bed. Marcel had brought two baskets of baby things and a proper little wicker crib.

"Madam, I go... I need work, but Colette, she stay with you," whispered Marcel, and then was gone.

Juliette whimpered, and Colette helped Prue prop herself up in bed, before she lifted the little one to Prue's breast. It worked as it was meant, and this made Prue feel she was now a real mother.

Following her short feed, Colette busied herself changing Juliette and as she did this, Prue looked through the selection of little garments and baby items. She could not believe how kind people could be. Colette then took charge, and Prue drifted away into a proper, much needed slumber...

After a while, Colette woke her gently and indicated she had to leave, "I come tomorrow... early, if you want?" she suggested.

"Oh, Colette, please do," replied a sleepy eyed Prue.

CHAPTER FORTY-THREE:

Jeanette drove Jim beyond the Green Plantation Road towards the Convent. He marvelled at the colour of the sea, and the raw beauty of the landscape. "Can we stop for a moment," he asked, "just until I gather my thoughts; I have to be prepared for whatever comes my way?"

"Of course, I understand," replied Jeanette, who was feeling nervous herself. She slowed the car, and came to a stop facing the ocean.

"Can I thank you again for looking after me in the manner you have?" said Jim.

"It's my pleasure," she replied. After a few minutes watching the mesmerising ocean, they continued towards the Convent, and when they reached their destination, he sprang from the car and raced around in time to help her out. Their hands lingered a fraction longer than necessary, and Jeanette's mouth felt dry…

He knocked with his knuckles upon the wooden Convent door, before he glimpsed the bell, whereupon he pulled upon its long chain. They were still smiling over this, when the heavy door opened. Inside was an anti-climax when Jim announced who he was, and who he'd come to see. They were told there was no one of that name here, and were about to be shunted back outside, when Sister Monique caught sight of Jeanette.

"Her father? Why that's wonderful," she exclaimed, after being introduced. She nodded at Jeanette and mouthed 'well done'. "I have news! Prue delivered a healthy baby girl yesterday in the Chapel of all places," she announced.

Jim could hear babies crying in the distance. He could not fully take in what she was telling them, only the part about him having a grand-daughter! After some pleasantries, Sister Monique directed them to the hospital.

Once back outside, Jim found himself hugging Jeanette, "I have a grand-daughter," he exclaimed, bouncing on the spot. "Can you imagine?"

"Yes, you have," she replied, "so let's go visit her."

However disappointment once more awaited them when they arrived at the hospital. They were informed that she had been a patient, but had been discharged late yesterday. They had no forwarding address, other than the Convent. Jim was distraught when he heard this, and his disappointment was compounded by the fact that Jeanette didn't know of any other possible address.

"She never did say where exactly she had lived, only that it was in a modern apartment, and I'm sorry to say that I didn't enquire further. What do you want to do next," she asked, "do you not have an address?"

He shook his head, ashamed. What sort of man was he who had lived his life not always knowing where his only child was? Jeanette could see his upset and reached out her hand tentatively in his direction. He took it and caressed it with his own. Jeanette had never felt such a thrill for years, that part of her, she thought, had died along with her late husband...

"No, we didn't have her address in *Sérénité*. Sometimes we had an address and other times we didn't, depending on where she and Michael were. Let's go back to the Convent, they must have an address for her there," he replied.

Disappointment followed yet again, when they learned that the Convent had no such information.

"Who brought her here?" asked Jeanette.

"Bernice, brought her," replied Sister Monique.

"Bernice?" exclaimed Jeanette. "You're not telling us it was Bernice Duval, surely?"

Sister Monique nodded, "Yes, it was my dear friend Bernice Duval who has now been dead for over three months."

"Are you telling us that Prue was here all that time?" queried Jeanette. Sister Monique nodded once more. "I see," Jeanette continued, "I'll explain to you later Jim, about Bernice."

"I'm so sorry, but I'm sure you'll find her soon, with it being such a small island," replied Sister Monique.

Jim thanked her for looking after Prue, which in turn made Jeanette feel extra bad at losing her. She had never thought of her being in the Convent Home. She was not the type normally found there, and instantly felt bad about herself for having that thought, as she had let herself be tainted in her thinking about the girls and women there by none other than *Docteur Gilles Charbonneau*!

*

Jeanette's apartment was empty when they returned, which meant that Paul had collected Francine, and Jeanette wondered what they would make of each other... two people each vying to be the centre of attention?

"What will we do now?" asked a subdued Jim.

"I'll make us coffee while we work that out. Let's sit out on the *terrasse*," she suggested.

"Jeanette, please don't you worry about this. This is my problem, not yours," he answered.

"I know, but I want to help," she replied. "I have an idea… I know someone who I think will know the location of her apartment. After coffee, I will go and see him… I don't want to ask over the phone."

*

Jim remained on the *terrasse* while he waited for her to return. He felt the sun's rays caress his face in a far gentler manner than in Somerset. He could smell the sweet scent from Jeanette's planters, which were stuffed with flowers as exotic as their colours. If only he could find Prue, then he knew he could feel happy and contented here. In the back of his mind he could still hear barking… a shrill, harsh bark that never stopped. He did not want to go back home to the farm and her incessant barking!

Jeanette returned with the information they required. The apartment was located within the Blue Ocean development, in an upmarket part of the island. Fuzz had yielded up this information without questioning why she wanted it. What she'd also heard on the grapevine was correct; the ladies were working side by side with him, and why not… to feel useful is very important. To serve, instead of being served, does wonders for self-confidence, and personal happiness.

It had become a topsy turvy world, this new *Sérénité*.

Jeanette reflected on this… it was a place to where a dead man would not be able to return. She was glad of this, and in this moment her knowledge and memory of the truth concerning Michael Lambasto died.

"Can we go there right now?" Jim asked impatiently. He took her hand briefly, and secretly she did not want him to let go… but he did.

"Whom did you ask?" he queried.

"It was a guy… a guy with whom Prue used to be friends," replied Jeanette.

"He's not the baby's father, is he?" asked Jim.

"No, the baby's father was her husband. Michael Lambasto was the father… she told me that herself," she replied.

"Well, that at least makes it more straightforward," stated Jim.

"The man's dead, how does that make it more straightforward?" asked Jeanette.

"I'm sorry, I didn't mean to sound so prudish. I sounded like my wife Elizabeth just then," he replied. That was the first time he had spoken her name. They looked at each other, and then diverted their eyes, each withdrawing into their own private thoughts…

*

Twenty minutes later, she stopped the car in front of the Blue Ocean Apartments, and they entered through the grand revolving doors. The Concierge appeared to be busy, and did not make eye contact with them, so they sat and looked at the sensational view, as they waited for him to come off the phone.

"Can I help you?" he asked finally, as he laid down the receiver.

Jim approached and asked for Mrs Lambasto.

"Can I tell her, who is here to see her?" he asked.

"Her father," he replied.

His conversation to Prue appeared rather lengthy... to have just conveyed the words to her that her father was downstairs? Eventually, he beckoned Jim over, and asked if the lady with him was his wife?

"No," was his answer, "she's a friend... not my wife." The Concierge then went back on the telephone, and was about to ask some more questions, when Jim grabbed the phone from him.

"It's me Prue, Dad... let me come up please, I've come all this way to see you," he asked.

The phone was thrust back into the hands of a far from happy Concierge, who then spoke to Prue. He next beckoned for a porter to escort them in the lift to the apartment, and as they made their way, he called out, "*Monsieur*, no more of that behaviour, or I will have to call the police," wagging his finger.

Jeanette was a little embarrassed, but thought they had made progress. Jim had just shown himself to be a passionate and caring man.

When they arrived outside Prue's apartment door, Jeanette experienced butterflies, and silently wished she hadn't come. The door opened, and a woman, around Prue's age, stood holding a sleeping baby in her arms, "*Monsieur* welcome, *Madame* welcome," announced Colette.

She led them into the stunning apartment's lounge, where seated on an armchair was Prue. Colette slipped Juliette into her arms. "Dad! Oh, Dad, it's so nice to see you," she exclaimed, reaching out to him with her free hand. Jim took it and kissed it. His eyes then strayed to the baby... "Juliette Monique, this is your grandad," she announced. "She is so beautiful."

"She sure is, Prue," he replied, with tears freely streaming down his ruddy weatherbeaten cheeks.

"This is Colette, Dad, *mon ami*," she added. Colette smiled in appreciation at Prue for calling her a friend.

Prue then noticed Jeanette, lurking in the background. She looked at her quizzically. Jim noticed this, and came to her rescue, "I'm only here because of Jeanette, she's the one who tracked me down and has been looking after me since I arrived," he hurriedly explained.

Prue smiled, and beckoned for her to come and see Juliette. "She's lovely, Prue… a perfect little girl," she said.

Colette then went through into the kitchen and brought back some glasses of lemonade. Prue handed the baby to her proud dad, who nervously took her in his arms, while smiling at Jeanette. "Suits you," said Jeanette, with a grin.

"Where are you staying, Dad? You can stay here, it's far nicer than any of the hotels," suggested Prue.

"I could… I suppose, as I'm putting Jeanette and Francine out at the moment. They're having to double up to accommodate me. That would be so good, Prue," he replied.

"Then I would have you here at night. Colette comes in the mornings, but has her own children to attend to, and can't stay all the time," explained Prue. "It's settled then, just stay on now. There are plenty of… Michael's things for you to use."

Jeanette felt deflated. She had lost him, although he had just arrived. It had felt homely with him around her apartment… in fact, more than homely. Now she would have Francine bouncing around with Paul, and would be a gooseberry in her own flat.

"Jeanette, would that be okay with you? I know you've put yourself out for me, and I really appreciate that, but Prue needs me here," asked Jim.

"Of course she does, it's no problem," she replied, her voice quivering. If he noticed, he didn't say. "I'll be off now Prue, that's him delivered."

"Thank you for everything," replied Prue, "Jeanette, before you leave… who's Francine?"

"Your dad knows all about her and can fill you in later on that score," she replied. She then waved in his direction, but he was too busy talking to Juliette and her mum to notice, so she just quietly slipped away…

CHAPTER FORTY-FOUR:

In the town Square, Paul and Francine were enjoying a cosy meal together in one of its most intimate eateries. "This is great Francine," he said, "my sister Amabel doesn't like me going out for meals without her."

"I thought she was just your sister? What is she… your keeper or your gaoler?" asked Francine.

"She'd like to be. She's two years older than me, and has always treated me like *son petit frère*," replied Paul.

"But Paul, you are *son petit frère,* although it seems absurd to me that she still likes to play these kind of games at her age," stated Francine.

"What games? I don't understand what you mean," he replied.

"*Petites filles* always like to play games that include bossing *leurs petit frères*. Most give up once they reach their teens," explained Francine. "*Ta seoul* has obviously not reached puberty yet?"

"Wait until I tell her that. That will be a bit of a shock... she's only fifty-nine after all," he replied. The two of them giggled and spluttered their drinks, which made them giggle even more.

Paul was around twenty years older than Francine, but it did not seem to faze her, and it certainly did not faze him. This holiday was looking up, now he had someone who appreciated his brand of chit chat and humour. He stretched his hand across the table and placed it on top of hers. She looked at his hand and for a moment he thought he had blown it, but no, she smiled and placed hers on top... and then squeezed his a little. The restaurant's beady-eyed accordion player saw this gesture, and rushed to their table, closely followed by the flower seller with her basket of exotic wares. Paul bought a rose for Francine and helped her pin it into her hair. The accordion player then serenaded them, until they burst out laughing. Paul slipped him something for his trouble, and once he'd left, they toasted each other.

"Just as well I answered the phone," said Francine.

"Just as well I called," he replied.

*

Back home at her apartment, Jeanette was taken over by a black anxiety attack. She was annoyed with herself for the way she had been behaving... the touching of hands, and the knowing looks... did not suit a women of her age. Her annoyance turned to shame... what kind of a woman was she? Just imagine, she had even eavesdropped at the partition wall to hear if he snored! She had sat and talked to him in the middle of the night, dressed only in a flimsy nightie, and her hand had lingered on his. He must have been so embarrassed by her actions... only he was too well mannered to let her know.

She was surprised at Francine, but not jealous. Oh no, she definitely was not jealous. Francine was after all only forty and well-schooled in looking after herself. She allowed herself a brief smile at the thought of Paul getting out of line, and Francine bringing her military training to bear on him...

She then went into Jim's bedroom, forgetting momentarily that it was actually Francine's. His few belongings were still there, neatly stored. He would have to return for them, or perhaps it would be more convenient for her to return them to him... only that would give the impression that she wanted rid of him... which she didn't. What she wanted was him back.

*

Jim had been so engrossed with baby Juliette and Prue, that he hadn't noticed Jeanette slip away. What must she think of him? She had opened up her home to him, and now he had led her to believe that he didn't appreciate it. He wanted to be here, but not because he didn't want to be there. He was thrilled with Prue and little Juliette, but he didn't want it to be at the expense of Jeanette. In truth, his world was in turmoil. He was far from what he knew, and thankfully from his wife… but was already feeling at home on this strange, bewitching island.

One thing he did know, was that he would rather be alone here, than at home with Elizabeth. He would have to deal with her though, and the going would get tougher before it got better…

*

Jeanette decided that she would not sit and mope, instead she made her way to the *Colonial Club* with the intention of putting her name down on their rota of helpers. She was recruited immediately, and was soon waiting her first table, which she found a strange but satisfying experience.

"I hope you didn't waste your time going to the Blue Ocean Apartments, Jeanette," stated Fuzz. "I was there recently, and she wasn't there."

"Well, she's there now. I've seen her and her daughter. The baby's name is Juliette," she replied.

There followed a stunned silence amongst all within earshot, with eyes fixed on Fuzz! He said nothing, but took a seat on a vacant chair.

"Who's the guy you've staying with you, Jeanette?" asked Amabel. "Paul says he was looking for his daughter… is there any connection?"

"Yes, he's Prue's father. His name's Jim Dibble," she replied. Fuzz looked at her in disbelief!

"He's a lovely man, although ashamed of not being more forceful with his wife and her actions over the years. He's with Prue now… in fact has moved in with her. She also has a young woman helping her called Colette."

"Well, Fuzz, what have you to say about that? She's now been found," announced Amabel.

"I haven't found her, other people have found her. She's surrounded with other people, and doesn't need me. They're all there for her," he replied, his eyes hot with salty tears.

"Fuzz, you've got to see her, you can't just let it go," urged Jeanette.

"Yes I can… just watch me," he replied. "Can you all manage without me for a while, I need some fresh air?"

"Sure," they told him.

When he'd left, the ladies raked over Jeanette's news and Fuzz's unusual reaction. "I didn't expect him to react like that," announced Jeanette.

"None of us did," added Amabel. "He loves her; the man's a fool to himself… bloody pride gets one nowhere!"

*

Baby Juliette was thriving. Colette came each morning, and Marcel called in whenever he could manage. Mum and Grandad muddled along fine, each learning on the job as they went along.

Around a week had passed, and Prue now felt back to her old self. Neither Jim nor she had left the apartment or *terrasse* throughout this time. Grandad just loved being there, and couldn't believe he had no recollection of Prue as a baby. He must have been excluded by Elizabeth, and wondered how that could have happened?

"Have you spoken to Jeanette to thank her for everything?" asked Prue.

"No, although I've phoned a few times, but she hasn't been home," he replied.

"Didn't you leave a message?" she asked.

"No, I don't like leaving messages," he replied, "not on strange machines."

Prue laughed, and shook her head. Jim's thoughts turned to Jeanette. He had tried to call her, and had thought about her, but really didn't like leaving messages on strange answering machines. They seemed so impersonal…

The void out there scares some folks. It's like talking to the wind, which then carries your innermost thoughts and words away to who knows where…

"Why don't you go and see her, she's probably at the *Colonial Club*… it's a small intimate café run by—" began Prue.

"Run by who?" interrupted Jim.

"You'll see, if you go," she replied. "Take my car, you can't miss the place, it's in the main Square beside the waterfront... opposite a large café called *The Coffee Palace.*"

"Thanks, I will," said Jim...

CHAPTER FORTY-FIVE:

Jim entered the *Colonial Club* and was surprised to see its clientele. He had expected them to be somewhat younger and not all female. He smiled over at Jeanette, as she came over to join him. "Girls, this is Jim Dibble… he's Fuzz's friend Prue's dad," she announced, "and has travelled all the way from Somerset, England."

"Fuzz?" exclaimed Jim. "Is that the friend we talked about… the one she'd been asking for… the one I thought might have been… where is he?"

"He's stepped out," replied Amabel. "He left in a bit of a mood."

"Is he going to visit Prue anytime soon?" he asked.

"I don't know, Jim. He wasn't very clear about that," replied Jeanette.

"Well, that's not what I came here for anyway. I came to thank Jeanette for all her help," said Jim, uttering what was a half-truth. "I've been trying to phone you but to no avail, and I don't like leaving messages on these answer machine things. Right, now that I'm here, which of you ladies would like to serve Jeanette and I?"

This request brought on a bit of shoving and pushing, as they each vied to reach him first. "For goodness sake, let's have some decorum ladies, please," called out Amabel. She looked at Jeanette and winked at her... he's very nice, she mouthed.

Jeanette sat beside him, and he nudged her with his knee under the table. She couldn't believe this was happening to her... not to staid Jeanette, a regular old frosty pants! "What would you like to drink," he asked, "and would you also like to go for a meal with me later this evening?"

"I'll have a black coffee, and I'd be delighted to have a meal with you later," she answered, nudging him back with her knee.

By the time Jim left with Jeanette to return to the Blue Ocean Apartments, there was still no sign of Fuzz.

"Where has he got to, the bloody fool of a man? Well, he can do the clearing up this evening on his own. He's done nothing else today," announced Amabel.

*

Prue was nursing Juliette, when her dad and Jeanette arrived back. She did not ask directly, but indirectly moved the conversation around to Fuzz, without actually mentioning his name.

"That chap you were friendly with, wasn't there," replied her dad. "One of the ladies mentioned that he was in some sort of mood."

"I think he may have just needed a break from all the women," suggested Jeanette.

"I never found him to be the moody type," replied Prue, then turned her attention back to Juliette, who had milk dribbling from her mouth and running down her lovely little dimpled chin.

"What a greedy little girl you are," laughed her grandad fondly.

Colette came and relieved her from Prue, "*Bébé* no greedy; *bébé* need *lait maternal*," she said indignantly, looking at Jim with disdain. Jim told her he was sorry, and that she was correct. Marcel arrived later, with more supplies, and a selection of *bébé* garments made by Dorothée.

"Thank her so much from me," replied Prue. "You must bring her to see Juliette."

Afterwards, Jeanette went home, Jim having arranged to pick her up around eight that evening. "You seem happy, Dad," stated Prue, "I think it suits you being here, away from the farm and… Mother."

349

"I am happy. I think it suits me here too, and I really like Jeanette. I feel like I'm starting over," he replied, with a slight blush.

Prue looked down at Juliette's sweet face, while she let these words sink into the inner depths of her mind. She too would like to start anew with her little daughter… and her dear friend… but how do you start anew? Simple… it suddenly came to her; what you do is you go back to the beginning and start over again, it's the only way.

"Dad… will you drive Juliette and I into town later?" she asked.

"Sure, just tell me when," he replied.

*

Just after five-thirty, they left the apartment, and Jim drove her into town. "Do you mind waiting outside, Dad?" she asked, once they had reached the town Square.

"Not at all, I'll sit and feast myself on the ocean view. Can I ask you where you're going? I don't want you to go missing again," he exclaimed.

"Dad, I'm going to try and catch Fuzz who ought to be clearing up at the *Colonial Club*," she answered. "A little bird called Amabel, phoned to tell me that he'd be clearing up by himself tonight."

"Oh, I see… well, I don't, but that doesn't matter, whatever you want to do is fine by me," he stated.

Prue pressed Juliette close to her breast, as she made her way to the cafe. It felt strange to be back... but also oh so right. Through the window she could see he had his back to her... and the sight of Fuzz's hair made her smile in the same way it had always done. Quietly turning the door handle, she slipped inside. "Do you have any spare seats?" she asked.

He knew it was her... not just from her voice, but by that something special that now hung in the air. He wanted to turn around, face her and rush to her side... but found he could not, as his feet were transfixed to the floor. There was so much at stake... his whole future happiness depended on what happened next... "How many of you are there?" he asked.

"Only two," she replied.

"Will that be two coffees then?" he asked.

"No... only one coffee please. One of us has brought her own supply," she replied. "You don't mind do you?"

"Of course not!" he exclaimed.

"Could I have something to eat?" she asked. "Wait, I'm sorry... I shouldn't have asked... it's far too late in the day."

"No problem... I can certainly rustle you up something," he replied. No problem, he thought? That was a laugh... he would have to switch to auto pilot.

"Do you not have any help with the clearing up?" she next asked. "I remember you used to have a girl."

"Oh... I got rid of her. She was cruel to my best customer, so had to go," he replied. "I do have my ladies who help, but because I've been moody today, they've decided to leave me to do it all by myself."

"What was making you moody. That doesn't sound like you?" asked Prue.

"I was more sad than moody. I wanted a certain lady so much, but thought she didn't want me," he replied.

There came a whimpering sound followed by a proper cry of... "I'm hungry Mummy, feed me," just as the air filled with the aroma of overdone toast.

He turned at that moment and came towards them carrying a tray with two mugs of coffee and two plates of burnt toast. He laid her's out in front of her, and was about to sit at another table, when she said, "Won't you join us? I've missed your company... and I've also missed you," she said.

"I'd love to join you," he replied, as he slid over beside her. "I've missed everything about you."

Juliette was now firmly fixed to Prue's breast, and Fuzz looked at the little miracle, as tears trickled down his cheeks... "And who is this little lady... I haven't been introduced?" he asked.

"Fuzz... this is Juliette Monique," said Prue... "Juliette Monique, this is your... daddy."

THE END

352

ABOUT THE AUTHOR:

Now getting on a bit, being seventy-three, I came late to both painting and writing. From where it manifested itself remains a mystery, other than it accompanied a prolonged period of ill health.

Having been blessed with four children, ten grandchildren and a lovely husband, I have to conclude that my inspiration and 'degree' must have come from the university of my life.